WHY THE WHALES CAME
MICHAEL MORPURGO
THE GHOST OF GRANIA O'MALLEY

EGMONT

First published in Great Britain in two separate volumes:

Why The Whales Came
First published in Great Britain 1985 by William Heinemann Ltd
Reissued 2001 by Egmont Books Ltd
Text copyright © 1985 Michael Morpurgo
Cover illustration copyright © 2001 Claire Fletcher

*To
Mark, Linda,
Geoffrey and Stewart*

My thanks to Marion and Keith Bennett
and Leonard Jenkins of Bryher,
and also to Roy Cooper of Tresco,
for their help in the writing of this book.

The Ghost of Grania O'Malley
First published in Great Britain 1996 by William Heinemann Ltd
Reissued 2001 by Egmont Books Ltd
Text copyright © 1996 Michael Morpurgo
Cover illustration copyright © 2001 Mark Bannerman

*To Alice and Lucie –
welcome to the world*

As she says herself, there are many spellings of Grania
O'Malley's name. The spelling used in this book is an
English translation of her name from the Irish language.

This omnibus edition first published 2001 by Egmont Books Ltd,
239 Kensington High Street, London W8 6SA

The moral rights of the author and cover illustrator have been asserted

ISBN 0 7497 4868 0

1 3 5 7 9 10 8 6 4 2

A CIP catalogue record for this title is available from the British Library

Printed and bound in Great Britain by Cox & Wyman Ltd, Reading, Berkshire

WHY THE WHALES CAME

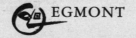EGMONT

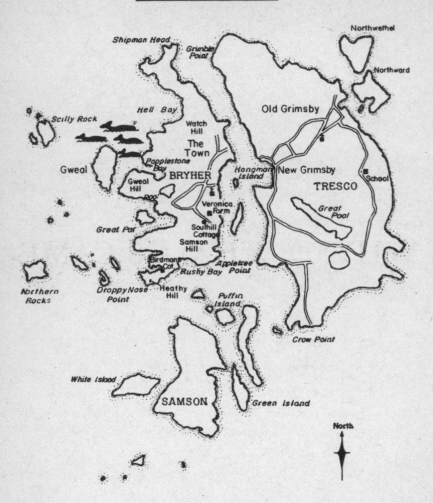

Scale in Miles

0   ½   1

Shipman Head

Grimble Point

Northwethel

Northward

Hell Bay

Old Grimsby

Scilly Rock

Watch Hill

The Town

Gweal

Popplestone Bay

BRYHER

Hangman Island

New Grimsby

TRESCO

School

Gweal Hill

POOL

Veronica Farm

Great Pool

Great Par

Southill Cottage

Samson Hill

Birdman Cot.

Appletree Point

Rushy Bay

Northern Rocks

Droppy Nose Point

Heathy Hill

Puffin Island

Crow Point

White Island

SAMSON

Green Island

North

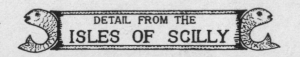

DETAIL FROM THE
ISLES OF SCILLY

CONTENTS

I was brought up on Bryher, one of the Isles of Scilly. You can find them on any map, a scattering of tiny islands kicked out into the Atlantic by the boot of England.

I was about ten years old when it all happened. It was April 1914.

Gracie Jenkins, 1985

1 Z.W.

'YOU KEEP AWAY FROM THE BIRDMAN, GRACIE,' MY father had warned me often enough. 'Keep well clear of him, you hear me now?' And we never would have gone anywhere near him, Daniel and I, had the swans not driven us away from the pool under Gweal Hill where we always went to sail our boats.

Daniel and I had built between us an entire fleet of little boats. Fourteen of them there were, each one light blue with a smart white stripe along the bulwarks. I remember well the warm spring day when we took them down to the pool in father's wheelbarrow. We had just the gentle, constant breeze we needed for a perfect day's sailing. We launched them one by one and then ran round to the far side of the pool to wait for them to come in. It was while we were waiting that a pair of swans came flying over, circled once and then landed in the middle of the pool, sending out great waves in their wake. Two of our boats keeled over and some were eventually washed back to the shore; but we had to wade in after the others to retrieve them. We tried shouting at the swans, we even threw sticks at them; but nothing we did would frighten them away. They simply ignored us, and cruised serenely around the pool, preening themselves. In the end it was we who had to leave, piling our boats into the wheelbarrow and trudging defeated and dejected home to tea.

For some days after that we tried to occupy our pool again, but the swans always seemed to be on the look-out for us and would come gliding towards us in a meaningful, menacing kind of way. They left us in no doubt that they did not want us there, and that they would not be prepared to share the pool with anyone.

So reluctantly we gave up and took our boats to nearby Popplestone Bay, but we found it was so windy there that even on the calmest of days our boats would be capsized or beached almost as soon as we pushed them out. And then one day the fastest boat in the fleet, *Cormorant* it was, was carried out to sea before we could do anything about it. The last we saw of her was the top of her yellow sail as she vanished in the trough of a wave. That was the last straw. After that we never sailed our boats from Popplestone Bay again. We were forced to look for somewhere else.

The beach on the sheltered coast of the island opposite Tresco would have been perfect, for the water was calmer here than anywhere else around the island, but there was always too much happening there. It was the hub of the island. Fishing boats were for ever coming in and going out, leaving great tidal waves behind them big enough to swamp our boats; and the children were often fishing off the quay or splashing through the shallows. Then there were Daniel's brothers and sisters, most of whom always seemed to be on that beach mending nets and lobster pots or painting boats. Of all of them, the one we most wanted to avoid was Big Tim, Daniel's eldest brother, and our chief tormentor; and he was always there. The one time we had tried to sail our boats there, he had come with his cronies and bombarded our fleet with stones. They had managed to break two of the masts, but to our great delight and their obvious disappointment, none of our boats was sunk. Even so, we did not want to risk it again. We had to find somewhere secret, somewhere where no one came and where the water was still enough for us to sail our boats. There was only one place left that we could go – Rushy Bay.

Rushy Bay was forbidden territory to us, along with most of the west coast of Bryher. The pool under Gweal Hill and the beach on Popplestones beyond was as far as any of us children were allowed to go in that direction. We never asked why, for we did not have to. We all knew well enough that the west coast of the island was dangerous, far too dangerous for children, whatever the weather. Mother and Father reminded me repeatedly about it, and they were right to do so. At Shipman's Head and Hell Bay there were black cliffs hundreds of feet high that rose sheer from the churning sea below. Here even on the calmest of days the waves could sweep you off the rocks and take you out to sea. I had been there often enough, but always with Father. We used to go there for firewood, collecting the driftwood off the rocky beaches and dragging it above the high-water mark to claim it for our own; or we would go for the seaweed, piling the cart high with it before going back home to dress the flower pieces or the potato fields. But I never went alone over to that side of the island, none of us ever did.

There was another more compelling reason though why we children were warned away from Rushy Bay and Droppynose Point and the west coast of the island, for this was the side of the island most frequented by the Birdman of Bryher. He was the only one who lived on that side of the island. He lived in the only house facing out over the west coast, a long, low thatched cottage on Heathy Hill overlooking Rushy Bay itself. No one ever went near him and no one ever spoke to him. Like all the other children on the island, Daniel and I had learnt from the cradle that the Birdman was to be avoided. Some said the Birdman was mad. Some said he was the devil himself, that he fed on dogs and cats, and that he would put spells and curses on you if you came too close.

The little I saw of the Birdman was enough to convince me that all the stories we heard about him must be true. He was more like an owl, a flitting creature of the dark, the dawn and the dusk. He would be seen outside only rarely in the daylight, perhaps out in his rowing boat around the island or sitting high on his cart; and even in the hottest summers he would always wear a black cape over his shoulders and a pointed black sou'wester on his head. From a distance you could hear him talking loudly to himself in a strange, unearthly monotone. Maybe it was not to himself that he talked but to the kittiwake that sat always on his shoulder or to the black jack donkey that pulled his cart wherever he went, or maybe it was to the great woolly dog with the greying muzzle that loped along beside him. The Birdman went everywhere barefoot, even in winter, a stooped black figure that lurched as he walked, one step always shorter than the other. And wherever he went he would be surrounded by a flock of screaming seagulls that circled and floated above him, tirelessly vigilant, almost as if they were protecting him. He rarely spoke to anyone, indeed he scarcely even looked at anyone.

Until now it had never even occurred to either Daniel or me to go alone into the forbidden parts of the island, nor to venture anywhere near the Birdman's cottage. After all, the island was over a mile long and half a mile across at its widest. We could roam free over more than half of it and that had always been enough. But Daniel and I had to have somewhere to sail our boats. It was all we lived for, and Rushy Bay was the only place we could do it. Even so I did not want to go there. For me it was far too close to the Birdman's cottage on Heathy Hill. It was Daniel who persuaded me – Daniel had a way with words, he always had.

'Look, Gracie, if we go up around the back of Samson Hill he won't see us coming, will he, not if we keep our heads down?'

'S'pose not,' I said. 'But he could if he was looking that way.'

'So what if he does anyway?' Daniel went on. 'We just run away don't we? He's an old man, Gracie, the oldest man on the island my Aunty Mildred says. And he limps, so he won't hardly be able to run after us and catch us, will he?'

'P'raps not, but . . .'

'Course he won't. There's nothing to be frightened of, Gracie. Anyway we'd have the whole of Rushy Bay to ourselves, nice calm sea and no Big Tim to bother us. No one's ever going to find us there.'

'But what if the Birdman does catch us, Daniel? I mean he's only got to touch us, that's what I heard.'

'Who told you that?'

'Big Tim. He said it was catching. Said the Birdman's only got to touch you and you'll catch it. Like measles, he said, like scarlet fever; and it's not the first time I've heard that either.'

'Catch what?' Daniel said. 'What do you mean?'

'Madness of course. It's catching, that's what Big Tim said anyway. Honest, you go loony, just like him if he touches you.'

'Tommyrot,' Daniel said. 'Course you won't. That's just Big Tim trying to frighten you. Don't you know him by now? He's full of stories, you know that. Honest, Gracie, you won't go mad or loony or anything else, I swear you won't. 'S not true anyway, and even if it was true he isn't going to get near enough to touch us, is he? Oh come on, Gracie, Rushy Bay's the only place left for us. We'll keep right to the far end of it, away from his cottage, so that if he does come we can see him coming and then we just run for it. All right?'

'What would Father say?' I asked weakly.

'Nothing, not if he doesn't know. And he won't, 'less you tell him of course. You wouldn't go and tell him would you?'

'Course not,' I said.

'Well that's all right then isn't it? Go tomorrow shall we?'

'S'pose so,' I said. But I was still not happy about it.

So we went the next day to Rushy Bay to sail our two fastest boats, *Shag* and *Turnstone*. It was a Sunday morning after church, I know that because I remember crouching in my pew beside mother that morning and asking God to protect me against the evil powers of the Birdman. When it came to the last words of the Our Father, 'And deliver us from Evil, Amen', I squeezed my eyes tight shut and prayed harder than ever before in my life.

As we crawled up through the heather on Samson Hill that morning I tried to turn back, but Daniel would not let me. He took my hand, smiled his sideways smile at me and said I would be all right because he was there and he would look after me. With Daniel and God on my side, I thought, my best friend on earth and my best friend in Heaven, surely nothing could go wrong. I was still trying to convince myself of this when we came over Samson Hill and saw the sand of Rushy Bay below us.

It was deserted just as Daniel had promised. We could

see the smoke rising from the two chimneys at either end of the Birdman's cottage and his two brown goats browsing in the heather beyond, but there was no sign of him anywhere. We sailed *Shag* and *Turnstone* until lunchtime. The wind was just right, blowing gently from east to west so that the boats fairly flew over the sea side by side. *Turnstone* was just that much faster – she always was – and I was worrying now only about the rigging on *Shag* which had somehow worked itself loose. I had already forgotten all about the Birdman.

When we went back for lunch we hid the boats in amongst the dunes; it would save us carrying them all the way home and all the way back again after lunch. But that afternoon when we returned to the spot we had left them, they were nowhere to be found. At first we thought we might both have been mistaken, that perhaps we had forgotten the exact place we had left them; but the more we searched the surer we were that they were gone and that someone must have taken them. I knew well enough who that someone must be.

I turned for home, calling to Daniel begging him to come with me. He was standing with his back to me on the top of the dunes, hands on hips, his shirt flapping around him, when suddenly he cried out and launched himself down over the dunes and out of sight. My mouth was dry with fear and I had a horrible dread in the pit of my stomach. But curiosity got the better of my fear and I followed him, even though he was running along the beach towards Heathy Hill, towards the Birdman's Cottage. All the while I called to him to come back, but he would not.

By the time I caught up with him he was crouching down on the sand just below the line of orange and yellow shells left by the high water. There were three boats lying at his feet in the soft white sand. I recognised them at once. There was *Shag*, *Turnstone* and beside them, *Cormorant*. Below them I could see two letters written out in orange shells: Z.W.

We both looked up expecting to see the Birdman standing over us, but there was no one. Smoke still rose from the chimneys in his cottage. The gulls ranged along the ridge of his thatch screeched at us unpleasantly. Then from the dunes close behind us a donkey brayed suddenly and noisily. That was enough even for Daniel. We picked up the boats and we ran; we did not stop running until we had reached the safety of Daniel's boatshed.

2   ISLAND OF GHOSTS

TEA WHEN I WAS A CHILD WAS ALWAYS FISH, FISH
and potatoes; and that evening it was mullet, a great pink
fish that stared up at me with glazed eyes from the platter.
I had no appetite for it. All I could think of were those two
letters in the sand on Rushy Bay. I had to know one way
or the other – I had to be sure it was the Birdman.

I forced myself to eat the fish for I knew mother and
father would suspect something if I did not, for mullet was
known to be my favourite fish. We ate in silence, busying
ourselves over the fish, so I had the whole meal to work
out how best to ask them about the initials in the sand,
without incriminating myself.

'Saw the Birdman today,' I said at last, as casually as I
could.

'Hope you kept your distance,' said Father, pushing his
plate away. 'With young Daniel Pender again were you?

Always with him aren't you?' And it was true I suppose. Daniel Pender and Gracie Jenkins were a pair, inseparable. We always had been. He lived just across the way from our front gate at Veronica Farm. Whatever we did, we did together. Father went on. 'Proper young scallywag his father says he is and I can believe it. You be sure he doesn't lead you into any trouble, my girl. Always looks like a big puppy that one with his arms and legs too long for the rest of him. Hair's always stood up on his head like he's just got out of bed. Proper scallywag he looks.'

'Looks aren't everything,' said mother quietly; and then she smiled and added, 'they can't be, can they, else how would I ever have come to pick you?'

'My beard, perhaps, Clemmie,' father laughed, and he stroked his beard and smoothed his moustache. He always called her 'Clemmie' when he was happy. It was 'Clem' when he was angry.

'You leave Daniel be,' said Mother. 'He's a clever boy, clever with his hands. You seen those boats he makes?'

'I help him,' I insisted. 'I paint them and I make the sails.'

'Been sailing them all day, I suppose,' said father. 'Out by the pool were you? That where you saw the Birdman?'

'Yes, Father,' I said; and then, 'About the Birdman, Father; everyone just calls him "The Birdman", but he must have a real name like other people, mustn't he?'

'Woodcock,' said father, sitting back in his chair and undoing a notch in his belt as he always did after a meal. 'Woodcock, that's what his mother was called anyway. You can see for yourself if you like – she's buried down in the churchyard somewhere. Last one to leave Samson they say she was, her and the boy. Starving they were by all accounts. Anyway, they came over to Bryher and built that cottage up there on Heathy Hill away from everyone else. The old woman died a few years after I was born. Must have been dead, oh thirty years or more now. The Birdman's lived on his own up there ever since. But you hear all sorts of things about his old mother. There's some will tell you she was a witch, and some say she was just plain mad. P'raps she was both, I don't know. Same with the Birdman; I don't know whether he's just mad or evil with it. Either way it's best to keep away from him. There's things I could tell you . . .'

'Don't go frightening her now with your stories,' said Mother. 'Anyway it's only rumours and tittle-tattle. I don't believe half of it. If anything goes wrong on this island they blame it on the Birdman. Lobsters aren't there to be caught – it's his fault. Blight in the potatoes – it's his fault. Anyone catches the fever – it's his fault. Dog goes missing – they say he's eaten it. Lot of old nonsense. He's just a bit simple, bit mad perhaps, that's all.'

'Simple my aunt,' Father said, getting up and going over to his chair by the stove. 'And what's more, it's not all tittle-tattle, Clemmie, not all of it. You know it's not.'

'There's no need to tell her any more,' said Mother. 'Long as she doesn't go anywhere near him, long as she keeps off Samson, that's all that matters. Don't you go filling her head with all those stories.'

'But they're not all stories, are they, Clemmie?

Remember what happened to Charlie Webber?'

'Charlie Webber? Who's he?' I asked.

'Never you mind about Charlie Webber,' said Mother; and she spoke firmly to Father.

'That's enough – you'll only frighten her.'

But Father ignored her. He leaned forward towards me in his chair, stuffing his pipe with tobacco. 'Charlie Webber was my best friend when I was a boy, Gracie. Got into all sorts of scrapes and capers together, Charlie and me. Nothing we wouldn't tell each other; and Charlie wouldn't ever have lied to me, not in a million years. He wasn't like that, was he, Clemmie?' But Mother wouldn't answer him. She walked away and busied herself at the sink. His voice dropped to a whisper now, almost as if he was afraid of being overheard. 'There's always been strange stories about Samson, Gracie. Course, people only half-believed them, but they've always steered clear of Samson all the same, just in case. But it was all on account of the Birdman and his mother that Samson became a place no one dared go near. They were the ones who put it about that there was a curse on the place. They were always warning everyone to keep off, so we did. They told everyone it was an island of ghosts, that whoever set foot on the place would bring the terrible curse of Samson down on his family. No one quite believed all that about ghosts and curses; but just the same everyone kept well clear of the place, everyone except Charlie.'

Father lit up his pipe and sat back in his chair which creaked underneath him as it always did whenever he moved. 'I never went over there, but Charlie did. It was a day I'll never forget, never, never – low tide, no water to speak of between Bryher and Samson. You could walk across. It was my idea, and not one I'm proud of, Gracie, I can tell you. It was me that dared Charlie Webber. I dared him to walk over to Samson. We were always daring each other to do silly things, that's just how we were; and Charlie Webber never could resist a dare. I stood on top of Samson Hill, and watched him running over the sands towards Samson, leaping the pools. It took him about ten minutes I suppose and there he was jumping up and down on the beach waving and shouting to me, when suddenly this man in a black sou'wester appeared out of the dunes behind him, came from nowhere. He began screaming at Charlie like some mad fiend and Charlie ran and ran and ran. He ran like a hare all the way back across the sand, stumbling and splashing through the shallows. By the time he reached me he was white with fear, Gracie, white with it I tell you. But that's not all of it. That very same night Charlie Webber's house was burnt to the ground. It's true, Gracie. Everyone managed to get out alive, but they never did find out what caused the fire; but Charlie knew all right, and I knew. Next day Charlie went down with the scarlet fever. I caught it after him and then near enough every child on the island got it. Aunty Mildred – you know Daniel's Aunty Mildred – she was just a baby at the time and she nearly died of it.'

'Did Charlie Webber die of it?' I asked.

'Now that's enough,' said Mother sharply. 'You've said enough.'

'Clem,' said Father, 'she's ten years old and she's not a baby any more. She's old enough to hear the rest of it.' He lit his pipe again, drawing on it deeply several times before he shook out the match. 'No, Gracie, Charlie didn't die, but he had to leave the island. His family was ruined, couldn't afford to rebuild the house. But before Charlie left for good he told me something I'll never forget. The day after the fire, Charlie was sitting on the quay when he felt someone behind him. He looked around and there was the Birdman. There was nowhere for Charlie to run to. He'd come, he said, to say sorry to Charlie, to explain to him that it wasn't his fault. There was nothing he could do once Charlie had set foot on Samson. He told Charlie that there was a curse on the island, that the ghosts of the dead haunted the place and could not rest, not until the guilt of Samson had been redeemed, whatever that meant. And when Charlie asked him why there was a curse on Samson, why the ghosts could not rest – this is what he told him. He was a little boy when it happened, younger than Charlie, he said. The people of Samson woke up one morning to find a ship run aground on a sandbank off Samson. Like a ghost ship it was on a flat calm sea. No fog, no wind, no reason for it to be there. They rowed out and hailed it, but no one answered; so they clambered on board. There was no one there. The ship was deserted. Well you don't look a gift horse in the mouth, do you? Every man on Samson, sixteen of them there were in all he said – every one of them was on that ship when it refloated at high tide. They sailed it off to Penzance to claim the salvage money, but they never got there. The ship foundered on the Wolf Rock, off Land's End, went down in broad daylight, mind you; gentle breeze, no fog. Every man on board was lost. The Birdman's own father went down on that ship, Gracie.'

'It's a horrible story,' said Mother, 'horrible. Every time I hear it it makes me shiver.'

'True nonetheless, Clemmie,' father said. 'And that wasn't the last of it. It seems things went from bad to worse on Samson after that. With no men left to go fishing or to work up the fields, the women and children soon began to go hungry. All they had to eat was limpets. The Birdman told Charlie that they even had to eat the dogs. It's true, Gracie, that's what Charlie told me. Then with the hunger came the fever, and the old folk and the babies began to die. So they left. One by one the families left the island until the Birdman and his mother were alone on Samson.'

Father drew on his pipe again and found it had gone out – his pipe was always going out. 'And I believe every word Charlie told me, Gracie. I don't pretend to understand the whys and wherefores; and I tell you straight, I don't know if it's him that's cursed or Samson. All I do know is that it's better to keep away from the both of them – that's for sure. So you keep well clear of him, you hear me now?'

I sat silent for some time lost in father's story, my head full of questions. 'So he can put spells and curses on people like they say he can?' I asked.

'Maybe,' said father, tapping his pipe out on the side of the stove. And I shivered as I thought of how close we had

16

been to his cottage that day, and how he must have been watching us on Rushy Bay. Then there were those letters in the sand. Perhaps they were initials, but perhaps they were part of some spell. I wanted to be sure.

'What about his first name, Father?' I asked. 'Do you know his first name?' But immediately I regretted it for I felt Mother looking at me. I was being over inquisitive, too interested; and she was suspicious.

'Why all these sudden questions about the Birdman, Gracie?' she asked. 'You've never shown any interest in him before.'

'Just saw him today, like I said. Just wondered, that's all. Daniel and me, we just wondered about him.'

Mother came over and stood in front of me. She took my chin in her hand and pulled it up so that I had to look her in the eyes. She always did this when she thought I'd been up to some mischief and she wanted to get the truth out of me. 'You haven't been speaking to him, have you Gracie? You haven't been over on Heathy Hill, have you? You know you're not supposed to go there, don't you?'

'No, Mother, course I haven't, honest I haven't.' It was just as well I did not have to lie, for Mother would have known. Father I could deceive any time I wanted, but Mother knew me far too well. She looked down at me out of tired kind eyes, a knowing smile on her lips, so knowing that I had to look away.

'You leave him to his birds, Gracie,' father said. 'You keep well away like I said. Promise me now. You be a good girl and stay away.'

'I promise,' I said. 'I'll stay away.'

And so I did, for a day or so at least. It took only that long for Daniel to persuade me to go with him back to Rushy Bay, that we had been silly to run away in the first place just because we'd heard a donkey braying. I told him everything Father had told me about the Birdman and Samson and Charlie Webber. He listened, but I could see he didn't really believe any of it. He said he had heard something about the fire before, and that it didn't matter anyway because we weren't going to Samson like Charlie Webber did. We were only going to Rushy Bay. And the Birdman might be a bit loony, but what did that matter? He just wanted to make friends, that was all. Why else would he give us back our boat? Why else would he be leaving messages for us in the sand? We didn't have to go anywhere near him, did we? Perhaps I agreed to go with Daniel because I was half convinced by his arguments, or perhaps I was inquisitive.

When I crawled up over Samson Hill with Daniel that next day I kept flat on my stomach in the heather until I was sure the Birdman was not down there on Rushy Bay waiting for us.

The Birdman was not waiting for us, but something else was. Lying on its side in the sand in almost the same spot we had found our boats the day before was a bird, a cormorant. At first we thought it had been washed up dead, for it lay amongst the flotsam at the high water mark. As we approached I could see it was small even for a young bird, and that the feathers were not oily black as they should have been. I thought it must have been blown off the rocks before it could fly.

Suddenly Daniel caught my arm and pointed further along the beach. A trail of footprints led right to where the cormorant lay and away again. At that moment I would have panicked and run as I had done before, but this time Daniel's hand was firm on my arm and he led me forward. In the sand above the cormorant, written out in orange shells were the letters I now expected to find: 'Z.W.' It was not until we were down on our knees in the sand beside it that I realized the cormorant's feathers were not stirred by the breeze as they ought to have been, that it was in fact made of wood. Then we noticed the shells. Only a few feet away the shells along the tide-mark had been rearranged to read: 'Stay and play. Your beach as much as mine.'

We scanned the dunes above us for any sign of the black sou'wester amongst the reeds, but all we could see of the Birdman were his gulls still lined up on the thatch of his cottage watching us. Thin wisps of smoke rose from the chimney pots at each end of the cottage only to be whipped away at once and dissipated by the wind. Daniel reached out and picked up the cormorant. The base of it was carved out as a rock, covered with limpets and barnacles, and the cormorant stood on his great webbed feet, head slightly lifted, almost indignant. He was leaning forward as if balancing himself against the wind. All his feathers were so finely crafted that I expected them to be soft to the touch. Daniel set the bird down in the wet sand facing out over the water to Samson and sat back on his ankles.

'You ever seen anything like it?' he said stroking the crown of the bird's head. 'Looks as if he could lift off and fly, doesn't he?'

'D'you think the Birdman's watching us?' I whispered.

' 'Spect so. Don't mind if he is. Look at this, Gracie. The man who made this isn't a madman; he just can't be. And he gave us back our boat, didn't he? It's like I told you, Gracie, he's trying to make friends with us. He likes us being here. I'm going to stay and sail our boats, Gracie just like he said we could, and what's more I'm going to say thank you to him.'

'Well I'm not going anywhere near that cottage,' I said, suddenly cold with fear at the very thought of it. 'Not in a million years.'

'We don't need to, Gracie,' he said. 'Look.' And he wrote in shells beside the Birdman's message: 'Thanks. Daniel and Grace.'

'No,' I shouted as soon as I saw my name in the sand. 'You can't, you can't! He'll know who we are if you do that, he'll come after us and put his curses on us.' And I lifted my foot and kicked the sand all over Daniel's writing until I had obliterated every last letter. I was crying in spite of myself. 'Father says he puts spells on people. We mustn't talk to him. We're not supposed to.'

Daniel looked up at me and I could see from the look in his eyes that he was disappointed in me. 'But we're not going to talk to him, are we?' he said. 'Look, Gracie, it stands to reason. If the Birdman had wanted to put a spell on us he could have done it already, couldn't he? Well he could, couldn't he?' I would not answer him because I hated to be wrong, and I knew well enough in my heart that I was. In my shame and fury I kicked the cormorant over on its side and ran off up the beach towards Samson Hill. Daniel called after me to come back and all my rage at my own humiliating fear burst from me.

'If you're so brave, Daniel Pender,' I screamed at him, 'then you can sign your silly name; but I'm not coming here again, never, d'you hear me? Never. You can keep your silly boats and your silly cormorant for all I care. I don't want it and I don't want ever . . .', and I would have gone on to say every hurtful thing I could think of, had I not caught sight of the Birdman's dog plodding purposefully along the beach behind Daniel, his tongue lolling out of his mouth. I tried to call out to Daniel to warn him but my voice would not speak as it should, so I just pointed and ran back down over the sand to warn him.

The dog paid us no attention but went straight to where the cormorant lay and sniffed it. Then, arranging his jaws with care around it, he picked it up and came and sat tidily at our feet looking very pleased with himself, his tail swishing the sand behind him.

The dog seemed to have no eyes, for they were covered by a curtain of matted black ringlets. 'He's giving it to you,' I said. 'He wants you to take it.'

'For us is it?' Daniel asked the dog and he took the cormorant out of its mouth. 'Did he send you then, did the Birdman send you?' And the dog licked his lips and shook the sand out of his mouth. Daniel patted him and parted the hair over his face to reveal two shining black eyes. 'How can you see through all this lot?' he said.

And then the dog pricked up his ears, stood up and

looked around towards the cottage. He stopped panting for a moment and listened. Before we knew it he was bounding away over the sand and had vanished into the dunes. Neither of us had heard a whistle, but neither of us had any doubt at all that he had been called back.

'Must have been watching us,' I said. 'He must have seen me kick it over, mustn't he?'

Daniel brushed the sand off the cormorant's head. 'See, I told you, Gracie, didn't I? He just wants to be friendly, that's all.' And he dropped to his knees in the sand. 'Come on. We've got to thank him, haven't we?'

We never spoke a word after that but knelt in the sand together and collected all the shells we were going to need. Then I wrote out in orange shells: 'Thanks for the cormorant.' And both of us signed our names in shells underneath.

We stayed all day sailing our boats on Rushy Bay and even when Daniel suggested the sea was getting too rough I insisted we stayed on, just to prove to myself, to him and to the Birdman that I was no longer frightened. True, I did keep my eye on Heathy Hill, but now I was almost hoping the Birdman would come down to the beach with his dog. He did not come however, and my new-found courage was not put to the test, not yet anyway. As we left the beach Daniel cupped his hands to his mouth and called out, 'Goodbye', in the direction of the cottage, and I waved with him because I felt sure that the Birdman would be watching us.

Back in Daniel's boatshed that evening we stood by his workbench and examined the cormorant closely. 'One day, Gracie,' he said, 'one day, I'm going to be able to make something like that.'

'What happens if someone finds it?' I asked. 'What are we going to say?'

'Just tell them I made it,' he said laughing. 'But they may not believe us, so better if they don't find it. I haven't got a room of my own to hide it and I haven't got anywhere to put anything, not anywhere private anyway. You got a room of your own, Gracie, you keep it. It'll be safer with you. If Father finds it, he'll only want to know where it comes from and Big Tim will torture me till I tell him.' And he handed the cormorant carefully to me. I already knew where I would hide it – I was only worried about how I was going to get it there without being discovered.

'I've been thinking, Gracie,' Daniel said. 'He gave us this cormorant to show us he was friendly, didn't he? So we've got to do the same, haven't we? We've got to give him something back so's he knows we want to be friends as well. I've been thinking. D'you think he'd like it if we made him one of our boats?'

'Could call her *Woodcock*, couldn't we?' I said. 'We've got to name it after a bird, like all the others are. Woodcock's a kind of bird, isn't it?'

'Never seen one,' said Daniel, 'but I think it is.'

And so I went home that evening with the Birdman's cormorant stuffed inside my blouse. Mother paid me no attention as I came in; she was busy over the stove and I reached the safety of my room without her even seeing me.

We built *Woodcock* together that spring, but it was nearly summer before she was ready for launching. We had never taken so much trouble over a boat as we did with *Woodcock*. Nothing was ever right until it was perfect. We took her to Rushy Bay for her trials and pushed her out towards Samson Island. She danced out over the waves, her sail catching the wind and leaning her over so that she sped out to sea. I think she might have gone all the way to Samson had we not waded waist high into the sea after her and brought her back. She was quite magnificent with her shiny blue hull, her white stripe and her brick-red sail. Daniel was satisfied. So we left her, beached well above the high-water mark; and we left too a long shell message for the Birdman in the sand. It read: 'We name this boat *Woodcock*. May God bless her and all who sail her'; and we signed it, 'Daniel and Grace'.

We waited until sundown in the purple humming heather on Samson Hill to see if the Birdman would come for it, but he never came. We could not stay any longer for mother always liked me to be home before dark. But first thing the next morning we went back to Rushy Bay and found the boat gone. In its place there was this message: 'Thanks. Beautiful.' And underneath, 'Zachariah Woodcock.'

3 MESSAGES IN THE SAND

I NEVER MUCH LIKED GOING TO SCHOOL. IT WAS A nuisance for it took me away from home and from everything I wanted to be doing. But that summer it was more than a nuisance, it was an intrusion into our secret life on Rushy Bay and I resented it more than ever. I feigned sickness successfully on a few occasions, until Mother discovered that Daniel always seemed to be ill on the same day I was and put a stop to it. Sometimes, though not very often for Mother would have suspected me, I was able to persuade Father he could not do without me on the boat and I managed to stay off school that way. I knew we would only be out lobster fishing for the morning, so Daniel and I could spend the afternoon down on Rushy Bay. Father was never that hard to persuade because he liked the company and it did help to have me handling the boat whilst he set or hauled the lobster pots, particularly when there was a heavy swell out around the Northern Rocks.

It was always a great deal easier for Daniel to stay away from school because no one much cared in his house whether he was at school or not, and his father was only too pleased to have an extra pair of hands in the boatshed. Whatever happened though we always went to school together or stayed away together. It was not a formal pact between us, there was never any need for that – it was just an understanding.

School was across the water on Tresco. About fifteen of us went across on the boat each day from Bryher and we often had to get out and push the boat when it became stuck fast on the sandbanks at low tide. All day at my desk I longed for lessons to be over so that I could get back to Rushy Bay. It was hardly surprising therefore that my teacher, Mr Angus Wellbeloved, was for ever reprimanding me for lack of attention. Mr Wellbeloved, or 'Welly Belly' as we called him, grew a crop of long white hairs out of his ears which he always twiddled to a point whenever he was reading to us, and his wiry eyebrows joined in the middle of his nose and hung around his eyes like a misplaced moustache. From an early age Mr Wellbeloved had condemned me as 'unladylike', 'untidy' and 'unteachable', mostly because I could never master my arithmetic. For Mr Wellbeloved, arithmetic was the yardstick by which he judged character. Sums or anything to do with figures had always induced in me a kind of panic. I raged then against their peculiar logic. I could never understand them and I cannot to this day.

Only Daniel made it all bearable. We sat side by side

and survived school together. He did not care for school or for Mr Wellbeloved any more than I did, but he was clever enough to succeed at his sums and was therefore the apple of Mr Wellbeloved's eye. I copied just enough of his sums to get by and in return he copied my spellings whenever he needed to. I was a genius at spelling and proud of it. So with Daniel beside me I made an adequate pupil, just satisfactory enough to avoid being kept in for detentions, and that was all that mattered.

I may not have liked Mr Wellbeloved – few of us did – but it has to be said that it was Mr Wellbeloved who warned us early that summer that there would be a war with Germany before very long. I asked father about it and he told me it was all nonsense, and that anyway it did not much matter whether there was a war or not because no war could ever touch us on Bryher. I did notice that mother pursed her lips at this and kept silent, a sure sign that she did not share his optimism.

But even when school was finished for the day, Daniel and I were not free to go at once to Rushy Bay, for he was always needed to sweep up in his father's boatshed; and father might well send me out to fish for wrasse for lobster bait, or there were always lobster pots to be mended. Sometimes it could be almost evening before we were able at last to set off together. Even so, every day without fail we managed to get to Rushy Bay, not so much now to sail our boats, although we did if the wind was right, but rather to see if the Birdman had left another message for us in the sand.

Some days, to our intense disappointment, there

would be nothing there but a jumble of seaweed and flotsam. On most days though we would reach the top of Samson Hill and see the Birdman's dog waiting for us on the beach below. Whenever he was there we knew we would find a shell message in the sand beside him, or the remains of one anyway. Often he would be sitting so close to the message that by the time we got there his ever-wagging tail had scattered the shells far and wide, leaving us the problem of trying to make some sense out of the few surviving but scarcely decipherable letters. And leading to and from the message we would find the Birdman's distinctive footprints, the right foot broad and heavy, the left just half a footprint, five toes and the ball of the foot. It was always this left foot which dragged a continuous furrow through the sand from one print to the next.

Our exchange of shell messages became like a long drawn-out conversation. The messages took a long time to write out, so we kept them as short as possible. We tried to discover all we could about the Birdman, but by the end of the summer we still knew very little about him. We did manage to find out that he was exactly eighty years old, that the birds on the island came to him because he fed them, because they knew he liked them and because they knew he would never harm them. We learned he had been carving birds as long as he could remember, that his father had taught him. It kept his fingers from going stiff like the rest of him, and it made him feel like God because he could make any creature he wanted. All he needed was the wood, and there was plenty of that washed up on the beaches. That was all he would tell us about himself. He would simply ignore many of the questions we left behind for him; either that or the dog had wagged them out and ruined them before the Birdman could read them. We were fairly sure though that he was answering only those questions he wanted to answer.

He seemed quite happy however to tell us about his animals, so that we came to know a great deal more about them than we did about him. The donkey was called Friend, he told us. He had bad feet and a bad temper, mostly because he was old. Friend lived only for carrots which the Birdman grew exclusively for him in the garden. Just to look at him, the Birdman wrote, was to know that there was someone worse off than oneself. And he told us a lot about his dog, Prince, about how he had found him washed up in Hell Bay one day. 'Been with me a long time now,' he wrote. 'Don't know what I'd do without him.'

As the weeks passed, the pattern of questions and answers between us changed. It became clear he wanted to ask questions but not to answer them. At first he wanted to know everything about us, all about our families. He wanted to know how old they all were, what they looked like, where they lived and what they did. 'Father builds boats.' Daniel wrote one day.

'What kind of boats?'

'Gigs. Luggers. Anything.'

'Building one now?'

'Fishing lugger – 14ft.'

'Flower crop good this year?'

'Fair.'

'Potatoes? Any blight?'

'Late crop. No blight.'

And when the messages were longer the Birdman used bits of wood, even seaweed, to make his letters. But he always signed them 'Z.W.' in orange shells.

His appetite for news became more and more insatiable. For Daniel and me it was like having to describe the world to a blind man. He wanted to know everything people said, everything they did. It was after we had told him about Big Tim, about how much we hated him, that he first began to talk to us through his messages rather than simply to ask more questions. 'Never hate anyone,' he wrote. 'Hate eats away at your soul.' And when one evening we wrote that Mr Wellbeloved thought there would soon be a war with Germany we found his reply the next morning. It read simply: 'I am sad today.'

There was no time to build boats any more now for Daniel was busy with his first puffin carving. He had originally meant it to be a standing shag drying its wings, but no matter how hard he tried he could not get the head quite right, so he cut off the wings in disgust and reduced it to a rather bulbous-looking puffin that seemed to me more like an owl, but I did not dare say so. As it turned out I did not need to, for he soon discarded it and began another.

It was hot that August of 1914, hotter than any summer I have known since. The sand on Rushy Bay was too hot even to stand on by midday, so we had to retreat to the shelter of the dunes. Here Daniel would sit cross-legged in the sand whittling away at his new puffin, and I would brush out Prince's matted fur and pick the burrs out of the hair behind his ears while he lay panting beside me in the heat. When the sand had cooled in the late afternoon Prince would come with us down to the sea and cavort clumsily in the waves. He would swim out towards Samson for the sticks we threw for him and then lie beside us on the beach as we composed and wrote out our message in the sand for his master. But when we left for home at the end of the day he never once attempted to follow us. From the top of Samson Hill we would see him sitting alone on the beach still watching us, or trotting away up through the dunes back to the Birdman's cottage.

From time to time we did catch sight of the Birdman himself, but always at a distance. We would see him emerging from his cottage door at dusk to feed the chickens or milk the goats, or we might catch a glimpse of his boat bobbing up and down as he rowed out towards Samson. In the early evening sometimes we might see him setting off with his donkey and cart, up towards Hell Bay, Prince following along behind; but the closest we ever came to actually meeting him was one day when that summer was almost over.

We had left the beach later than usual that evening and were on our way back over Samson Hill when we saw him rowing out around Droppy Nose Point and into Rushy Bay itself. Above him flew his usual escort of shrieking, wheeling gulls. Prince was sitting where we had left him on the beach below. We shouted and waved but the Birdman had his back to us and never turned round. We felt sure he must be able to hear us for we heard his whistle clearly and saw Prince bounding down the beach and into the water. He paddled out through the sea towards the boat, his small black head rising and falling with the waves. We watched as the Birdman shipped his oars, leant down over the side and bundled him up into the boat. We saw Prince shake himself and heard the Birdman laugh and begin to talk as he took up the oars again. Prince stood up like a figurehead in the bow of the boat as it moved slowly out towards Samson, the flock of gulls circling above. All the while we could hear snatches of the Birdman's voice from across the water. He was too far away for us to hear what he was saying but we listened all the same, straining to pick up the sense of it over the sound of the surf.

'What d'you think he goes over to Samson for?' said Daniel. 'Nothing there 'cept empty houses and sand.'

'P'raps he goes fishing over there,' I said.

'He doesn't fish,' said Daniel. 'I've never seen him fishing, have you? And it's strange, Gracie, you only ever see him out in his boat in bad weather. Doesn't seem to bother him. You noticed that? I've seen him out in gales before now. He'll go out in any weather. Funny that, don't you think?'

I looked over towards where Samson lay brooding darkly under gathering storm clouds. About it the sea, blood-red with the evening sun, surged and heaved. 'Island of ghosts,' I said. 'Don't care what you say, Daniel, I tell you there's ghosts on Samson just like father said there was. You only got to look at it. It's cursed, Daniel, I can tell it is.'

'Don't believe in ghosts,' said Daniel dismissively, and he turned away. 'And I don't believe in curses either.'

'Well I do,' I snapped, suddenly angry at him, and we walked on down through the heather in silence.

The first few drops of rain were so huge and heavy that they hurt the top of my head. We began to run. The rain pounded us all the way home, stinging our eyes and ears. By the time we got there we were soaked through and dripping from our noses and chins. The houses all round were dark and quiet, unusually so. Only one light glowed at our kitchen window. 'Strange,' said Daniel, 'there's no lamps lit in my house. Everyone's out by the look of it. No one about, is there? Can't think where they could all be. Can't see anyone in the boatshed either. Can I come in with you, Gracie, till they get back?'

I knew full well how much Daniel hated to be alone in the dark. He was brave about everything else except the dark, and that always made me feel good because the dark had never bothered me. We shook ourselves in the porch and went in together.

Mother was sitting in the kitchen, her chair rocking back and forth. The lamp was on the table beside her and her sewing lay in her lap. I expected a wigging from her for being out after dark but she looked up vacantly at us as we came in and seemed neither annoyed nor surprised that we were late.

'Well,' she said, a weak smile on her face. 'You're back.' And then, 'I'm afraid your Mr Wellbeloved was right after all, Gracie. I thought he might be you know. I didn't want to believe him, no one did, your father least of all; but he's an educated man, Mr Wellbeloved, he could see it coming.'

'Right about what, Mother?' I asked. 'What's happened?'

'Where is everyone?' Daniel asked. 'Can't find anyone at home.'

'They've all gone to a meeting in the church, Daniel. Father's gone too, Gracie. They called an island meeting as soon as they heard the news this afternoon.'

'It's the war, isn't it?' Daniel said. 'They've started the war, Gracie, like old Welly Belly said they would.' And mother nodded and lowered her head.

There was such a storm that first night of the war, a violent thunderstorm that flashed and rolled around the island as if it wanted to uproot it from the sea. The wind moaned and howled horribly through the house. White sheet lightning turned the night to day outside my window heralding each new rumbling crescendo of thunder.

I was still awake when Father came in later that night. I heard him talking on and on about the war and about how the Germans had it coming to them, about how they had bitten off more than they could chew, about how we were better sailors than they were because we were an island race with the sea bred into us. It would not take long to finish them, he said, and we were going to do our bit on Bryher. By day there would always be someone on the look-out for submarines up on Watch Hill; and by night there were to be no lights showing on the island, all curtains were to be drawn and the island blacked out completely. All the while I never heard Mother speak a word. But what kept me awake had nothing to do either with the war or the storm, for I had no idea then what a war really was. I thought the war like the storm would pass soon enough. I lay there all that night thinking only of the Birdman and Prince out in the tiny boat, and I prayed and prayed that they had not been caught out in the open sea when the storm broke.

4 THE BIRDMAN

DANIEL WAS WAITING OUTSIDE MY FRONT GATE early the next morning. He too had scarcely slept for worrying about the Birdman and Prince. 'I just hope he reached Samson and stayed the night there, that's all,' he said. 'He wouldn't have had time to get there and back. I know he wouldn't. P'raps it's all right though. After all he must know that stretch of water better than anyone. Come on, Gracie, let's hurry.' And we ran all the way up over Samson Hill and only stopped for breath when we could see Rushy Bay below us.

By now the force of the storm was spent and the wind had died, but the sea was still seething and angry. The waves rolled into the bay from Samson, gathering and rearing as they neared the shore before they curled over to hurl themselves into the hissing sand. The beach was empty. There was no Prince waiting for us and we could find no message in the sand. We could see the storm had thrown up a line of debris high under the dunes and must certainly have washed away any message the Birdman might have left behind for us. Nonetheless we had to be sure, so we searched the thin strip of dry clear sand under the dunes, just in case. That was how we came across the oar, half-hidden under a tangle of seaweed.

Daniel helped me to pull it clear and we carried it up onto the clean sand. 'Could be anyone's, couldn't it?' I said, but Daniel said nothing. We scoured the beach together, picking over the flotsam, hoping against hope we would not come across what we were now both expecting to find, the shattered and torn timbers of the Birdman's boat. We found wood enough and plenty but it was white, wave-washed and smooth. There was no trace either of his boat nor of the other oar. I was relieved and heartened enough by this time to imagine that all must be well, that we had indeed found an oar from someone else's boat, but Daniel insisted that we should go over to Great Par, the beach on the other side of Heathy Hill where we knew the Birdman always kept his boat.

'If they are back safely like you say they are,' said Daniel, 'then the boat will be there, won't it, and we won't have to worry any more, will we?'

We left the oar lying on top of the dunes and made our way through the reeds towards Great Par. We walked on together in silence, and all the while I dreaded we might find nothing there, that my worst fears would be realised. As we came to the top of each dune more and more of the beach came into view, and still there was no boat to be seen. We were passing just below the Birdman's cottage when Daniel stopped suddenly and caught my arm. 'There's no smoke, Gracie,' he said, his voice hushed to a whisper. 'Look, can't you see, there's no smoke coming out of the chimneys. There's always been smoke before, I know there has. And there's no gulls either, there's no gulls on the roof.' I looked up at the cottage which was almost camouflaged against the background of heather on Heathy Hill and I could see Daniel was right, that the place was indeed deserted. The front door banged in the wind and no one came to shut it. A corner of the thatch had been ripped away by the storm and lay strewn around the potato field below the house. There was no sign of life on the hill except for the Birdman's two goats that clambered amongst the rocks at the top of Droppy Nose Point. Then a solitary gull flew over and hung on the wind above the cottage. It circled once above us and then flew on out over the sea towards Samson.

I knew at that moment what was going through Daniel's mind and knew I had to forestall him. 'There's no one in there, Daniel,' I said quickly. 'You can tell there's no one there. Let's go on and see if the boat's in Great Par. No need to go any closer is there? Well I'm not going up there, that's for sure.' And suddenly all those terrible fears of the Birdman welled up inside me once again.

'You can stay here if you like,' Daniel said ignoring my protests, 'but I'm going to find out if he's in there. What's the matter with you, Gracie? What's he ever done to hurt you? I mean we know he's not mad now, don't we? Come on, Gracie, it'll be all right.'

I found myself following him reluctantly up the hill, through head-high bracken and heather into the biggest and best-kept vegetable garden I had ever seen and past a pair of white beehives that stood like sentries on either side of the track. Several brown hens ran squawking towards us out of the heather and then followed us up the path at a discreet distance. We slowed, almost tiptoeing as we reached the front door that blew shut in our faces just as we reached it. Daniel knocked once. No one came. He knocked again.

'See?' I said, pulling him back. 'He's not there. I told you, didn't I? I told you he wouldn't be.' But Daniel paid me no attention. He lifted the latch on the door, took my hand firmly in his and we stepped together into the darkness of the cottage.

It was one long room with an unmade bed at one end by the fireplace, and an ornate black stove at the other. And above the stove on the mantlepiece stood *Woodcock*, the bright blue boat we had made for him. At the back of the fireplace was a pile of dead grey ash that the wind from the open door was whipping about the room. Daniel shut the door behind us to keep the hens out. Almost the entire room was taken up by a long trestle table that was covered from end to end in carvings, bird carvings, finished and unfinished, and around each one of them was a group of pencil sketches pinned to the table. Some of these had been torn away by the wind and a few of the carvings had been blown over onto the floor. The floor itself was a mat of wood shavings and sawdust, and the stone walls around were lined from the ceiling to the floor with shelves that bellied under the weight of hundreds of carvings. We were being watched by a silent audience of gulls and kittiwakes, petrels and gannets, merlins and puffins and plovers. Some were diving, some were preening themselves, but most stood glaring angrily at us from the shelves as if we had interrupted a secret meeting of bird conspirators.

To one side of the stove were the only shelves in the room not filled with birds. Instead on each of the four shelves there was a loaf of bread. I noticed that not much was left of the loaf on the bottom shelf. I was glad to have Daniel's hand to hold, nothing could have persuaded me to let go. He led me over to the stove and felt it. 'Cold,' said Daniel. 'They haven't been back all night. We won't find his boat in Great Par, Gracie; we won't find it anywhere.'

'They could still be on Samson,' I whispered. 'Couldn't they? I mean that's what I'd do; I'd wait there till the sea was calm and it was safe to come back. That's what you'd do, isn't it?'

Daniel shook his head. 'The oar, Gracie. Where did the oar come from if they're still on Samson?'

'But it needn't be theirs, need it?' I said. 'Could be someone else's, couldn't it?' Daniel did not answer me. A sudden gust of wind shook the cottage, rattled the windows and whistled down the chimneys disturbing the ash in the fire grate. I moved closer to Daniel who had picked up the end of the loaf on the bottom shelf to smell it.

'Wonder why he keeps four loaves?' he said. Then, as if they were all answering together, the birds lining the shelves began to shriek and scream at us. That was more than I could take. Dragging Daniel behind me I ran for the door which opened in front of us just as we reached it. Prince was suddenly around our legs, jumping up at us and shaking himself all over us; and blotting out the light from the doorway was the black, hooded silhouette of the Birdman with a kittiwake perched on his shoulder. Above him I could see the sky was white with screeching gulls. Daniel and I backed away towards the stove knocking over a chair as we went. Prince followed us sniffing at the bread in Daniel's hand.

'Hungry, were you?' came the voice from inside the sou'wester. 'Plenty of bread, always make plenty of bread. Bake one a day. Always have plenty in reserve in case I get ill. I keep the freshest till last, on the top shelf – you can have some of that if you like.' The kittiwake lifted off his shoulder and landed clumsily amongst the carvings on the table, knocking one of them over. He hopped on one leg; the other seemed curled up and stunted and he would not use it. The Birdman shut the door behind him, pulled off his sou'wester and shook it dry.

'Bit of a bluster out there I can tell you,' he said. The words he spoke were unformed and unfinished. They seemed yawned out rather than spoken and then thrown out from the top of his mouth. He heaved his black cape off his shoulders wincing as he did so, folded it and laid it carefully on the floor. All his movements were painfully slow and stiff. He whistled sharply and Prince left us at once and sat down on the cape, looking from the Birdman to us and back again as if waiting for someone to say something, but no one said a word.

We must have spent a full minute looking at each other. The old man I saw in front of me was not at all as I had expected him to be. All my life I had thought he would have the predatory look of an ancient crow under the shadow of his sou'wester. I could hardly have been more wrong. Only the tired stoop of his body and the loose, mottled skin of his forearm betrayed his age. His face was the colour of a well-worn polished brown boot. The skin was creased but still young and supple – not that you could see much of his face for it was almost entirely hidden by a head and beard of wild white hair. But it was his eyes that marked him out from any other man I had ever seen for they drew you into them somehow so that you could not look away even if you wanted to.

'So, at last we meet,' he said, breaking the long silence. 'I'm glad you came. I was afraid you never would you know. 'Course I could have gone down to the beach I suppose, but then you'd have run away soon as you saw me coming, wouldn't you? Not allowed to get too close to me are you? "Keep your distance" – is that what they told you? I don't blame them. Everyone runs away from me. I'm quite used to it by now; but I didn't want to risk that, not with you. That's why I sent Prince here down to see you and I hoped he would bring you home with him one day, but you never came. I thought of inviting you, of leaving a message in the sand asking you to come and visit; but then I thought that might frighten you away and you'd never come back.'

Still neither Daniel or I spoke. The kittiwake on the table glared evilly at us first with one eye, then the other.

The Birdman shook his head. 'Bit of a mess in here, isn't it?' he said. 'Course if I'd have known you were coming today I'd have tidied the place up a bit. Mother always said there was no one as untidy as I was; but I haven't had anyone up here in this house since she died, and that's nearly thirty years ago now. Nothing much to tidy up for if you never have visitors, is there? I mean they don't mind, do they?' And he laughed, looking around the room at the birds on the shelves. 'The wind blew the door open again by the look of it; ash everywhere. Still, not too much harm done though. One day I'll have to get round to mending the latch on that door. Been meaning to, but there always seems to be something else to be done. Never enough hours in the day.'

He stood looking at us and a smile opened his mouth. He did not have many teeth. 'What a gale that was last night, wasn't it? I can tell you I was lucky. Half-way across to Samson I was when it hit us. Came in faster than I thought it would. Only just made it. The dog came with me of course – always does, don't you boy? He always likes to go over to Samson. Likes the rabbits he does, and there's rabbits everywhere over there, great big black ones. Oh, he loves his rabbits. Course I don't often go out in the boat nowadays, only across to Samson when I have to. I can't pull against the wind like I used to – getting old you know. I spent the night over there like I usually do. Only one cottage left with a roof on it now, not like it used to be I can tell you. Made a fire, kept ourselves warm, didn't we, Prince?'

At the mention of his name, the dog looked up from

cleaning a paw, his wet tail slapping against the wall behind us. 'Then this morning, first light, with the wind around behind us and the worst of the storm blown out I thought we'd try to row back. Thinking about it now, I suppose I should have waited an hour or two but I had the goats to milk, and the hens to feed. Had to get back for them, poor old things. And if I leave Friend alone for too long he goes off all over the island looking for me. All the way up to Shipman's Head he goes – dangerous up there, even for a donkey. So I had to get back. I tell you though, I never had to pull so hard in all my life, did I, Prince? Then this old wrist had to go and give up on me.' He held up his left hand and flexed his gnarled fingers slowly. 'It just seized up, nothing I could do about it. Couldn't hold onto the oar any more, couldn't grip it. Worst of getting old – your body won't do what you tell it any more. It was just off the Point out there. We nearly ended up on the rocks after that, didn't we Prince? I had to paddle my heart out with one oar. Don't know how we managed it, but we did, and the waves brought us nicely into Popplestones. I looked up and there was old Friend himself waiting for me, as if he knew I was going to beach there all the time. So I had a ride home and here I am. And I'll tell you something else for nothing, I wasn't the only thing washed up on Popplestones. I've never seen anything like it. The whole beach is covered with timber, great thick pine planks they are, finest looking timber I've ever seen; and no sign of a wreck that I could see, just the timber.'

'Gracie found the oar,' Daniel said, but the Birdman

did not hear him. He raised his voice a little. 'She found the oar, Mr Woodcock, the one you lost. It's still down there in the dunes; we left it there. We thought you were done for, didn't we, Gracie?'

A sudden troubled look had come over the Birdman. The smile that had lit his face until now trembled and vanished, and he turned away from us while Daniel was still speaking. He lowered himself carefully onto his knees by the fire and began to break up the pile of lightings. Daniel and I exchanged glances. 'That's why we came up here, Mr Woodcock,' Daniel went on, 'to see if you and Prince were all right, because we knew you went off to Samson yesterday. We saw you rowing out there. Then when the storm came last night we thought . . .' The Birdman still had his back to us and seemed intent on lighting his fire. The paper flared and he bent down to blow on it until the flames were shooting up through the lightings into the chimney. He sat back on his haunches and watched it. I nudged Daniel, willing him to go on talking, but he shook his head. I mouthed to him silently, 'The war, tell him about the war.'

Daniel nodded and tried again. By this time the Birdman was sitting on the corner of his bed holding his hands out and rubbing them together in front of the flames. 'Mr Woodcock,' Daniel began, even louder now to be sure he was heard, 'you know we told you what Welly Belly said? You remember he thought there was going to be a war soon? Well they started it, Mr Woodcock, just like he said they would. They started it yesterday. It's all right though. Everyone seems to think we'll win it fairly quickly, but we've got to be on the look-out now for ships and submarines and things just in case we get invaded – that's what my father told me. And we're not allowed to show any lights at night. We have to draw the curtains.'

The Birdman looked up, his face filled with resignation. He put his hands on his knees and pushed himself up until he stood looking down at us again. 'You can talk all you want, Daniel, but I won't hear a word of it, not a word. These old ears of mine don't work like they should, haven't done since I was a boy. Mother always said it was the fever that did it, the fever I caught the day we left Samson. All I remember was the ringing in my ears and the roar of an endless wind blowing through my head. I could hear after the fever went, but the world was always muffled to me after that. As the years passed I heard less and less, and now these last couple of years I can't even hear my gulls. All I can hear is an empty silence. I'm as deaf as my wooden birds over there, Daniel. I can read though – Mother saw to that – but you know that already, don't you? So if you've got something to tell me, you'll have to write it down or draw it. Got plenty of paper – keep it for drawing the birds.' And he reached into the drawer of the little table by his bed and took out a pencil and a sheet of paper and put them down on the table beside us.

'You spell better,' said Daniel, handing me the pencil. 'You tell him.' So I wrote in my best writing: 'They began the war yesterday.' And Daniel turned the piece of paper round so that the Birdman could read it. When he looked up again there was anger in his eyes.

'It's wrong,' he said. 'It's all wrong. All killing is wrong, I tell you; I should know better than anyone. I should know. I should know.' And then as if he had suddenly had enough of us. 'Time you were going. I've got my goats to milk and my hens to feed, and you'd better get back home and quickly. Must have been in the sea some time already that timber, maybe most of the night. Doesn't do it any good to stay in the sea any longer than it's got to you know. So you get back home now and tell them all to get out to Popplestones as quick as they can. There's cartloads of it there, I tell you, 'nough to build ten houses. You'll have to hurry else it'll be too late. Soon as the Preventative hear about it – and they always do – they'll be crawling all over the island. Off with you now.'

We were almost out of the door before he called us back. 'Children,' he said, more gently now. 'That cormorant I gave you must be getting lonely all by himself. I think perhaps you ought to have another one to keep him company – token of your first visit.' And he picked up one of the carvings off the table, brought it up close to his eyes to examine it. It was a crying gull with its wings half-opened and a flatfish on the rock under its feet. 'I don't think I can do much more with this one. Like to take it with you?'

Daniel took it from him with great care and he looked up at the Birdman, pointed at his own lips and mouthed slowly and silently, separating each word, 'It is beautiful, thank you.'

'Thank you,' I said, following Daniel's example. And the Birdman understood and laughed aloud.

'You'll come back and see me tomorrow if you can?' he said. 'Now get along with you and get that timber hidden away before the Preventative find it.'

5 THE PREVENTATIVE

WE HID THE BIRDMAN'S GULL UNDER A PILE OF RAGS on the workbench in Daniel's boatshed – it was the only place we could think of – before running back to the house to break the news about the timber washed up on Popplestones. Within a few minutes the word had spread and every cart and wagon on the island was hitched up and hurrying towards Popplestones. It was only then when I was sitting up beside Mother and Father on the cart that I wondered whether Daniel and I should have gone out to Popplestones first to be sure the Birdman had not been exaggerating, but my first glimpse of the bay was enough to reassure me. I could see the Birdman's little boat hauled up on the dry sand, and from one end of the beach to the other the sand was littered with timber. Some of it had been smashed against the rocks and lay splintered in the water, but most of it was scattered across the beach in untidy piles and was still quite undamaged. In the farthest corner of the bay by the rocks the sea itself was smothered under a heaving, groaning blanket of boards.

Any thoughts of the war were forgotten now in this new heady excitement. No one could remember a harvest such as this, and for us on the island that is exactly what it was. Life there was never easy. We lived only on what we grew, on what we fished out of the sea, on what we made and sometimes by what we found on the beaches. Whatever was washed up by the sea on Bryher was as much ours as the fish we caught or the crops we grew. It was the way we lived, the only way we could live. Just as the seaweed and driftwood belonged to whichever of us were fortunate enough to find it and carry it above the high-water mark, so it was part of the same ancient tradition that anything, any wrecks, any cargo, any trove washed up on our shore belonged to us by right. But every child knew well that the Customs Officers over on St Mary's – the 'Preventative' as we called them – had different ideas and they would do all they could to stop us from keeping such a windfall; and there was nothing that united the islanders so much as the prospect of a visit from the Preventative. Everyone knew that morning on Popplestones that the Preventative would be coming sooner rather than later – they always did.

So all that day we loaded timber onto the carts and wagons, and they went back and forth along the track under Gweal Hill to every farm and every house on the island. Many of the men, Father amongst them, were neck high in the seething sea throwing hooks and anchors over the jammed timbers to pull them apart. Then we would grab them and haul them up out of the sea and onto the dry sand. No one even stopped to eat at mid-day. No one stopped for anything, except for a few of the smaller children who soon tired of the work and set up a see-saw with one of the planks over a rock. No one minded that for they were too little to be of much help and anyway it kept them out of the way. By late afternoon the planks were all gone and only a few of us stayed behind on the beach to tidy up, to remove all traces of the day's work. Using seaweed for brushes we swept the beach from end to end, walking in a line backwards so that we covered our own tracks as we went. We smoothed over all the tell-tale footprints, hoofprints and wheelprints that had criss-crossed the sand. We had not quite finished when the Preventatives' boat was sighted by the look-out on Watch Hill, but by the time their boat reached the quay we were ready for them.

There must have been at least half a dozen Preventatives, all of them dressed in their dark blue uniforms done up to the chin with bright brass buttons. The peaks of their caps rested on their noses so that you could not see their eyes. Most of them I noticed seemed to have long black moustaches, almost as if it was part of the uniform. They spoke to no one, but began by combing the island from Shipman's Head to Rushy Bay; and then, as we knew they would, they visited every house on the island.

We did not have long to wait before our turn came and we saw one of them opening our squeaky front gate and coming up the path. Father met the Preventative officer at the door and I was relieved to see that Father was the taller and broader of the two men. I felt very proud as I always did of Father and very safe under his protection. I could tell from the way Mother's hand was shaking that she did not feel quite so secure. I stayed with her at the sink peeling potatoes as we had planned, and I listened.

'Mr Jenkins, isn't it?' said the Preventative officer.

'That's me,' said my father. 'You looking for something?'

'This is a serious matter, Mr Jenkins, not a matter for levity. It so happens we had a few timbers – nice ones they were too – washed up on the west coast of St Mary's this afternoon, Colombian pine planks. Good sound timber, about fifteen foot long, a foot wide and three inches thick. Seems like they came in from the west during the storm last night. Well they must have done, mustn't they?' I could tell from his voice that he knew we knew, and that he knew we knew he knew. It was a kind of game but a serious one.

'If you say so,' said Father.

'I do, Mr Jenkins, I do. And we think it's likely that more of this timber was washed up on the west coast of Bryher. Stands to reason, doesn't it?'

'Ah well,' said Father, 'I wouldn't know about that. You see I hardly ever go over that side of the island – no one does – dangerous over there you know. Anyway I suppose you've had a good look over there yourselves, haven't you?'

'We have indeed, Mr Jenkins.'

'Find anything did you?'

'No, Mr Jenkins.'

Father shook his head and tutted. 'That's a pity,' he said. 'That's a terrible pity. Still perhaps all there was came up on St Mary's. Perhaps that's all there is.'

'I don't think so, Mr Jenkins, and it's my duty to remind you that any such timber would be the property of the Crown and it would be a felony to remove it or conceal it from the proper authorities. A criminal offence, Mr Jenkins, a criminal offence. And we are the proper authorities.'

'But there isn't any timber, is there? I mean you couldn't very well miss great planks of wood that size, could you?'

'No, Mr Jenkins, you couldn't.' And the Preventative officer straightened his shoulders and stretched himself to his full height before he went on. 'I have to ask you formally, Mr Jenkins, whether you have come across any such timber?'

'I wish I had, and if I had you'd have been the first person I'd tell, you know that. I'm a law-abiding man – we all are on Bryher.'

'Of course, Mr Jenkins, I've never been on an island more law-abiding than this – that's if you can believe what I've been told on every doorstep I've visited. No one I've spoken to has seen anything. But I wonder if your little girl here can help us? Children have such keen eyes, don't they, Mr Jenkins? Perhaps she's seen something you might have overlooked. Come over here little girl, don't be frightened.'

Mother took my shoulders and turned me round to face him. The Preventative was quite portly and almost purple in the face, whether with fury or exertion I was not sure. I was nervous certainly but not frightened, for Father was there behind him smiling over his head at me and I was confident I could play my part in the conspiracy. All I had to do was to keep a straight face and play ignorant. But it was then that I saw the white mess on the top of his cap and the dribble of it running down his left shoulder. One gull at least disliked Preventatives as much as we did. I did try not to laugh, but I did not succeed. A stifled squeak came out rather than a laugh, but it was recognisable as a laugh and quite enough to upset him.

'There something funny, little girl?'

'No, sir,' I said. It was not only the bird-spattered cap that made me quite unable to control myself, it was the thought of those hundreds of pine boards lying hidden under the pathways in the flower pieces and potato fields all over the island. It had been Father's brilliant idea and it must have worked, for otherwise the Preventative would not still be searching. Every sixth row in the daffodil piece was left as a path. It was here, and in between the rows of potatoes that the boards had been laid end to end and covered over. The flower pieces were untended and weed-covered at this time of year so they had even replanted the weeds to make it look right – the first and last time, Mother had said, that she would ever do that.

The Preventative officer's face had gone a deeper shade of purple. 'This is a serious matter,' he said. 'There is nothing funny about this at all.' And with some effort he crouched down in front of me so that our faces were on the same level. He forced his face into a kind of smile; but it looked to me more like a snarl than a smile. 'You can tell me where they've hidden them, can't you, little girl?'

Again my lips would not obey me and I could not hold my laughter back. His face darkened with anger. It was Mother who saved the situation.

'It's your cap,' she said sweetly. The Preventative officer took it off and it was clear he was not at all amused by what he found, but it seemed it was enough to explain away my laughter. Mother tried to make amends by taking it from him and wiping it with a wet cloth. However, the man's dignity had been ruffled and he was not finished with us yet.

'Well if you've nothing to hide, Mr Jenkins, then you won't mind will you if I search the house?' And he took his cap back from Mother and set it firmly over his eyes again.

'What? Search my house for fifteen foot wooden planks?' Father said. 'Where on earth are we going to hide things that size in a little place like this?'

'Oh you'd be surprised, Mr Jenkins,' he said. 'You'd be surprised at the places I've found things, I can tell you. I'll start like I always do, start with the roof and work downwards. Plenty of room under the thatch, I shouldn't wonder.'

'Well you won't find a thing up there,' Father said, 'except perhaps a few dead birds and mice. You'll find mice all right. But you're welcome to look anyway, I've nothing to hide. The trap-door is in my daughter's bedroom, just above her bed. It's the only way into the roof. Nothing to hide, have we, Gracie?' And Father smiled reassuringly at me as he led the man upstairs.

But my laughter had died suddenly inside me. Until they mentioned the roof it had simply never occurred to me the Preventative officer might want to search there. The roof was the only secret place in the house, the only place no one ever looked into, the only place I could hide anything I wanted and be sure it would never be discovered. That was why I had hidden the Birdman's cormorant up there. It had been the perfect place for it, hidden yet available. Every evening before I went to sleep I would climb up onto my bed, lift the trap-door and take it out to look at it and touch it; and whenever Daniel came to the house we would take it down and admire it together in the secrecy of my room.

I could hear them walking now across the bedroom floor above my head. The boards creaked and I knew exactly where they were. 'It's all right, Gracie,' Mother said putting her arm around me. 'He'll soon be gone.' Then I heard the trap door grate as it was lifted off and waited for the cormorant to be discovered. I did not have long to wait.

'Well, and what have we here, Mr Jenkins?' came the Preventative's voice. 'Didn't you say there was nothing up here?'

There was a long, long pause and then father began to speak in a voice so low that I could not hear a word. They talked together for some time up there before I heard the trap-door drop back into place and their heavy tread coming down the stairs. Father came first holding the cormorant in both hands and he was laughing as he came into the room. 'Well, I did say there were only dead birds up there, didn't I? Look what we found, Clemmie,' he said. 'Quite a surprise after all these years, isn't it? It's been lost for so long, we'd almost forgotten we had it. God knows how many years it must have been up there in the roof, and if you hadn't come here today looking for those planks we'd never have found it again. I'm very grateful to you, sir. You haven't seen this before, have you, Gracie? My father, your old grandfather, made this over fifty years ago now. Never thought I'd see it again, never thought I'd see it again. You remember it Clemmie, don't you?' Mother seemed stunned for a moment. All she could manage was a weak smile and a nod, and then I looked away from her for fear of catching her eye.

After that the Preventative made only a half-hearted search under the settle and under the table and then, feeling perhaps that his honour had been sufficiently restored, he left us. Father shut the door after him and turned round to face me. I looked from Mother to Father and back again. Of the two I think Father looked the more angry, but I always feared Mother's silent disapproval more than his roaring anger.

'Well?' he said, holding the cormorant out under my nose. 'And where did you get this from, Grace Jenkins? I want the truth now mind, none of your stories.'

'Daniel and me, we made it,' I said.

'You made this?' Father said, his voice rising to a shout. 'You don't expect me to believe that do you?'

'Honest,' I insisted. 'We did, we did. You can ask Daniel if you like. He'll tell you.'

Mother took the cormorant out of Father's hands and looked at it closely. She handled it gently. 'Gracie,' she said quietly, 'how can you say such a wicked thing? You know Daniel couldn't make this. I know he's clever with his hands but he's not that clever. This is the work of a craftsman, a real craftsman. Daniel couldn't do this.'

'And anyway,' Father went on, 'what was it doing hidden up in the roof? Answer me that if you can, Grace Jenkins.' Father's brow was furrowed and I could see his anger taking hold.

I was crying anyway by now, so the tantrum I threw came easily to me, as did the lie. 'All right then; if you don't believe me, I'll tell you. It was going to be a Christmas present and I hid it up there so you wouldn't find it and so it would be a surprise and I wish I'd never done it now and I never will again and I'll never give you anything else ever again.' I ran crying up the stairs, leaving my mother and father silent in the room behind me.

They left me where I was, sobbing noisily on my bed. Then almost at once I heard the front door open and shut and Father's footsteps going away down the path. From my bed I could see him striding along the escallonia hedge down towards Daniel's boatshed. I buried my head in my pillow again, knowing that this was the end of it all, knowing that I would have to tell them everything now about the Birdman and about Rushy Bay. Once they discovered I was lying I would have no other choice. I could just see the shed door from where I was. I lay there on the bed and waited for Father to come out. When he did, Daniel was with him and Father was carrying the seagull the Birdman had given us in both hands.

'Clemmie isn't going to believe this,' I heard Father say. 'She's not going to believe this when she sees it. Clemmie! Clemmie!' he called and Mother came out of the house and met him half-way down the path. Father held out the seagull and she took it carefully and turned it over and over in her hands. 'He made this too, Clemmie,' Father said. 'Daniel made this one too.'

'You make this yourself, Daniel?' she asked.

Daniel nodded. 'I can't do puffins though,' he said sweetly. 'I keep trying to do a puffin. I started six of them now but I can't ever get them right. Look.' And he held out his half-finished lumpy-looking puffin. He had contrived a look of bemused bewilderment as if he could not understand what all the fuss was about.

'And you made the other one too, Daniel, the cormorant?' Mother asked. I could hear she was still not convinced.

'Well not on my own; Gracie helped me of course,' said Daniel. 'You know, like she helps me with the boats.'

'I should have thought puffins would be easier to carve than cormorants or gulls,' Mother said. 'And who taught you to carve like that anyway?'

'Taught myself,' Daniel said.

'That's just how they are when they've caught a fish and they're trying to keep it for themselves,' said Father stroking the raised wing of the seagull. 'You ever seen anything like this before, Clemmie?' But Mother never answered.

'Can Gracie come out now?' Daniel asked. 'Everyone's going down to the quay to see the Preventatives off.'

'I'll call her,' said Father. 'Gracie,' he shouted up to me. 'Daniel's here.'

I came slowly down the stairs rubbing my eyes, still sniffing as convincingly as I could. Father was waiting for me by the door. He put his arm round me as he led me outside. 'Been a bit of a misunderstanding, Gracie,' he said. 'Perhaps you'd better go and put that cormorant of yours back in the roof. We'll pretend we never saw it, shall we? And we'll have it for Christmas just like you planned. I never would have believed you two could make something like that. Forgive and forget, eh?' And he hugged me tight, and kissed me with his tickling beard that always smelt of smoked fish and pipe tobacco.

All the way down to the quay I never spoke a word to Daniel. I hardly dared look at him, for I knew Mother must still be suspicious and that she would detect any flicker of collusion between us, but I could not resist just one quick glance. Daniel looked back at me po-faced but I recognised the glee in his eyes. He blinked at me once. Daniel always blinked when he meant to wink – he never could shut one eye at a time.

When we reached the quayside the Preventative boat was just weighing anchor and half the island was there to watch them leave empty-handed. We stood in the silent crowd until the boat was well out into the channel, and then a spontaneous cheer of relief and triumph went up and did not stop until we knew they could hear it no longer. I think I must have cheered louder and harder than anyone else there, but then I did have more to cheer about.

6 THE KING'S SHILLING

THE ELATION THAT FOLLOWED THE DISCOVERY OF the timber on Popplestones did not last for very long, for as the months passed the shadow of the war grew ever closer to the islands and began to darken all our lives. Talk of the Front in France soon became as common as talk of pilchards or crayfish, lobster or potatoes, and as important to all of us on the islands as the weather itself.

At home, as the news came in of more ships sunk and more retreats on the battlefields in France, Father became ever more despondent and angry. All the joy and exuberance he breathed into our lives at home vanished during that first year of the war. He rarely smiled even at me and he never set me up on his shoulder as he used to do on the way back home when we had been out fishing together. Indeed he took me out with him less and less now. He said it was too dangerous with the German submarines lurking out there in the Atlantic – and it was true they had been sighted quite close to the islands – but that was not the reason, and I knew it. He just wanted to be on his own. At home in the evenings he would scarcely ever speak to us and when he did he often spoke harshly to Mother. I had never before heard him speak unkindly to her. He would sit in silence by the fire, rolling his pipe in his teeth, staring vacantly into the flames, and the house became a place of gloom around him. Mother tried her best to lift Father's spirits and to placate his rages, but could do neither. No more could I.

It was from Mr Wellbeloved at school that I learnt about what was happening at the battlefronts in France. Frequently now the blackboard at school became the battlefield of the Western Front. I welcomed these extended lectures on the progress of the war because at least it meant we might be missing an arithmetic lesson. Like some omnipotent Greek god, he pushed and wheeled the great armies to and fro across the blackboard, forecasting with great conviction our inevitable and total victory. He told us that even if we were not winning yet we soon would be because God was on our side. Mr Wellbeloved talked with great pride and fervour of the bravery of our little army holding its own against the German hordes sweeping through France. We could help our soldiers, he said, by making blankets and socks for them; and so we did. I remember he wrote out messages of exhortation and stuffed them down the socks we had made before packing them away in boxes to be sent off to the Front. But socks, he said, were not enough. We had to be vigilant, and report at once anything, anything at all that looked suspicious. Invasion, he said, was always possible. We had to be prepared.

Whether it was Mr Wellbeloved's words that inspired the war games, I am not sure; but I do know that it was Big Tim who organised them up on Watch Hill. With rifles and bayonets whittled from driftwood, the two armies, one British and one German, would be drawn up opposite each other on either side of the hill. Big Tim would blow a blast on the battered bugle his uncle had brought back from the Boer War, and that was the signal that would send the two armies screaming towards each other over the heather. The battle that followed was always swift and the outcome always the same – after all it was Big Tim that picked the sides and he made quite sure the British always won. Either the Germans would run away or they would fall, dying noisily on the spongy grass around the rabbit warren at the bottom of the hill; and Big Tim, dressed in his uncle's pith helmet and waving the union jack, could always be seen standing triumphant on the battlefield at the end of the day.

Of course they tried to make us join in, but we had no wish to be cannon fodder in Big Tim's war games and besides we were always far too busy building our boats and sailing them – that was what we told everyone and they had no reason to doubt us. In fact, of course, we slipped away as often as we dared to the Birdman's cottage on Heathy Hill.

For Daniel and me his cottage became a second home

during the first year of the war. I was happy enough frolicking with Prince along the sand on Rushy Bay, or kneading the Birdman's dough for him in the wet weather when his fingers were too stiff and painful. The Birdman never asked for help. He was just the kind of person you wanted to help. I suppose that was why I offered to milk his goats for him. It looked simple enough, and I had milked a cow before after all. A goat was smaller than a cow, so it had to be an easier job I thought. I was wrong, very wrong. Goats know. They know everything. You can see in their eyes they know everything. They knew I was clumsy and inept and they made it as difficult as possible for me. One of them, Bertha it was, always walked away whilst I was milking her; and Betsy would turn around and chew my hair, pulling at it until I had to stop milking her because it hurt me so much. Only then would she let go. I was determined to master the Birdman's goats; but they knew that too and so I never did. All summer I tried. I tried gentle persuasion, I tried bribery, but milking always became a trial of will and strength which I invariably lost.

Sometimes Daniel would come with Prince and me down to Rushy Bay and we would sail our boats together as we had always done, but more often than not now he would stay inside the cottage with the Birdman and work on his carving all day long. I would leave them sitting side by side at the long table, chiselling away at an unpromising block of driftwood only to return some hours later and find the beginnings of a gannet or a plover or an oystercatcher hatching out of the wood. To me it was always a miraculous metamorphosis. They worked together with great concentration, even urgency, for Daniel was ever eager to practise and to learn, and the Birdman seemed equally anxious to teach him. I remember him saying once: 'I want to pass on all my father taught me whilst my fingers still obey me, and they won't for much longer.' The more Daniel improved the more he seemed to enjoy it and the more time he would spend carving with the Birdman. As they worked the Birdman would talk and talk. He was making up, he said, for all the years he had only had the birds, the animals and himself to talk to.

I myself was never comfortable talking to the Birdman in those early days for he would stare uncannily at me whilst I was speaking, trying to read the words as they came out of my mouth. So I would resort almost immediately to pencil and paper, partly to avoid those piercing eyes of his. Daniel never did that. Right from the very start he mouthed the words, contorting his lips into extravagant shapes. He made letters out of his fingers and spelled out the words. He drew shapes in the air; indeed sometimes he did all three at once and talked aloud at the same time. If at first the Birdman could not understand – and he often did not – then Daniel would persist resolutely until he did. Sometimes this might entail acting out a complex charade, and both of them would end up helpless with laughter at his antics and the misunderstandings they created.

It took some time and it was gradual, but Daniel invented that year a whole new private language of signs, pictures and signals that the Birdman could recognise and understand immediately, so much so that I sometimes found the Birdman could understand what Daniel was saying now before I could. I remember that at one time I began to feel a little excluded, even hurt by this; but the Birdman seemed to sense my unease and took great delight in teaching me the new sign language he was learning. We became so used to using the new language that in time Daniel and I could talk to each other without uttering a word, and we would use it at home now instead of whispering whenever anyone else might be about and we wanted to talk about the Birdman or Rushy Bay. In time though the Birdman learnt how to read our lips well enough to understand most of what we said. We had to speak slowly of course and make sure he was looking at us before we began. We still used our secret language, but he needed it less and less as the months passed.

We found out early on that there were some things you just did not talk about to the Birdman. Any mention of the war for instance, any talk of the latest outrage or offensive Mr Wellbeloved might have told us about, and he would simply turn his back and walk away. It seemed to plunge him into a deep despair and so we learned never to talk of it. Neither, we discovered, would he ever talk about himself. If we asked him about his mother or his father he would just turn his head away and pretend he could not hear us.

Then one day Daniel asked him about Samson. 'It's not really true there's ghosts on Samson, is it, Mr Woodcock?' The Birdman stared at him. 'You know,' Daniel said and he put a blanket over his head and drifted around the room arms outstretched, his muffled moanings and groaning interspersed with giggles. 'Like this, Mr Woodcock. Ghosts. Gracie believes in them, but they're not true are they, not really?' It was the only time I'd ever seen the Birdman angry. Terrified at this sudden fury, I backed away until I felt the wall behind me and could go no further. He advanced on Daniel, pulled off the blanket, took him roughly by the shoulders and shook him.

'Ghosts!' he cried. 'Ghosts! Do you know what a ghost is? Well I'll tell you. A ghost is a soul so darkened with shame and sin that it can never rest. It is a spirit condemned to wander the earth until the end of time. Yes, there are ghosts on Samson. You cannot see them, you cannot hear them, but I know they are there. They are all there, all the guilty men of Samson, my father with them.' His voice was full of anguish as he went on. 'His spirit is still there on Samson. They all are and they always will be unless the curse of Samson can be lifted, unless I can save them. Until then that place is cursed, so keep away from it. Stay away both of you.' After that I never dared mention Samson again, and nor did Daniel.

For fear of discovery we could not spend as much time as we would have liked with the Birdman. We knew it strengthened our alibi if we were seen from time to time to be sailing our boats on the pool under Gweal Hill; and now the swans had finally left we could do that again. In Daniel's boatshed that first spring of the war I busied myself repairing and repainting our fleet of boats whilst Daniel worked tirelessly on yet another puffin carving.

This was the seventh; he had rejected all the others. It would be finished, he said, only when it was perfect, quite, quite perfect. Each of them seemed to me to be more puffin-like than the one before and I would have been proud to have made any of them, but he was never satisfied. He made endless puffin sketches and pinned them to the table in the shed just as the Birdman had taught him he should.

It was while we were working side by side in the boatshed one drizzling May morning that we heard a distant dull boom. We took very little notice of it at the time. We thought that perhaps one of the Navy ships might be firing a practice salvo out to sea – we had heard them often enough before – and we had seen several grey warships cruising in and out of the islands of late, their turrets bristling with guns. Not until Father brought back the news the next day was I to find out what it was.

He had been off to St Mary's that morning to sell our catch of lobsters and crayfish as he always did on Wednesdays providing the sea was calm enough. Mother and I were down on the rocks fishing for wrasse when we saw him bringing the boat in over the sandbars towards the quay. We watched him throw out the anchor and leap down into the shallows. We could see as he came along the beach towards us that a change had come over him. He walked briskly over the sand, jumping from stone to stone and hurdling the ropes and anchor chains as he came. I could feel Mother's arm come around me, and I knew she was bracing herself for something, but I had no idea what it might be.

'Clemmie,' he called as soon as he was within ear-shot. 'Clemmie, I've done it and I feel ten years younger for it. Should have done it long ago.' He was smiling now as he used to and I wondered why it was that Mother was looking away from him as if she did not want to hear what he was about to tell her. 'You remember that explosion we heard yesterday morning? Well, they sank another freighter, Clemmie,' Father went on, 'not five miles from here it was. Submarine again. Just waiting out there they were, and they picked her off and sent her to the bottom. All good men, all gone. They told me all about it over on St Mary's as soon as I arrived this morning. I saw for myself a couple of lads laid out there on the beach. Washed up on the tide this morning they were. They were young lads, both of them, barely out of school, half my age, Clemmie. Well that was it, that was enough. I decided there and then I wasn't going to stand by any more and just watch. It isn't right, Clemmie, you know it isn't. They need sailors and I'm a good one, better than most. We Scillonians are the best navigators in the world; we have to be, don't we? So anyway, I went and signed the papers, Clemmie. There's a dozen or more joining up from all over the islands, but I'll be the first from Bryher. It's all done. I joined the Navy. I've taken the King's Shilling.'*

Mother's arm tightened around my shoulder and I looked up at her. She was smiling at him. 'I'm not going to argue with you,' she said. 'You wouldn't listen to me

* To 'take the King's Shilling' is to join up. In fact, volunteers received a day's pay when they joined up, which was about a shilling.

anyway, would you? I knew you'd be going sooner or later, I knew it had to come.'

'You won't go short, Clemmie,' said Father. 'I've worked it all out. I'll be sending money home all the time. Pay's not bad you know, one and a penny a day. You and Gracie won't even need to work the flowers and potatoes if you don't want to. There'll be enough for the both of you, don't you worry.'

'I'm not worried about that. I'm not worried about the money,' said Mother. 'Gracie and me can manage till you get back, can't we, Gracie? We'll see to the flowers and potatoes; might even catch a few lobsters, you never know. It's not just men that can catch lobsters you know. No, it's you I'm worried about.'

'Me?' said Father. 'Stuff and nonsense.' And he picked me up and set me high on his shoulders. 'Getting heavier by the day, Gracie,' he said as I put my arms around his neck. 'You used to hang on to my beard when you were smaller, remember? It's a wonder I've got any left.' And we walked back up to the house, happy together for the first time in months. 'Don't you worry about anything, Clemmie,' he said. 'I'll be back before you know it. Won't take long this war, not now I'm in it.'

'No dear,' said Mother. 'Not now you're in it.' And she put her arm around him and laid her head on his shoulder.

'When will you be going to the war, Father?' I asked from high above them.

'Soon,' he said.

And it was soon, all too soon. Only a week later

Mother and I were standing on the quayside at St Mary's and Father was hugging me to him. He looked so fine and grand in his blue uniform. Maybe it was my pride in him that stopped me crying like everyone else seemed to be. I tugged his beard when I kissed him goodbye and he laughed and then whispered, 'Take care of your mother for me, Gracie.' I remember thinking that was all the wrong way round, for Mother had always been the one to take care of me. And then he laid a hand on Mother's arm, brushed her cheek gently and said, 'Bye, Clemmie. Chin up.' And he was gone, up the gangplank and into the ship.

We waited until the ship was so far out that we could no longer distinguish him from the others waving beside him on the deck. 'At least he's his old self again,' said Mother, taking my hand and leading me away. 'At least he's happy now.'

'They won't sink his ship, will they?' I asked Mother on the way back across the water to Bryher.

'Course not, Gracie, don't even speak of it. He'll be back, you'll see.'

I told the Birdman the next day that my father had gone to be a sailor in the war and he smiled sadly and put his hand on my head. 'Daniel and me will look after you,' he said. 'We'll look after you and your mother, won't we, Daniel? I'll be your father till he gets back home again; how would that be?'

'That'll be fine,' I said. 'Just till he gets back though.'

7 SAMSON

NOTHING WAS EVER TO BE THE SAME AGAIN AFTER Father left. I basked briefly in the reflected glory of a father away fighting in the war, but the void he left behind him grew wider and deeper as time passed. The glory soon faded as it always does, and when other fathers went off to the war I found I was no longer even very special.

At first we did manage well enough on our own, Mother and I. She insisted everything had to go on just as before. 'One day soon,' she told me, 'any day now, your father will come in through that gate and up the path and I want him to find everything just as he left it. Meanwhile we have to live, don't we?'

So to that end she toiled all day and every day working up the fields and planting, bringing in the seaweed to dress the flower pieces and often going out lobster fishing alone in the boat whilst I was at school. I begged to be allowed to stay away from school to help, but perhaps she suspected my reasons were not entirely unselfish for she would never hear of it. She sent me off to school every day that summer. So I had to endure Mr Well-beloved whether I liked it or not, and I left Mother behind to do both her work in the house and Father's work outside all on her own.

There was less time than ever now to go visiting the Birdman and Prince and no time at all to sail our boats on the pond. The boats gathered dust and cobwebs in the back of Daniel's boatshed, and when Daniel was not helping us out in the fields – and he often did – he went by himself to the cottage on Heathy Hill. I tried to console myself with the thought that at least I would not have to milk those horrible goats, but there was little enough comfort in that. I missed Prince and I missed the Birdman. Each time I saw Daniel go off alone I longed to go with him, but I knew I could not. My place was at home now alongside Mother, so I stayed behind.

As summer passed into autumn Mother became ill. The long hours of work in the fields and out in the boat were taking their toll of her strength and her cough settled on her chest and forced her to stay indoors in the warm. I could see her back was troubling her as well. She found it difficult even to let herself down into her chair at the end of the day. She tried to disguise it from me of course, but she could not. Only Father's letters, infrequent and brief as they always were, seemed to brighten her life and keep her from despair. She would read them aloud to me over and over again and then put them up on the mantleshelf over the stove beside the Birdman's cormorant I had given them for Christmas. I often noticed that she would look up at them during the long dark evenings as if she were trying to draw strength from them.

It was on those rare happy days when Mother had just received a letter and when all the work was done that I felt I could leave her and go up to the Birdman's cottage with Daniel like we used to. Whenever I went there now the Birdman would greet me like a long lost friend, sitting me down on the edge of his bed by the fire and feeding me a great feast, a cup of warm goat's milk and all the bread and honey I could eat – and I could eat plenty. Every mouthful seemed to give him as much pleasure as it gave me, if that were possible. He would sit opposite me in his chair nodding and smiling until I had finished every last crumb. I remember that kittiwake on his shoulder watching me enviously with his beady sideways eye. I did not care for that bird and I could tell from the way he looked at me that the feeling was mutual. I would suck the honey deliberately noisily off my fingers so that the kittiwake would know what he was missing.

The Birdman was as good as his word. He was indeed a father to me, looking after Mother and me like some anonymous guardian angel. Often, first thing in the morning when Mother went down to open the door, she would find a loaf of bread on the doorstep, or perhaps some eggs or potatoes or milk, and occasionally a huge jar of honey. 'Manna from Heaven,' she would say, dipping her little finger into the jar and licking it. 'Manna from

Heaven. People are so kind. But we can't live on charity, Gracie. Your father wouldn't like that, wouldn't be fitting.' I longed to tell Mother who our benefactor was, but I dared not for fear she would forbid me from ever going to see him again.

I often tried to thank the Birdman for his kindness, but either he pretended not to understand or he seemed to sense what I was about to say and would turn away and ignore me. In the end I had to write it down on paper for him and make him read it.

'Thanks for the honey,' I wrote in big letters, and drew a swarm of bees over the top.

He smiled at me. 'Thank the bees,' he said.

'Thanks for the eggs.'

'Thank the hens,' he replied.

'Thanks for the milk.'

'Thank Betsy and Bertha,' he replied. And I made a face at that and held my nose.

'Thanks for the bread,' I wrote.

'Thank God for that,' he said.

Daniel would bring us back the occasional fish he had caught off the rocks at Droppy Nose Point, so thanks to the two of them we never went hungry, Mother and I. But winter was coming on and Mother was worried; and it was not just about whether we would have enough food to last. 'It's the money, Gracie,' she confessed to me one night, lying beside me in bed – we had taken to sleeping in the same bed since Father left. 'Your father sends me all he can, but one pound and ten pence a month just isn't enough. I had to buy in seed potatoes and bulbs this year, and then there were those repairs to the boat. I've got to keep the boat going, Gracie, for your father when he gets back. And the lobster catch was poor for everyone this year. The few I did manage to catch no one wanted to buy. There's no market for them now. It's the war I suppose. Oh, Gracie, how I hate this war for what it's doing to us all. And then there's still the rent to pay. I could manage if only I was strong enough to go out and do a bit of fishing. A few good catches a month and a bit of luck and I could sell enough fish to bring in enough money to keep us going.'

'I could do it, Mother,' I said sitting up beside her. 'I could go fishing, course I could. Daniel would go with me, Mother. We'll take Father's boat out and we'll bring back all the fish you need. I've done it with Father often enough, haven't I? I know where to go. And Daniel can handle a boat as well as anyone; you know he can, Mother.'

'No, I can't let you,' Mother said. 'And Daniel's too young anyway. You're both too young to go out fishing alone. We'll manage, I expect. We'll be all right. When I get stronger, Gracie, we'll go out together.'

'Please, Mother.'

'No, Gracie,' she said. 'It's out of the question. It's October already. Summer time it would be different perhaps, but if you get out there this time of the year, and the wind gets up you'd not come back. We'd lose you and the boat and then what would I tell your father when he comes back home? No, you're not to do it, Gracie. You hear me? It's too dangerous.' But I knew there was no other way to find the money she needed, and I knew Daniel would need little persuasion.

The next evening, a still overcast evening with the sea the same soft grey as the sky, Daniel and I took out one of his father's boats. It was smaller than ours, a fourteen foot lugger that Daniel thought we could handle more easily. We said nothing and told no one for we knew they would forbid it. We waited until the beach was deserted and slid the boat out gently into the water. We set sail as soon as we were round the point and out of sight of the houses, and then made out past Samson round Droppy Nose Point towards Scilly Rock. 'Best place for pilchards,' Daniel said. 'Father always says so. We'll be back before dark and no one will ever know we've gone. You can always tell your mother I caught them off the rocks, can't you?'

So we baited our hooks, let down the lines and within half an hour we had caught more fish than we had ever dreamed of. Two dozen pilchard or more and one large bass. We were fishing midway between Gweal and Scilly Rock. Perhaps it was the one big bass that tempted us to stay just a little longer to see if we could catch another even bigger. Whatever it was, we were so intent on our fishing that we never even noticed the weather coming in behind us. We were fishing with our backs to Scilly Rock and the open sea. The boat lolled beneath us, lapped by a listless sea. I had just hooked my biggest pilchard when I noticed a wisp of mist above our heads. I looked around over my shoulder. Scilly Rock had vanished as had the sky and the sea as well. A grey wall of fog was rolling in towards us over the sea. There was nothing we could do, for it was already too late to do anything. It was over us and all around us before Daniel could even haul up his line. Gweal and Bryher beyond it were not there any more and we were left alone and lost on a silent sea. What little breeze there was had gone and we found ourselves quite becalmed. I remember we spoke in a whisper, as if the fog were a living creature that might be listening to us. I was not too worried though, not at first, for the sea slapped so softly against the sides of the boat and seemed to hold no threat for us. Besides, I had Daniel with me. Both of us had been out in fog before, and both of us thought we knew the waters around Bryher quite well enough to get home.

'As long as we keep Scilly Rock astern of us we can pull home easily enough,' Daniel said softly.

'But how are we going to do that if we can't see it?' I whispered, taking the oar he was handing me. 'I can't see it any more.'

'We can hear it though, can't we?' he said. 'Listen.' And certainly I could hear the surge of the sea seething around Scilly Rock as it always did even on the calmest of days. 'Hear it?' he said. 'Just keep that sound astern of us and we'll be able to feel our way home. Gweal must be dead ahead from here. There's no swell to speak of, so we won't go on the rocks. All we have to do is to hug the coast all the way round and that'll bring us nicely into Popplestones.'

And so we began to row, only a few strokes at a time, stopping to listen for the sea around Scilly Rock. It was not long though before I began to think that Gweal was not at all where it should have been. We had already been rowing quite long enough and hard enough to have reached it by now. Then I thought that perhaps the current must have dragged us off course, that we must be somewhere between Samson and Bryher, that I could still hear Scilly Rock somewhere astern of us and distant, but Daniel was no longer even sure of that. We pulled until our arms could pull no longer, but still no land loomed up out of the fog as we expected. Within half an hour we had to admit to each other that we were quite lost. We sat over our oars and drifted, straining our ears for the wash of the sea against the rocks, anything to give us some idea of where we were. The fog though seemed to obscure and shroud the sounds of the sea just as it was hiding the islands that we knew lay all around us. Even the piping of invisible oystercatchers was dulled and deadened as the dark came down through the fog and settled around us.

Strange as it may seem, the darkness came as a kind of comfort to us, for at least it was the kind of blindness we were accustomed to. Even Daniel who was never fond of the dark seemed relieved at the onset of night. We searched now for some crack in the blackness about us, a glimmer of a light from the shore that would guide us safely home. We sat beside each other huddled together and silent, the damp jibsail wrapped around us to keep out the cold, peering constantly into the impenetrable night and listening, always listening for the hiss of surf on the shingle or the distant muted charge of the waves against the cliffs.

Often during that long, long night our hopes were raised by the whisper of waves on some far shore, and we would row frantically towards it for a few minutes and then sit silent and listen again, only to discover it had been nothing but wishful thinking, a trick of the mind. Either it was that or we had simply been rowing the wrong way – we could never be sure which. In this dense darkness all sense of direction, time and space seemed to be distorted. Each time our hopes were raised only to be dashed, and each time the disappointment was all the more cruel and all the more lasting.

The cold had numbed my feet up to my knees and my hands could no longer feel the oar I was pulling. I wanted so much just to go to sleep, to give up and go to sleep. But Daniel would not let me.

'Got to keep moving, Gracie,' he said. 'We don't know where we are, do we? We only know that we're cold and that we're going to get colder if we just sit here, so we're going to row. We're going to row till we warm up and then we'll rest and then we'll row again. We might be rowing out to sea but at least we'll keep warm. We can't just sit here.' And so we did, Daniel calling out the rhythm to keep us together.

I discovered that night that you can sing almost everything there is to sing to the rhythm of the oars, that is if you change the rhythm of the song. We were half-way through 'Ten Green Bottles' for the second time when I saw the light and stopped rowing. It was a flickering prick of light, the kind you see when you close your eyes tight shut and look into the back of your eyelids. I did not believe it at first for I did not want to be disappointed again, but when Daniel saw it too, I knew my eyes were not deceiving me. Then at last we heard the welcome sound of the sea running back over the sand.

The boat beached even before we saw the shore, the bottom grating and growling to an abrupt halt in the surf. We jumped out and pulled her out as high as we could on the next wave and then dropped the anchor into the sand. Both of us believed that we were on Popplestones until we discovered there were no pebbles above the line of sand as there should have been. We found instead we were climbing in amongst dunes. Then hand in hand we were stumbling up through dead bracken and heather towards the light that shone in the sky ahead of us like some glowing orange moon as we approached it. Daniel stopped often to call out, 'Is there anyone there? Anyone there?' But his voice was deadened by the fog-black night, any echo stifled. I heard only one reply, the single bark of a dog somewhere far away in the darkness.

'Prince?' I called out. 'Is that you, Prince?'

'You're imagining things,' Daniel said. 'It was nothing, I never heard anything. Come on, let's get up to that light.'

It was a long, painful climb. The sharp heather tore at my legs as I followed Daniel up the hillside. The dark shape of a cottage grew out of the gloom and we ran towards it; but there was no door, no windows and no roof. Just an empty shell was left, the walls, a fireplace at each end and the window-ledges. Through one of the windows I could see the light flaring high above us. As we came out of the cottage and turned towards the light, our footsteps were suddenly loud in the night, crunching over what we found to be a mound of limpet shells. I thought at first that what I was hearing must be the freak echo of the crackling of the shells under our feet, but then I smelt the smoke and I saw the first lick of orange flame flickering up into the blackness. Our light had become a great spitting beacon of fire and we ran towards it, caring no longer now for our sore legs, and calling, calling to whoever was up there. But no one was. The fire was a towering teepee of flame that was gradually falling in on itself as we watched. The heat from it sent shivers of welcome warmth through our cold aching bodies and we jumped up and down in the light of it and laughed aloud with joy and relief.

It was some time before we had warmed up enough to collect our thoughts and begin to worry again. We were sitting cross-legged up-wind of the fire, revelling in its heat when Daniel said, 'Gracie, I don't think we're on Bryher. I mean, d'you know any cottage on Bryher like that one we saw down there, that one without the roof? You seen one like that on Bryher?'

'P'raps we're on Tresco then,' I said.

'Gracie,' Daniel went on, breaking a stick and throwing it onto the fire, 'there's only one island where there's houses like that. Samson, Gracie. I think we've landed on Samson.'

Until then I hadn't given a thought as to where we might have landed. I had not cared. I was happy just to be safe, alive and warm again. 'It can't be,' I said, moving nearer to him; and as I looked around me, the darkness seemed to close in on us. 'You sure?' I whispered.

'I'm sure,' he said.

8 CASTAWAYS

THE FIRE WAS OUR ONLY COMFORT THROUGHOUT the long and dreadful hours of the night. Each new settling of the burning embers sent an explosion of sparks high into the sky until all that was left was a perfect circle of glowing embers. Only fear kept us awake, fear of the unknown out there in the dark around us, and fear that one of us might fall asleep and leave the other to face the night alone. Every rustle behind us in the heather, the sudden squawking of a disturbed gull, even the soft groaning of a seal in the bay somewhere below us kept us both taut with terror. We talked all night long, as much as anything to keep out the noises of the night around us. I sought endless reassurances from Daniel and he did indeed seem to have an answer for everything. It was just that sometimes I found it difficult to believe him.

'You think the Birdman's here then?' I asked. 'How do you know it was him that lit the fire?'

'Well, he's the only one who ever comes to Samson, isn't he?' Daniel replied. 'And someone built this fire, didn't they? It has to be him, stands to reason. And remember you were the one that said you heard Prince barking just after we landed. They're here somewhere, got to be. Soon as it's light, we'll find the house he stays in – the only house on the island with its roof on still – that's what he told us, remember? All we've got to do is find it and he'll be there. He can't leave the island in this fog any more than we can, can he? Don't worry, Gracie.'

'But I still don't see why he lit this fire,' I went on. 'Not unless he's signalling to someone out at sea. P'raps that's it, Daniel. P'raps that's what he's up to. He could be, couldn't he, Daniel? I mean that's what those smugglers and wreckers used to do in the old days, isn't it? That's what I heard.'

'A smuggler?' Daniel laughed. 'The Birdman a smuggler? Don't be silly.'

'Could be,' I said. 'Why not?'

'Gracie,' Daniel said. 'If you were a smuggler and you were signalling to a ship out there, would you do it in thick fog?'

'All right then,' I went on. 'If you know so much then, you tell me why he's gone and built a fire in the middle of nowhere?'

'Who knows?' Daniel shrugged his shoulders. 'P'raps he's frightened of the dark. I know that's what I'd do if I found myself alone here in the middle of the night.

Anyway, it's his island, isn't it? I mean he lived here, didn't he? He can do what he likes. He can build fires anywhere he likes. You still don't trust him, do you, Gracie? Not after all he's done for us, you still don't trust him.'

'And what if he isn't here at all?' I said. 'What if we don't find him in the morning? I mean you'd think Prince would have heard us by now and come and found us, wouldn't you?'

'He's here, Gracie, honest he is. You'll see.'

'But what if those stories are true?' I said, lowering my voice to a whisper. 'What if all Father told me is really true and Samson does have a curse on it, like Charlie Webber told him. What's going to happen to us then? You've only got to set foot on the island and you'll be cursed for ever. That's what he said. That's what hapened to Charlie Webber.'

'Tommyrot,' said Daniel. 'It's all tommyrot. Everyone knows it's just stories.'

'Then why doesn't anyone else ever land on Samson if it's all stories?'

'They're just scared, that's all,' Daniel said. 'Just scared.'

'Well so am I,' I said. 'It's this place, Daniel, it doesn't feel right. And it's not just the dark either. I'm not the one who's scared of the dark, am I? There's ghosts here, Daniel. I can feel them all around us. The Birdman told us, didn't he? And one of them's his own father. That's what he said, didn't he?'

'Just imagining things I expect,' said Daniel. 'I mean if

you were alone on this island for long you'd begin to imagine things wouldn't you? And after all he is old, isn't he? Anyway he never said he'd *seen* a ghost, did he?'

'No, but . . .'

'Well then,' Daniel said. 'Listen, Gracie, you ever seen a ghost? Have you?'

'No.'

'So if you've never seen one, how do you know they exist? You don't, do you?'

'P'raps not, but . . .'

'Well then, if you've never seen them and you don't believe they exist, you know he was just imagining things. Must have been, mustn't he? And all those stories your father told you about curses and houses burning down and the scarlet fever, they're just stories, Gracie. I mean everyone thinks the Birdman's mad, don't they?'

'Yes.'

'Well, is he?'

'No.'

'And Big Tim said you'd catch his madness if you touched him. Well you've touched him, haven't you, and have you gone mad?'

'No.'

'Well then. Stands to reason, it's all just stories like I said. I mean, you can't believe in anything you can't see, can you? Well can you?'

'Anyway p'raps we've got nothing to worry about,' I said. 'P'raps we're not on Samson at all.' But I knew full well we were. I could feel it. I could feel the ghosts watching us. They were out there in the darkness. I knew they were. I huddled closer to the fire hugging my knees, and prayed and prayed.

It seemed that on Samson it was the terns that decided when morning should come. It was they who announced the dawn even while it was still dark, filling the air with their raucous racket. If other birds joined in, we did not hear them. Terns ruled on this island, and the night knew it of old and left us swiftly. We had hoped that the fog might be gone by daybreak so that we could get back home, but there was no wind to blow it away and we knew well enough that autumn fog could hang about for days at a time over the islands, particularly over Samson. But it was not as thick as it had been the evening before. At least now we could see quite clearly for ten paces or so ahead of us. The terns flew shrieking in and out of the fog above our heads, fleeting pale grey shapes that seemed startled and angry to find us there; and once they found us out they never left us alone diving out of the fog at us until they drove us away from our dwindling fire. Neither of us wanted to leave it and face the dank cold of the island and I more than Daniel dreaded our meeting with the Birdman. I knew how angry he would be to find us on Samson. I was for getting back to the boat at once and making for Bryher and home, whatever the weather.

'It'll be easy enough now we know where we are, won't it?' I said. 'After all, it's only a narrow channel between Samson and Bryher.'

'Gracie,' Daniel said. 'If we get out in that fog again it'll be like yesterday all over again. You think you know where you are but you don't. We can't go, not yet. Father would kill me if I wrecked his boat. I'd prefer to face the Birdman, even if he is cross with us. But he won't be. I know him. We'll tell him we couldn't help it. And we couldn't, could we? After all, we didn't mean to land on Samson, did we? It's not as if we were snooping or anything, is it? It just happened; he'll understand. Come on, let's find him. Let's find that cottage, he's bound to be there.' Daniel was adamant. There was nothing I could do when Daniel was adamant and I knew it.

We began by whistling for Prince, hoping his bark might lead us to them and save us the trouble of searching the entire island, but only the terns replied. We tried calling, hands cupped to our mouths, but there was no answering bark. So we started to search. We followed the hill upwards from the fire and searched the higher ground first, for the fog seemed to be less thick up there. Every cottage we came to we found deserted and roofless. Fog curled out of gaping windows and doors so that each one looked like some ghostly apparition. They were elongated human faces that breathed out smoke from staring eyes and gruesome grinning mouths. I refused to go inside any of them. I would wait outside on the huge mounds of limpet shells that we found outside each cottage, while Daniel went in on his own to see if the Birdman was there, but he never was. All he ever found were a few rusting kettles and pots, a pair of shoes white with mould and some broken clay pipes. Of the Birdman and Prince there was no trace.

Every ruined cottage we came across gave me fresh

hope, hope that we might not be on Samson after all. If it was Samson, then there had to be a cottage with its roof still on – the Birdman had said as much – and we had not found one. So when Daniel emerged from yet another crumbling cottage saying he was sure we must have searched every cottage on the island by now, I spoke out. 'Then p'raps you're wrong,' I said. 'P'raps this isn't Samson at all. Could be it's St Martin's or St Agnes for all you know.' But Daniel answered me by pointing over my shoulder into the fog behind us.

I turned round and there not more than twenty paces away over the bracken I could just make out the outline of a cottage, a cottage with a roof and two chimneys. 'That's it,' Daniel said. 'That's his. That's the Birdman's cottage. Don't know how we missed it before.' And he ran past me and into the bracken, fighting his way through until he reached the cottage and threw open the door. 'Prince!' he called out. 'Prince!' I stayed where I was, and not just because I was fearful of the Birdman's anger. I was seized with a sudden terrible foreboding. My last vestige of hope had been wrenched from me. We were on Samson. There could be no possible doubt about that, not now. I was cold and tired but the shudder that went through me had nothing to do with that. It was as if some cold hand had touched me and left its curse on me. I could hear Daniel walking about inside the cottage. No Prince ran out to greet me, nor were there any gulls lined up along the roof as there most certainly would have been had the Birdman been there.

'He's not here,' Daniel said from the doorway. 'There's

no one here. He's been here, though. The ashes in the fireplace are still warm and I can smell Prince. And there's something else here, Gracie. Come and look, quick,' he said, and he went inside again. I hesitated. 'Come on, Gracie,' he called out. 'Come on.'

Inside, the cottage looked almost the same as the Birdman's cottage on Heathy Hill. There was one long table, a fire at one end and a stove at the other; but here there were two beds, in opposite corners of the room. One bed was unmade and the mattress rolled up, and on the other the blankets were thrown back against the wall. There were shelves all around the room, but they were empty. 'Look,' Daniel said, pointing to the mantelshelf above the fireplace.

It rested above the mantelshelf on wooden supports. At first glance I thought it was a lance or a spear of some kind. Thick as the handle of an axe at one end, it spiralled towards a sharp point at the other. It reached across the entire width of the cottage, overlapping the mantelshelf at each end. As I came closer it seemed to me to have been carved from a paler wood than the carvings back in the Birdman's cottage on Bryher. The surface gleamed in the cold light as if it had been varnished. 'What is it?' I asked.

Daniel reached up and touched it gently, almost tentatively. Then he ran his fingers along the horn from end to end. He did not turn round. 'Come and feel it, Gracie,' he said.

I knew as I touched it that it was not made of wood – it was too smooth and too cold. We looked at each other. 'That's real bone isn't it?' I said. And suddenly I saw what it was. 'It's off a unicorn. It's off a real unicorn.'

'Couldn't be,' Daniel scoffed. 'Couldn't be off a unicorn. There's no such thing.'

'Then what else could it come from if it isn't a unicorn?' I asked.

'Well I don't know, do I?' said Daniel, and he reached up again and tried to lift it off the supports. He could hardly move it. 'But I can tell you one thing for sure, Gracie, it's not off a unicorn. Too big for a start. Only place you'll see a unicorn is in pictures and storybooks, and I've never seen one big enough to have a horn this size. And don't tell me it's off a giant unicorn 'cos I don't believe in giants any more than I believe in unicorns. The Birdman will know. He'll tell us what it came from.'

'Where is he?' I said. 'He's not here, is he? He's not on the island.'

'Doesn't look like it,' Daniel said, still preoccupied with the horn.

'Then who lit the fire?' I asked. But he did not answer.

He turned to face me. 'I'm thirsty,' he said suddenly. 'You thirsty? People lived on this island once,' Daniel said, 'so there's got to be water hasn't there? Must be a well somewhere; only got to find it. Come on, Gracie.' And he walked out of the cottage, not even looking behind him to see if I was following. I took a last look behind me at the horn above the fireplace and ran out after him.

We searched all over the hillside around the cottage but could find no well; so we were forced to look further afield. The longer we looked, the more thirsty we became. There was no talk any more of curses or ghosts or unicorns. We argued only over where it might be best to look next, for we were now craving for water and could think of nothing else. We must have trudged the length and breadth of that island several times that morning. From the top of the hills where the fog was beginning to clear we could now look down and recognise Samson below us. Fog still covered the neck of the island, so it looked as if the twin hills of Samson were two tiny islands surrounded by a sea of fog.

The search proved fruitless. We were sitting dejected and silent on the top of a hill looking over to where we knew Bryher must be, hidden under the fog. I was thoroughly exhausted and miserable by now and could summon up neither the strength nor the enthusiasm to continue the search. I just wanted to go home.

'Let's go back to the boat, please Daniel,' I begged. 'Let's not stay here any more. I hate this place. Let's go back to the boat, please.'

'Gracie,' he said suddenly, and he was hauling me to my feet. 'That's it, that's it. Why didn't I think of the boat before? All right, so we can't drink; but we can eat, can't we? Look, Gracie, we can't leave till the fog lifts, you know we can't; but we can't just sit here and wait, can we? So why don't we have breakfast?'

'Breakfast?' I said.

'Pilchards, or bass,' Daniel said, a triumphant grin on his face. 'Take your pick. We've got a fire, haven't we? Still hot enough to cook on; bet it is. And we've got fish, back on the boat, haven't we?'

The promise of food was enough to banish at once

both my thirst and my exhaustion, and we ran together down through the high heather towards the fog-covered beach below where we had left the boat the night before. The hill was so steep and I was running so fast that my legs finally could not keep up with me any longer and I tumbled headlong into the heather, rolling over and over until I came to rest at last in a clearing of soft grass covered in a sprinkling of rabbit droppings. When I sat up I saw Daniel on his hands and knees beside me. He was not at all concerned with my welfare; but was parting the bracken in front of him.

'It's a well, Gracie!' he called out. 'It's a well! We've found the well.'

It had been dug at the foot of the hillside and was lined all around with stones. Together we peered over the edge, but it was too dark to see anything. I reached down with my hand to touch the water, but there was nothing there. Daniel picked up a large stone and dropped it down, but there was no answering splash. We heard it bounce once, twice. It was stone on stone. The well was quite dry. Daniel sat back on his heels. 'P'raps that's why the people left here,' I said. 'You can't live on an island without water.' And then Daniel was on his feet again.

'Never mind,' he said, 'we've still got the fish.'

We chose to eat the pilchards because they were small and would cook quickly we thought, but the smell of them was so good and we were so ravenous that we only half-cooked them, eating the outside of each one and throwing the rest to the gulls and terns to keep them happy. I never much cared for pilchards and I haven't ever since, but that day on Samson we ate them until we were full and no fish ever tasted so good. I think we ate as much wood ash as we did fish but neither of us cared.

I was wiping my hands on the grass when I first noticed the rabbit. It was sitting looking at us out of the bracken only a few feet away, and it was perfectly black. It seemed quite tame so I thought I would try to get closer. I was crawling slowly towards it and was within inches of touching it when Daniel shouted out, 'Gracie! Gracie!' The rabbit bolted into the bracken and disappeared. Daniel was on his feet and laughing. I was surprised and angry at him for frightening the rabbit away. 'It's going, Gracie, it's going!' he shouted.

'Course it's going,' I stormed at him. 'What d'you expect a rabbit to do if you shout at it like that?'

'Not the rabbit,' he said. 'Not the rabbit, Gracie, the fog! The fog! Look, Gracie, it's going!' And sure enough below us was the infinitely wonderful sight of the sea shimmering blue through the mist below us.

'Let's go home, Gracie,' said Daniel. And he did not have to ask me twice.

9 31ST OCTOBER 1915

WE COULD NOT LEAVE SAMSON BEHIND US QUICKLY
enough, although now with the sunlight on it, it had lost its
haunted look. It was only now that I was on the way back
home that it occurred to me how worried Mother must
have been all this time. How I longed to see her again. I
thought no more of ghosts or curses but only of the joys of
being home with her again, of how I would drink and drink
and then climb into bed and pull the blankets up over my
ears and go to sleep for as long as I wanted.

We both knew though the kind of welcome that was
awaiting us. We knew the anger and the inquisition that
we would have to face, so our relief that we were at last off
Samson was tempered with a certain reluctance to arrive.
I remember there was precious little wind that day, only
the gentlest of breezes; so we did not bother even to set
the sail. The warmth of the sun was lifting the last

remnants of the fog off the sea as we rowed slowly down the channel past Puffin Island towards Bryher and home.

'Father's going to strap me, he always does,' said Daniel. ' 'S'pose I can't expect him not to, not after I took his boat; but it'll only make it worse if I tell him we were on Samson. He'd burst his boiler if he thought we'd been anywhere near the place, you know what he's like about rules.'

'What are we going to tell them then?' I asked.

'The truth,' said Daniel, 'only we just leave out the bit about Samson. Went fishing and got lost in the fog; that's all there is to it. Well, we did, didn't we? Didn't know where we were so we just sat it out until the fog lifted and here we are. Keep it as true as you like, Gracie, but for goodness sake don't ever let on we were on Samson.'

'Then we don't have to tell the Birdman either, do we?' I asked. 'I don't want to tell him. He'll be angry, I know he will be; and I don't like the look of him when he's angry. And he warned us not to go there, didn't he?'

Daniel thought for a moment. 'He's about the only person in the world I would never lie to. He's the only one I trust, Gracie, 'cept you of course. I'm going to tell him, Gracie, I'm going to tell him just the way it happened. He won't mind, honest. I know he won't.'

'Well you can tell him by yourself,' I said. 'I'm not going to see him, not until I know he isn't angry with us. And ask him about that thing we found in the cottage, that unicorn's horn or whatever it is.'

'All right,' said Daniel. 'I'll go. I'll ask him. Let's pull a bit slower, Gracie; I'm in no hurry to get home.'

They spotted us as we came over the sandbars past Puffin Island. Everyone came running down onto the beach. You could see the news spreading through the island. People were running from cottage to cottage, and then they were hurrying down towards us, so that by the time I threw out our anchor almost everyone on the island must have been there to meet us. I could see Mother in amongst them, looking pale and tired under her dark shawl. I waved to her but she did not wave back. Daniel's family were there too, Big Tim in amongst them, and it was Big Tim who came wading out into the shallows to help us haul the boat up onto the sand.

'You're for it now,' he said, and the smile on his face was more one of menace than of welcome. 'You're really for it.'

There were tears of relief at first. Mother held me to her briefly then she took me by the arm and led me away through the crowd. She did not say a word to me. I saw Aunty Mildred covering him with kisses in spite of Daniel's efforts to escape her clutches. But any tears of joy soon gave way to rage and Daniel was subjected to a barrage of furious questioning. He was immediately surrounded by his brothers and sisters, and as Mother led me up off the beach I heard behind me his father's thunderous voice. 'You wait till I get you home. You just wait. How dare you? How dare you take out one of my boats without asking me first. I'll teach you a lesson you'll never forget.' And when his mother intervened on Daniel's behalf he roared again. 'It's as much your fault as his, letting him run wild; and now look what he's done.

Every boat on the island's been out looking for him and he comes back here bold as brass after all the trouble he's caused. I'll tan him black and blue, you see if I won't.'

Mother waited until we were far enough away from the crowd before she said a word. I had shamed her in front of everyone, she said. How was she ever to hold her head up again on the island after this, with everyone thinking *she* had sent me out fishing for her at my age! But gradually her grip on my arm relaxed and we walked on side by side in silence for some time. 'I thought I had lost you, Gracie,' she said. 'I didn't think I was ever going to see you again. I spent all last night wondering how I was going to tell your father when he got home.' She stopped, put her hand on my shoulder and then lifted my face to look into hers. 'I know why you went out in that boat, Gracie Jenkins. I can do without the money,' she said, 'but I can't do without you. If needs be I can sell the boat. We'd have enough then to pay the rent for a year or two, and we'd be able to buy in all the food we need for the winter. Your father can always build another one when he gets back. You won't ever go off like that again, will you, Gracie? Promise me you won't. Never again.'

'I promise,' I said and she kissed me on my forehead.

'You're cold,' she said. 'You're ice cold.'

'I'm more thirsty than cold, Mother,' I said. So I had my water at last, three mugs of it brimful and wonderful. She put me to bed after that with a hot stone bottle at my feet and she sat down on the bed beside me. I waited for her questions to come; but she said nothing more about it, only that for the first time since Father left she was glad he was not at home. 'He'd have hit the roof,' she said. 'But then I suppose you'd never have gone out fishing in the first place if he had been here, would you? There'd have been no need for it, would there? And if he knew why you'd gone out, Gracie, he'd have been proud of you, that's for sure, like I am.'

'He'll be back soon,' I said. 'Won't be long, Mother. The war can't last for ever, can it?'

'Can't it?' she sighed as she got up to go, gathering her shawl around her. 'Gracie,' she said, 'best not to go and play with Daniel for a bit. You're not the most popular girl on Bryher just at the moment, you know. There's plenty of people, Daniel's mother amongst them, think you've been getting Daniel into mischief. Personally I think it's six to one half a dozen of the other, don't you?'

I rarely dream, and if I do I can scarcely ever remember them; but I dreamed a dream that night after my return from Samson that was so vivid I have never forgotten it. I saw through a sunlit fog, fleeting glimpses of Father riding over the sea on a bright white unicorn. He was in his sailor's uniform and he rode so fast that his hat fell off. He was laughing when he jumped down to retrieve it. Then the unicorn galloped off into the fog and left him alone, standing on the sea. He looked everywhere for his hat but he could not find it. It did not seem to worry him though because he was laughing, laughing all the time. As he sank into the sea he was still laughing and waving at me. All that night I kept waking up and falling asleep again only to dream the same dream again and again.

I wanted to tell Daniel about my dream – he was the only one I could tell, but there was no opportunity to do so. He had been forbidden to play with me and so we only saw each other now when we went to school, and then there always seemed to be other children around us. Even in playtime at school we were not left alone. Overnight, it seemed we had become famous. We were the heroes of the hour and constantly surrounded now by admirers who wanted to find out everything that had happened to us when we'd gone missing in the fog. However much we told them, they wanted to know more and so Daniel invented more. Each time he told the story he filled it out with colourful and often inconsistent embellishments, but no one seemed to notice. They hung on his every word.

I noticed though that Big Tim and his friends never came to listen to Daniel. They stood in a huddle in the furthest corner of the playground, whispering to each other and glowering over their shoulders at us. I did try to warn Daniel that I thought they were up to something, but he ignored me. Indeed as the days passed I felt Daniel was hardly even listening to me any more. I did not know why, but Daniel seemed quite unlike himself now since our return from Samson. It was not that he avoided me. On the contrary, he stayed so close to me all day that I began to feel he was trying to protect me from something; but he had become distant towards me, almost cold. He hardly ever spoke to me and when he did it was in monosyllables, and he kept looking around him all the time as if he were expecting something to happen. Even on the way back from school, coming down our lane when we were quite alone at last, he seemed to prefer to walk beside me in stony silence. I could have told him then about my dream; but there were more important, more urgent things I had to know.

'You been to see the Birdman yet?' I asked, and not for the first time. He shook his head and looked away. 'When you going then?' I went on. 'You said you were going to ask him about that horn thing in the cottage, you said you would.'

'Soon,' he said, and he walked on down the lane towards home, his hands deep in his pockets.

'Your father strap you?' I asked him. He nodded, but said nothing more. 'Does it hurt still?'

'Bit,' he said. 'See you tomorrow.' And he ran off up the path towards his house.

'Watch out for Big Tim,' I called after him. 'He's hatching something, I know he is, Daniel.' He waved his hand over his head and went inside.

At the time I put it down to the beating his father had given him. It had to be that; I could think of no other reason why he should suddenly have become so quiet and so sad.

Terrible things happen on quite ordinary days and there is never any warning. It must have been a week, I suppose, after we came back from Samson. I met Daniel as usual at the gate that morning and we walked together up the lane to catch the boat to school. We always went the long way because Big Tim and his friends went the short way and we always liked to keep well away from them. It was a gusty autumn morning with the leaves chasing each other in crazy circles down the lane. I remember Daniel was behaving even more strangely than usual. He kept glancing behind us, and then just before we joined the others on the boat he said quietly, not looking at me at all, 'Gracie, if anything happens at school today, just keep out of it. Don't say anything no matter what happens, understand?' There was no time to ask any whys or wherefores, no time even to reply.

It was a rough, buffeting crossing to Tresco, but I liked it that way. It took longer and there was always just a chance that if it got worse in mid-channel we would have to turn round and go back home again, but it did not. Big Tim sat in the bow of the boat with his friends as he always did; but then I saw that he was staring at us and grinning. They all were. There was menace in their eyes. I looked at Daniel and found him glaring back at his brother. There was a look of utter contempt on his face.

In assembly, Mr Wellbeloved thundered his daily tirade against the brutal German enemy, and we all sang 'God Save the King' as lustily as usual. Then in his arithmetic lesson we all had to recite our seven times table aloud. Of all of them this was the one I loathed and dreaded the most. I managed to stutter my way through it but it was not good enough and he told me to stay in after lunch and write it out twenty times. At break-time I followed Daniel out into the playground. We went and sat down together, as we often did, by the coalshed. I tried to ask Daniel again about the Birdman. 'You told the Birdman yet about Samson? You asked him what the fire was for?' But he never had time to answer me. They were all around us, about ten of them in all; and Big Tim stood above us against the sky, his thumbs hitched over his belt. His head was in the sun, but I could see the cruel grin was still on his face. I had never really looked at Big Tim until then, not closely. I suppose that was because I had grown up with him and was too used to him to notice him. Above his high collar his face had the look of a sweating red pudding; but as I got to my feet it was not his face I was looking at, but the massive fist clutching his belt. He grinned at me and pushed me back against the wall. Daniel stepped between us.

'Leave her be,' he said. 'She's nothing to do with it.'

'You're in it together,' Big Tim said. 'You're always together, isn't that right? If you're guilty, she's guilty.' And there was an ugly chorus of agreement from his friends behind him.

'Guilty of what?' Daniel said. 'All right, so you saw me coming out of the Birdman's cottage last night. What's the harm in that?'

'But that's not the half of it, is it, Danny boy?' Big Tim went on, an unpleasant sneer in his voice. 'A Hun-lover, that's what you are. I've got a Hun-lover for a little brother. No use denying it, Danny boy.' And he put a hand on Daniel's chest and pushed him back against the wall beside me. 'We saw you. We seen you often, haven't we? And not just last night, Danny boy. Keep a good look-out, Welly Belly said, for King and country, and so we did; and what did we find but my little brother running down along Rushy Bay and up into the Birdman's house on Heathy Hill. A stroke of luck really you see, 'cos we been watching that house the last few days, keeping an eye on him. Do you know why, Danny boy? Well of course you do. That friend of yours, that Birdman, he's the only one on Bryher who doesn't close his curtains at night like he should. Now why d'you think that is, eh?' And he pushed Daniel harder against the wall. 'Well I'll tell you why, it's because he's a spy. He's a Hun-loving spy and he's signalling to German submarines out at sea, that's why; and that makes you the friend of a spy, doesn't it, Danny boy?'

'Don't be silly,' said Daniel, 'he wouldn't do that. He doesn't even like the war. Says no one ever wins a war anyway, so there's no point in fighting it. He doesn't want anyone to win it.'

'Doesn't he indeed? So he's a Hun-lover just like I said he was, a Hun-lover and a spy.' Big Tim's friends closed in around us. He went on, 'Father's going to find this all very interesting when I tell him. He'll tan you again, Danny boy; that's after I've finished with you.'

'You can tell Father what you like,' said Daniel, 'but you can't prove anything. Just leave the Birdman alone. He hasn't done anyone any harm. Leave him alone, d'you hear me? The only reason you can see lights from his cottage is 'cos he hasn't got any curtains, that's all.' Big Tim looked a little taken aback at this.

'No curtains?' he said. 'That's no excuse. Got blankets, hasn't he? Everyone's got blankets. He could put up blankets. He's a spy right enough and you're in it with him, both of you are.'

'Can't you understand?' Daniel said. 'He hates the war,

says it turns men into savages. He doesn't even care who wins or loses.'

'Doesn't care, eh?' said Big Tim taking Daniel by the ear and twisting it viciously. 'So he doesn't care who wins the war? That's what we thought, isn't it, lads? So here's what we're going to do, Danny boy. When I get home I'm going to tell Father all about you and the Birdman, and he'll tell the Navy and they'll come and search his place and question him till he tells everything. And if he doesn't come up with the right answers then you know what happens to spies, don't you? They shoot them, them and their friends.' And he twisted Daniel's ear even harder, forcing him down onto his knees. The silent tears on Daniel's face at last spurred me to action and I threw myself at Big Tim, lashing out with arms and legs; but it was to little effect. He did have to let go of Daniel but then he just held me out at arm's length and laughed at me as I flailed pathetically, my arms far too short even to reach him. Then someone called out that Mr Wellbeloved was on the prowl; so he grabbed my arm, twisted my wrist up behind me and pushed me to the ground beside Daniel.

'That's where you both belong, in the dirt like all Hun-lovers. You won't see him again; he'll confess and tell them everything. I shouldn't like to be in your shoes when you get home this afternoon.' And he was gone.

Daniel helped me to my feet. 'I told you to stay out of it,' he said, his hand cupping his ear. 'I told you, didn't I?'

'But they won't shoot him, will they?' I said.

'Course not, Gracie. They'll find out he didn't do anything, not on purpose anyway; they're not stupid like

Big Tim. But we're both in trouble now. Big Tim will tell everyone all about us and the Birdman, and they'll try to stop us from ever seeing him again – you can be sure of that.'

'Daniel,' I said, brushing myself down, 'why did you tell me you hadn't been to see the Birdman?' He didn't answer me. 'You told me you hadn't been and you had.' He looked at me and then looked away again quickly.

'I didn't want to have to tell you, Gracie.' He spoke quietly, almost as if he were talking to himself. 'He was going to tell you himself, Gracie,' he said. 'It's about the curse, the curse of Samson. It's like you said. It's like your father told you. It's all true, but there's more . . .' And just then Mr Wellbeloved appeared round the corner.

'Anything the matter?' he asked.

'No, Sir,' said Daniel.

'Then run along in. Break's over. Bell's going.'

After lunch I had to stay in to write out my seven times table twenty times; and Mr Wellbeloved kept me at it all afternoon, sending me back and back to do it again until I got it right. But I never did get it right. I kept making small mistakes, for my mind was not on my work that day. I was not thinking of Big Tim and having my arm twisted again, I was thinking only about the curse of Samson. Would it be me or Daniel to suffer the curse first? I wondered if the house would be burnt down when I got home. I wondered if Mother would be sick with the fever, or whether we would drown on the way back to Bryher. I would have to tell Mother, to warn her. I would have to tell her before someone else did, all about the Birdman and Samson; and I knew how hurt she would be that I had deceived her all this time. How I dreaded going home that afternoon.

The boat from Tresco dropped us at the quay as usual and we took a different way home up through the town for fear of meeting Big Tim and his friends. As we passed the houses we noticed that people were gathered whispering in their doorways and they would disappear indoors as we approached. We saw them peering out at us through their windows. Even the Vicar looked away and did not speak to us as he hurried by in his billowing black cassock, and that was most unusual for him.

When we reached my front gate Daniel's mother was waiting there and she took him roughly by the arm and whisked him away into the house. 'What's the matter?' he asked. 'What've I done now?' but she said nothing, and I noticed she seemed not to want to look at me.

Mother was sitting in her usual chair, but it was not usual for her to be sitting down at this time of the day. 'Come here, Gracie dear,' she said, her voice an unnatural whisper. When she lifted her head and looked at me I could see she had been crying. 'We've lost your father,' she said.

'Lost him?' I said.

'He's missing, Gracie,' she said and she held up a letter and handed it to me. It was a brick red envelope that I held in my hand and the address on the outside was in pencil, as was the writing on the letter I took out. It read: 'The Lords Commissioners of the Admiralty regret to inform you that J591671 Able Seaman Peter Jenkins of

HMS Louis was reported missing in action on 31st October 1915.'

'That means he's not coming back, doesn't it?' I said.

'Oh why him?' Mother said. 'Why us?'

I knew well enough the answer to that question.

10 DAWN ATTACK

I GRIEVED THAT NIGHT AS ANY CHILD WOULD WHO
had just lost a father; but when I cried it was as much from
guilt as from sorrow. From the moment I read the letter I
had little doubt in my mind that I had been the cause of
my own father's death. It was I who had set foot on the
forbidden island and brought the curse of Samson down
on our heads. I lay awake beside Mother all night long
trying to convince myself that there was at least a
possibility it had not been *all* my fault, that after all
thousands of soldiers and sailors were dying in the war.
But no matter how I reasoned I could not get it out of my
mind that it was I and I alone that had been responsible.

Mother lay awake beside me like a statue that night
consumed by her own silent, private agony. She held my
hand and squeezed it whenever I began to cry but neither
of us talked. I was tempted to confess everything, but I

could not bring myself to do it. Anyway, I thought, there was no point in it; not now. It would not bring Father back and that was all she wanted. It was all I wanted.

The day after the letter came was a wretched day of endless visitors. Friends and relatives from all over the islands came to pay their respects. They all brought little gifts, a posy of flowers or a pot of jam; and they all smiled sweetly, said how sad they were and left as quietly as possible, some on tiptoe as if they were in church. They were all of them kind, but it seemed to me as I stood behind Mother's chair witnessing this procession that Father's death had altered every one of them, for none of them really talked to us as they used to do. They made short, hushed speeches, their eyes lowered, and then they became impatient to leave. It was as if we had contracted some dreadful contagious disease; they were sympathetic but they were keeping their distance just to be sure they would not catch it.

Only Daniel's voluminous Aunty Mildred, the aunt who was for ever kissing him, stayed to drink the cup of tea Mother offered everyone, and she talked just as she always talked. She was the only one I remember who actually mentioned Father. 'Of course,' she went on, after first saying how sorry she was, 'of course he was a fine man your Peter, good fisherman, brave man; but I always said he should never have left you and little Gracie like he did to go off to the war. I told him so at the time. I said, "Peter," I said, "you're too old to be going fighting wars at your age, there's plenty of younger ones should go first who haven't got wives and children." ' She sighed, sipping her tea daintily. 'But they never listen, do they, dear? They always think they know better, don't they? You can't tell them, can you?' And when she got up to go several cups of tea later it was already dark outside the window. She hugged me to her so long and so hard that she almost smothered me. 'Poor little mite,' she said, kissing me on the head. 'Poor little mite. Anything I can do to help, you know where I am.' And she was gone.

When I shut the door behind her and turned round I saw that Mother was smiling, the grief lifted from her face for the first time that day. 'Thank God for Aunty Mildred,' she said and she closed her eyes and put her head back against the chair. 'It's a funny thing, Gracie, but I never liked that woman, not until now. Neither did your father, come to that.'

Then came a knock at the door. 'Someone else,' Mother said. 'People are kind, Gracie, they're so kind, but I don't know if I can face anyone else. I'm tired, I'm so tired.'

'Could be Daniel,' I said. 'He hasn't been yet.' But even as I was opening the door I had the feeling it wasn't Daniel. The Birdman stood there in the darkness. He smiled at me, but there was not a flicker of recognition in his face; and then Prince was jumping up at me and squeaking with excitement.

The Birdman and mother looked at each other across the room. Mother had sat up in her chair and had her hand to her mouth. The Birdman held out a pot of honey for her. 'Heard about your husband,' he said. 'I heard what happened. I've come to tell you I am sorry. Believe me, Mrs Jenkins, I am so sorry.'

'It's Mr Woodcock, isn't it?' said Mother rising from her chair and taking the honey from him. 'And I think I have more to thank you for than just this one pot of honey, haven't I? It was you wasn't it? It was you all along. You were the one who's been so kind to Gracie and me all this time.' But the Birdman was already walking out of the door, Prince following at his heels. 'Mr Woodock,' Mother called out after him, 'I've a cup of tea for you; it's still warm.' But the Birdman never even looked round. He disappeared down the path and into the darkness.

'Well,' Mother said, 'so now we know who it was. But why, Gracie? I don't understand it. I've never even spoken to him before this evening. Worse than that, I've avoided him all my life and Father always kept well out of his way too.' She was looking directly at me now, the honey still in her hand. 'He speaks so strangely. It may only have been the way he talks, but I felt that he meant what he said more than anyone else today. It was almost as if he felt responsible somehow, as if he was apologising.'

To my great relief Mother said no more about it until we were in bed later that night. 'I've been thinking,' she said, 'about that dog, the Birdman's dog. You ever seen that dog before, Gracie? Have you? He certainly looked as if he knew you, jumping all over you like that, just like you were old friends. Gracie? Gracie?' But I was as fast asleep as I could pretend to be, my breathing so deep and regular that pretence must have given way to fatigue and I was soon well and truly asleep.

I was woken suddenly. I thought at first it might be a

gull tapping on the window, but when I looked there was nothing there. The night sky was already grey with morning. I could see the branches of the tamarisk tree outside my window shaking in the wind; but there was no gale blowing and it was only in a gale that the twigs scraped against the window pane. I sat up in bed slowly so as not to wake Mother, who lay on her side facing away from me. Then I heard it again and this time I knew it for what it was, for I heard the pebble fall back and bounce on the path outside. I eased myself carefully out of the bed and crept over to the window. Daniel stood on the path looking up at me and he was beckoning me to come down. I dressed quickly at the bottom of the stairs, wrapped myself against the cold of the morning and stole out of the house.

Daniel said nothing. He put a finger to his lips to prevent me even from whispering. We stole down the path and out of the gate and then we began to run. We ran all the way up to the top of Samson Hill before we stopped to rest. I looked across to the Birdman's cottage, but everything was dark on Heathy Hill. I flung myself down exhausted in the heather and Daniel crouched down beside me. 'Won't help saying anything I don't s'pose,' he said, 'but I am sorry, Gracie, honest I am.'

'It was the curse of Samson, wasn't it?' I said, and he nodded. 'My father's dead and all because we went on that island, isn't he? It's all true, isn't it?'

'The Birdman told me everything,' Daniel said. 'But it's not his fault, Gracie, and it's not your fault. He's done all he could.'

'What do you mean?'

'Tell you later Gracie. There's no time now. We've got to warn him; we've got to warn him quick.'

'Warn him?' I asked.

'It's Big Tim and his crowd,' Daniel went on. 'I heard them planning it. Dawn attack they called it. You remember what he said at school, don't you? Well Big Tim went and told Father, just like he said he was going to. He told him I'd been over to see the Birdman and all that tommyrot about the Birdman being a spy and signalling to German submarines. 'Course Father believed him, Father always believes everything he says. He strapped me again and then shut me in my room – that was Big Tim's idea so's I wouldn't be able to warn the Birdman that they were coming to search his cottage. And they did come, police from St Mary's, yesterday afternoon. I heard them talking to Father outside the window when they came back from the Birdman's cottage. Course they didn't find anything and they were angry. They told Father not to waste their time in future. Said they had better things to do than go visiting madmen. A lot of silly nonsense, they said. How could anyone think that a mad old fool like that could be a spy? Didn't even understand the questions they asked him. All he'd do was smile and nod his head – couldn't even speak properly, they said. So anyway, when they left, Father turned on Big Tim and gave him a piece of his mind for making him look a fool. They let me out at teatime and I went over to see the Birdman straight away to tell him about your father. He was so upset, Gracie. Said he had to go and see you and your mother. I tried to stop him; but he had to go, he said. He had to see your mother and tell her face to face how sorry he was. Blames himself, see. I warned him you'd be in trouble if he looked as if he recognised you in front of your mother. I told him he mustn't recognise you.'

'Prince did,' I said, 'leapt up on me he did, just like he always does. Mother knows something's up, I think, but she's not sure what. I think she's too tired to care. You could have warned me,' I went on. 'You could have warned me he was coming, couldn't you?'

'I was going to, Gracie,' Daniel said. 'I was on my way back from Heathy Hill to tell you he was coming, and then I heard them.'

'Who?'

'Big Tim and everyone, like I told you. Must've been about a dozen of them there, outside the boatshed; and I could hear Big Tim planning this dawn attack, just like he was a general or something. He said they should never have sent out the police to question the Birdman. They should have sent the navy, he said. They'd have got the truth out of him. He said he knew the truth anyway. The Birdman was a spy, had to be; and of course they all agreed. If no one else would do it then he'd do it himself. He was going to teach the Birdman a lesson. The last thing he said was that they'd meet at dawn and ransack his cottage. They want to drive him off the island for ever, Gracie.'

'Didn't anyone try to stop him?' I asked.

'No one argues with Big Tim, you know that. They're all frightened of him,' Daniel said. 'So that's why we've got to get there first whilst there's still time. We got to warn him, Gracie.' And he pulled me to my feet again and we began to run down towards Rushy Bay and up over the dunes towards the Birdman's cottage. Already there was a glimmer of daylight creeping over the sea.

When we got there the cottage was quite empty. The two goats came to nuzzle us as we searched outside and it was then that Daniel noticed that the cart was not in its usual place. 'He's off collecting wood somewhere I expect,' he said. 'Popplestones or Hell Bay. We've got to find him.'

We were passing the pool under Gweal Hill when I happened to look over my shoulder and saw them, shadowy figures against the skyline, flitting through the undergrowth high on Samson Hill. 'It's them. They're coming,' I said. 'What can we do?'

'Nothing,' said Daniel taking my arm and pulling me on. 'It's too late and there's too many of them.' We ran on down towards Popplestones.

The donkey and cart were by the rocks at the far end of the beach, moving from time to time as the donkey browsed along the line of seaweed, and for a moment that was all we could make out, until we heard Prince barking. We could see the Birdman now, standing in the shallows. A flock of gulls lifted off the water and circled shrieking overhead. Then we saw a long dark shape lying at the water's edge and the Birdman kneeling in the water beside it. As we ran across the sand we could see he was trying to roll it over and that it was clearly too big for him to move. It could have been mistaken for a great log but for the fact that it moved – it moved of its own accord. It had a huge fan-shaped tail that lifted and fell, slapping the water as we came towards it. The Birdman heaved again and the creature writhed once more and lifted its head. Until that moment the horn had been camouflaged from us because it was almost the same colour as the sand. The creature, whatever it was, possessed a long, pointed horn that protruded from just below the dome of its blunt black head. It was only when we came closer that we saw how vast the creature was. From tail to head it was the length of a small boat, perhaps fifteen feet, and the horn itself half as long again. It looked more like a whale than anything else. The fine tapering horn seemed an unnatural and incongruous addition to the clumsy bulk of its body.

'The horn, Daniel,' I said. 'That's just like the horn we found in that cottage on Samson, isn't it?'

'It's just like he told me,' Daniel said quietly. 'It's just like the Birdman told me.'

'What d'you mean?' I asked, but Daniel was running on ahead of me.

The Birdman got slowly to his feet as he saw us coming. Prince had stopped barking and growling, and was bounding up the beach towards us.

'Thank God you've come,' the Birdman called out. 'I can't do it on my own, not strong enough. Been here all night trying to roll her back into the sea, but she's too heavy for me.'

'What is it?' I asked, reaching out to touch it and then not daring to do so. It was speckled black all over, but darker along the ridge of the back than anywhere else.

Daniel pulled at the Birdman's sou'wester so that he should turn and look at him while he was speaking. 'It's like the ones they killed on Samson isn't it?' Daniel asked. 'It's the same, isn't it, Mr Woodcock?'

'Just the same,' he said. 'It was me that found the first one that day too.' And he looked out to sea. 'The others will be out there at sea just like they were before and they'll come in just like they did before. They think they can help, you see, but they can't. We've got to get her back in the water before they come else they'll beach themselves just the same. We've got to do it before anyone comes, I tell you. If they find her here that'll be the end of Bryher. It'll happen all over again.'

'What will?' I shouted. 'What's going on? What are you talking about? I don't understand what's happening. Please tell me, please.' I was crying now, out of grief and bewilderment, out of anger and frustration.

The Birdman looked down at me and spoke more softly and clearly than I had ever heard him speak. 'After what happened to your poor father,' said the Birdman, 'you have more right to know about the curse of Samson than anyone else, and you shall know. But I haven't much time to tell you, so listen well, Gracie. It was all a long, long time ago but I remember it as if it were yesterday. Samson was always a poor place when I was a boy, little enough food to go round and life was hard. But we survived well enough until the day the whales came. I found the first of them lying on the beach early one morning, crying out for help. Mother and I tried to roll it back into the sea, but we couldn't move it.'

The whale shifted again on the sand and the Birdman looked round. 'Just like that one, just the same,' he said. 'And by daybreak the whole island was there, but they wouldn't help us, not even Father. And do you know why not?' I shook my head. 'Well, I'll tell you, Gracie. You see, there were more whales out in the bay and the more the stranded whale cried out, the closer the others came to the beach. The people only had to wait and they knew it. By noon all the whales were stranded on the sand, calling out to each other, crying pitifully. Mother begged them not to do it, I begged them not to do it, but it was no good. They had all made up their minds. They said there was enough ivory in the horns to make us all rich for life. So they butchered them on the beach in the sunshine, and the blood stained the sand and ran out into the sea. The sea was redder that evening than any sunset I've ever seen. The very next morning, Gracie, we woke up to find a ship out in the bay, stuck fast on a sandbank.'

'The ghost ship,' I said. 'The ghost ship Father told me about.'

'Ghost ship?' the Birdman said. 'Maybe it was. It was deserted that's for sure, not a soul on board. They couldn't believe their luck – ivory one day and a fine ship for salvage the next. They floated her off the sandbank on the morning tide and sailed for Penzance. Every man on the island went, Father too, and they took the horns with them to sell on the mainland – all except one. We found it later, Mother and me, half buried in the sand.'

'That's the one we found over on Samson,' Daniel said.

The Birdman went on, hardly pausing for breath. 'They none of them came back. I never saw Father again. The ship went down with all hands. Every man on Samson was gone. Mother said the island was cursed because they had massacred the whales, but no one believed her. They said she was mad. And they didn't believe her in the years that followed when ship after ship was wrecked on the rocks off Samson. Over fifty people have died in those wrecks, Gracie. Even the few that crawled ashore never survived. Everyone said it was just bad luck, but Mother and I knew it was the curse. When the hunger came and the disease we knew what it was, and still no one believed us. All we had to eat were limpets and a few wild rabbits.'

'Did you eat the dogs?' I asked. 'Father said you had to eat the dogs.'

The Birdman nodded. 'When you're starving you eat anything,' he said. 'One by one the other families left. For two years Mother and I lived alone on the island. Mother wouldn't leave; she didn't want to leave Father's ghost on the island. Said she owed it to him to stay. We would never have left at all if the well hadn't gone dry. Never failed before, that well. Wet summer it was, too. No, it was the curse that dried that well, Gracie. It was the curse that drove us off the island.'

The Birdman looked up towards the black hills of Samson in the distance. 'All my life I've tried to lift the curse. All my life I've tried to keep everyone away from Samson. That's why I row out there whenever there's a storm threatening, whenever I see the fog rolling in. It's to light a beacon on the clifftop to warn the ships to keep away.'

So it *was* you,' I said. 'It *was* you over on Samson that night Daniel and I got lost in the fog.'

'Yes, it was me,' he said sadly. 'And I wish to heaven I'd never done it. It was my fire drew you to Samson, Gracie and brought the curse down on you. And now your poor father's dead.'

At that moment we heard the first blood-curdling yell up on Heathy Hill behind us. We turned round. 'Look!' Daniel said, pointing up toward the hillside where we could just make out Big Tim's soldiers moving like shadows through the dark of the heather for their dawn attack on the Birdman's cottage. We saw the goats bolting up the hillside bleating in terror, and then came the sound of squawking hens and crashing glass.

'We're too late, Gracie,' Daniel said. 'We came to warn you, Mr Woodcock. It's Big Tim and his friends. Like I told you, he thinks you're signalling to German submarines. Thinks you're a spy or something.'

'Spy?' the Birdman did not seem to know what the word meant. He seemed more hurt and puzzled than angry. 'It doesn't matter, anyway,' he said, turning away. 'All that matters now is the whale. She must not be allowed to die. She must not. The tide is already on the ebb so if we don't get her back in the water soon it'll be too far to drag her and then it'll be too late.'

'They're inside the cottage now, Mr Woodcock,' Daniel said. 'I can't see any of them outside any more.'

'Let's hope they stay inside,' the Birdman said. 'It's

getting lighter all the time. If they see us here I'm afraid that'll be the end of it, just like it was on Samson when the whales came before.'

However hard we pushed and shoved, the whale always rolled back to where it came from. Daniel and I tried to ignore the sounds of destruction coming from the cottage as we threw ourselves time and again against the side of the whale. Desperately we dug the sand away from one side and tried to roll it over, but it would only go so far before the fin on the far side would push it back towards us again. All we had managed to do it seemed was to make matters worse, for the whale now lay half buried in a deep trough of wet sand, and all the time the tide was taking the sea away from us.

We sat back to regain our strength and to take stock of what could be done. We knew it was useless to try again, but we steeled ourselves for one last attempt. Kneeling in the sand, our shoulders against the side of the whale, we heaved together, once, twice; and then felt the great weight of the creature falling back on us. As it came back it fell heavily into its ditch in the sand almost trapping my arm underneath it. I was sitting breathless in the sand when I heard Big Tim's voice behind us.

'What've you got there?' They were coming towards us across the beach.

'Look at the size of it!' one of them said; and they stopped several yards away from us. Big Tim was the next to speak.

'Well, what is it?' he asked.

'It's a whale,' said Daniel, 'and we've got to get it back

into the sea before it dies. We've got to. Because if it dies the Birdman says we'll all be cursed on Bryher just like they were on Samson. You got to help us, Tim. If you all help we can roll it back, easy.'

'The Birdman says,' Big Tim mimicked, and his friends laughed in unison around him. 'The Birdman says. He's a Hun-lover, Gracie I told you, Gracie, he signals to German submarines, maybe to the very one that killed your father. Well, we've broken every window in his cottage and we've pulled down his henhouse, and there's a few of those wooden birds that won't fly again; and if he stays we'll be back again, and then it won't be just his windows we'll break – it'll be him. D'you hear that, you mad old fool? You clear out; you're not wanted on this island.'

The Birdman got slowly to his feet and limped towards Big Tim. Prince followed growling at his heels. As he came towards them Big Tim and his friends backed away. 'You must be Big Tim,' he said. 'I think I recognise you. Daniel told me all about you. I tell you, if we do not get this creature back into the sea before she dies, then this island will die like Samson did. Do you hear me? Do you understand what I'm telling you? If you love your island, help us while there is still time.'

'Help you?' said Big Tim still backing away. 'Why should we help you after what you've done? Anyway that whale or whatever it is doesn't belong to you; it belongs to all of us. If you want it for yourself, you'll have to drag it up above high-water mark, and you're too old and feeble to do that, aren't you? And these two aren't much use, are they? So it's ours as much as it's yours; all of ours, isn't it?

It's no different to the timber washed up here last year. We shared it, didn't we? Everyone shared it. That's worth a bit too, by the look of it. Never even seen a fish that big; and I've seen some big ones. 'S a monster of a fish. That horn's worth something too, I shouldn't wonder.'

'You can't, you can't kill her,' cried Daniel, appealing not to Big Tim now but to his friends. 'You can't let him do it. You heard what the Birdman said. It's all true, and I know him. He's a good man. He's not a spy like Big Tim says. Why should he lie? Can't you see he's trying to save us?'

But they were not listening, none of them were. They were staring out over the sea, a look of utter astonishment on every face. There was nothing there but the sound at first, a curious roaring and crying from the open sea beyond Popplestones that became a crescendo of thunderous snorting and whistling. Within minutes Popplestones was alive with whales. Great spouts of water shot into the air. Everywhere you looked in the bay shining black backs broke the surface, rocked a little and then rolled forward and vanished again under the water. All of Big Tim's friends had already fled up the beach, but he stayed with us as mesmerized as we were. Beside us, the stranded whale writhed and rolled in its grave of sand its tail thrashing in fury and frustration, its own whistling cry joining the chorus of the others out in Popplestones.

'They've come,' cried the Birdman. 'It's too late, too late!'

'What a catch!' shouted Big Tim. 'What a catch! There

must be dozens of them out there. Can't do it on our own though; we'll need help. I'm going back for help.' And he ran up the beach to join his friends. 'We're going, but we'll be back and we'll kill every one of them, Birdman.'

'What does he say?' the Birdman asked Daniel. 'I don't understand what he's saying. Is he going for help? I can't see what he's saying; he talks too fast for me. Is he going for help?'

'No,' said Daniel, 'He's going to fetch the whole island down here, but they won't be coming to help. They'll be coming to kill, Mr Woodcock, and we can't stop them. There'll be too many of them.'

'Not again,' said the Birdman. 'Oh please God, not again. We have to stop them, we have to stop them.'

11 LAST CHANCE

WE DID ALL WE COULD TO DISCOURAGE THE whales from coming in too close to the shore. Shouting and screaming at the water's edge, we hurled stones and driftwood at them but most fell far short and those few that did hit them did not seem to deter them. The Birdman's flock of gulls wheeled noisily overhead, but the whales took no notice of them either. All the time they were drifting closer and closer to the beach and disaster. Every faint whistle from the stranded whale seemed to drive the others out in the bay to distraction, sending them rolling and plunging in amongst each other and precipitating a chorus of thunderous snorting and whistling that subsided only when the whale lay still and silent again on the sand. But each furious flurry of activity left them that much nearer the shore and there seemed nothing we could do now to stop them beaching themselves.

'Gracie,' said the Birdman, 'you go back to the whale and try to keep her happy. Stroke her, Gracie. Talk to her, sing to her, anything so's she doesn't call out.' And he took off his sou'wester and handed it to me. 'It won't do to let her get too dry either, Gracie. You can use this for a bucket.'

So I went back and forth from the water's edge to the whale with the Birdman's sou'wester full of water. I began at her head, pouring the water all over her eyes and mouth. She seemed to relish it, blinking and rolling her head from side to side as the water ran down over her skin and into the sand, and all the while I talked to her quietly. I remember thinking as I looked into her eyes that she could understand me, that she could understand every word I said.

I was kneeling in the sand beside her head, stroking her behind the blowhole above her eyes, when I saw them coming back. They were hurrying along the path under Gweal Hill, Big Tim running out in front. It looked as if he had brought most of the island with him. Everyone had a weapon of some kind in his hand, a fork, an axe, a hoe or a scythe; and Daniel's father carried a harpoon over his shoulder. I looked for Mother amongst them but could not pick her out. The Vicar was there, his cassock tucked up into his trousers and Mr Wellbeloved was there too, striding out with his stick alongside Daniel's father.

'Stay where you are, Gracie,' the Birdman told me, 'and keep her quiet if you can.' By the time they reached the beach, the Birdman, Daniel and Prince stood between them and the stranded whale. No one spoke for a moment. They all stood looking incredulously at the Birdman and the whale, at Daniel and me, whispering anxiously amongst themselves. It was only when they noticed the rolling black backs breaking the water out in the bay that they began to talk aloud.

'See,' Big Tim shouted in triumph, pointing his machete. 'Didn't I tell you? Didn't I tell you? There's dozens of them out there. I said there was.'

'It's a narwhal,' said Mr Wellbeloved. 'Yes, I do believe it's a narwhal. Well I never. Only the males have tusks, you know. He's a long way from home. That's the kind of whale that the Eskimos hunt off Greenland. Quite what he's doing here I cannot imagine. If I might take a closer look . . .' As he stepped towards us Prince began to growl, his lip curling back above his teeth, his neck tense with fury. Mr Wellbeloved stopped where he stood.

'Look here, Mr Woodcock,' Daniel's father said, taking Mr Wellbeloved's arm and pulling him back, 'we don't much care what this thing is. Whale, narwhal, it doesn't matter to us. All that matters is that there's meat on it and ivory too by the look of it. That's money to us, Mr Woodcock. Anything washed up on our beaches is ours by right, always has been, Mr Woodcock; you know that.' The Birdman said nothing but looked along the ranks of islanders that faced him. 'And as for you, Daniel Pender,' Daniel's father went on, pointing at Daniel, 'you can come right back over here, else I'll take a strap to you right here and now in front of all these people. You've no business to be here with this man. You've been told time and time again.' Daniel stayed where he was alongside the Birdman.

'You can strap me all you want, Father,' he said, 'but you got to listen to Mr Woodcock. You got to listen to him. If you don't, then we're done for, all of us. You got to do what he says, Father.'

'Mr Woodcock,' Daniel's father said, his patience fast vanishing, 'are you going to move that dog or am I? Now I don't want anyone to get hurt . . .'

'He can't hear you, Father,' Daniel said. 'He's deaf. Gracie and me, we're the only ones he can understand.'

'Deaf?' said Daniel's father, and he was clearly taken aback. 'All right then, you tell him for us, Daniel. You tell him that the whale belongs to all of us and we aim to kill it and those out there in Popplestones as well. They're ours by right and he can't stop us. Tell him to stand aside.'

Daniel interpreted quietly and the Birdman nodded his understanding, putting his hand on Daniel's shoulder. He straightened up and faced Daniel's father. 'Then you will have to kill me first,' he said. 'This whale must go back to the sea where she belongs. Then we must drive them all back out to sea. If just one of them dies, the curse that fell on Samson when I was a boy will fall on you, and Bryher will be cursed forever. You must help me before it's too late.'

'Oh come on,' said Big Tim pushing his way through. 'We don't have to listen to this old fool. Those whales out there could turn round any minute and head back out to sea and we'd lose the lot of them.' And the crowd began to move slowly in towards us.

'Stand aside, Mr Woodcock,' said Daniel's father. 'You know we're within our rights. Out of the way now.' At once Prince was on his feet and the growl had turned to a snarl. Those just in front of him fell back, but the rest kept coming until we were almost surrounded. At that moment the whale must have sensed danger for she raised her head and whistled again, twisting and turning and thrashing the ground behind her. Popplestones Bay suddenly boiled with life.

'Don't do it, please Father,' cried Daniel backing down towards me. 'Don't do it. Listen to him. He's telling the truth. I know he is.' But I could see from the hardness in the faces around me that they were ignoring him, that they were no longer even listening as they closed in around us.

'Wait!' It was a voice from the back of the crowd, a voice I knew well. 'Wait!' Everyone looked round. They hushed instantly, and then stood to one side as my mother came forward, Aunty Mildred beside her. Mother looked first at me and then at the Birdman. 'You were up early this morning, Gracie,' she said. 'I wondered where you'd got to.'

'Had to go, Mother,' I said, standing up. 'I had to. Daniel came for me. Big Tim and all of them, they were going to attack the Birdman's cottage. Daniel heard them planning it, so we had to warn him, didn't we?'

'Were they indeed?' said Mother, looking around her. There was a hard edge to her voice I had never heard before. 'Did you know that, Mr Pender?' she asked, and Daniel's father looked hard at Big Tim.

'Well he deserved it,' said Big Tim. 'He was signalling to German submarines, I know he was. We seen him, didn't we?' But none of his friends supported him now.

Mother walked across to Big Tim and looked him in the eye. 'You know nothing, Tim Pender; because you don't think, you never have. You know only what you want to know. You're a bully and a coward and you should be ashamed of yourself.' And she turned and spoke to the crowd. 'This old man helped me and Gracie. He left honey and milk and bread on my doorstep when we needed it most. Just like you, I've known him all my life and never spoken to him, but in all that time I've never known him harm anyone. Yes, every one of us is frightened of him and we tell our children to keep out of his way; but what has he ever really done to harm any one of us?' There was silence. Mother came over to me and took me by the hand. 'I don't know what Gracie and Daniel have been up to, and I don't know why Mr Woodcock wants to save these creatures. I do know we owe it to him and to the two children at least to listen to them, to hear them out. If after that you still want to kill the whales, then you can. They'll still be here.' She did not wait for approval, she assumed it. She turned to Daniel. 'Tell us, Daniel. Tell us all about it.' And not a word was raised against her.

I wondered at the time that she was able to command such instant obedience. On reflection I think everyone was as shocked as I was at the sudden transformation in her. I certainly had never seen her so authoritative and passionate. All I know is that without a murmur, even from Big Tim, they all backed away and waited shamefaced for Daniel to begin.

Daniel turned to Mr Woodcock. 'Shall I tell them?' he asked, and the old man nodded.

'Tell them,' he said, 'tell them everything. But hurry, Daniel, hurry. There's no time to lose.'

They listened intently as Daniel told them of how the Birdman and his mother had witnessed the massacre of the whales on Samson all those years ago, how they had tried to stop it and failed, that it was the islanders' greed and cruelty that had brought the curse down on Samson. He told them the whole terrible story of the death of Samson, of the ghostship, of the starvation and disease that followed, of all the ships drawn to their destruction on the rocks off Samson, of the dogs the people had to eat to survive.

As the truth behind the age-old rumours came out, the islanders listened all the more closely. They heard how the people left one by one until finally the well had dried up and forced the Birdman and his mother off the island.

For some time no one said anything. They looked at each other uneasily, and then it was Big Tim that spoke up. 'So what? We don't know that any of it's true, do we? He could be making it all up, couldn't he? Where's the proof?'

'The proof's on Samson,' Daniel said. 'I've seen it – and Gracie's seen it too. We've seen the horn, haven't we, Gracie? In Mr Woodcock's cottage on Samson it was, hanging above the stove. Just like that one it is,' he said, pointing at the whale.

'You been over there, Gracie?' Mother asked me. 'You been over to Samson?'

'We couldn't help it, Mother,' I said. 'It was that night we went out fishing and the fog came down. Never told you before 'cos I knew you'd be angry. Didn't know where we were, Mother, honest. Couldn't see a thing. Then we saw this light and rowed towards it. We thought it was Bryher at first, but it turned out it was the Birdman's fire on Samson. He lights a fire on Samson whenever there's bad weather. It's to keep the ships away from the rocks.'

Suddenly Mother was beside me. Hands on hips, she faced the crowd. 'Well?' she said. 'What are you waiting for? If we don't hurry, every one of those whales will be on the beach and then we'll never be able to get them off. We need a sail to roll her onto and we need ropes. We'll need a horse, or a donkey, both maybe to haul her back into the sea. Hurry now.' This time there were no arguments. On the contrary there was a sudden stir of excitement. Somehow, Mother had galvanised the whole island into action. The Vicar and Aunty Mildred organised every spare man, woman and child into an extended line at the water's edge. There must have been a hundred people there advancing into the sea to keep the whales from coming in. Waist high in the water they were whistling and shouting and splashing, whilst behind them the rescue began.

It was Daniel's father who directed the delicate task of engineering the stranded whale back into the sea. 'Got to launch her gently, just like she was a boat,' he said. They dug a deep trench to one side of her and when the sail came they laid it in the bottom. Then they dug away the side of the ditch she was lying in and eased her sideways, rocking her gently until she slid down onto the sail. It took twelve men pushing, the Birdman, Mr Wellbeloved and Daniel's father amongst them, before the whale was finally in place.

All through the rescue I stayed by the whale's head whilst an endless relay of children with buckets, Big Tim and his friends mostly, fetched and carried water to keep the whale's skin wet. She was tiring quickly now. Her flourishes were less and less frequent and she had fallen almost silent. She moved quietly from time to time, her tiny eyes often closing for minutes on end so that sometimes I thought she might be dead. A bucket of water poured gently over her head seemed to revive her, but each time it took longer. She would open her wedge-shaped mouth under the horn and allow the water to trickle in through her teeth. I talked to her all the while, reassuring her as well as I could that it would not be long now before she was back with her friends and out at sea again. I could feel her breath on my fingers as I stroked the top of her head around her blowhole. She was breathing less often now and more deeply, almost as if she were going to sleep. Or was she dying slowly?

Friend and another donkey were hitched up already to the sail. At first it looked as if they would not be strong enough for the task. Their feet sank deep into the sand as they pulled and the whale did not move. What the Birdman said into Friend's ear no one knows, but whatever it was was enough, for they were soon hauling the whale down across the wet sand towards the sea. There were a dozen men or more straining at the sail at each side, so that the whale was returned to the water cradled in a kind of hammock. I stood back and watched with the others as the waves washed over her and she gradually came back to life. On the Birdman's advice we left her there wallowing in the shallows for some time, giving her time to regain her strength, to feel her buoyancy. Then to our delight she began to heave and thrash again and she let out a long wailing whistle. That seemed enough to satisfy the Birdman and we gathered around her and pushed her through the water towards the others that lay waiting for her out in the bay. There was a flurry out in the middle when she joined them and much rolling and groaning and whistling, an exultant chorus of joy at their reunion. Then she became one of them, and I was never sure which she was after that.

I thought, as everyone thought, that the job was done then, that once reunited they would turn for the open sea; but for some reason they seemed reluctant to leave the bay in spite of all we did to frighten them away. Big Tim it was who suggested that banging on tin trays and corrugated iron might do the trick, so we children were all sent home to fetch back any bit of sheet metal we could find that would serve as a drum. It was a good idea and the first time we all thundered on our makeshift drums it seemed to have an effect, for they turned and swam away; but then they stopped at the mouth of the bay and turned back again setting up such a row of whistling, whooping and snorting so that you would almost have thought they were talking back to our drums. Far from driving them away, the drumming only seemed to interest them and excite them.

All day long the islanders sustained this frantic effort. Everyone took turns in the water now, for it was too cold to stay there long. Hot soup and bread were brought out to the beach and kept warm over a fire in one corner of the beach, so that a ready supply of food was on hand all day. We had one brief taste of success when a pair of the whales was spotted swimming out to sea, past Gweal Rock. However the others did not follow, so that by nightfall most of the whales were still trapped in Popplestones, unable or unwilling to find their way out.

The Birdman, Daniel and I were sitting drinking our soup by the fire when the Birdman had the idea. His face was ashen with cold and exhaustion, but suddenly there was an urgency in his voice. 'Look where they are,' he said, getting to his feet and pointing out into the bay. 'Look at them.' The whales were lying together in a pack in the dark waters on the far side of Popplestones. 'It's the fire,' he said. 'It's the fire. They're as far from the fire as they can be. They don't like fire.'

Flaming torches, oil lamps, piles of burning brushwood and driftwood, we used anything, anything that would burn. We lit fires all along the rocks around the bay; and then the Birdman, with a long line of islanders on either side of him waving their torches above their heads, waded out into the sea towards the whales. We children were told to stay on the beach. It was too dangerous now, out in the dark water with the whales' flailing tails and the sea whipped up into a frenzy by a fresh offshore wind. So we stayed and watched the line of torches as they moved out into the bay.

Only minutes later they brought the Birdman back, Daniel's father and the Vicar carrying him out of the sea. A wave had knocked the breath out of him, Daniel's father said as they laid him down by the fire beside us.

'I'll be all right,' the Birdman said, struggling onto his elbows. 'Let me get out there. We need everyone out there.'

'I think you've done enough, Mr Woodcock,' said the Vicar. 'They're going, they're turning. We can manage without you now. You nearly drowned out there. You stay here and rest.' And much against his will, he did. Mother put a blanket around him and Daniel and I huddled close to him, and Prince came to lie down at our feet. 'Maybe it'll be all right, children,' the Birdman said.

'Maybe it will be, after all.'

It was the line of flaming torches that at last made the whales leave for the open sea; for with a final flourish of triumphant whistling and snorting, and shooting great fountains into the air, they swam out past Gweal Island and left us in the gathering dark. A great cheer went up all around the bay, but beside us the Birdman was still not happy. He was on his feet again by now. He made everyone build beacons all along the beach to be sure they did not come back during the night; and even when almost everyone had left Popplestones for home he still would not go.

Mother asked him to come home with us. She begged him to come. 'Tell him it's a cold night, Daniel, and he can't sleep in a house with no windows. He's soaked to the skin. Tell him he must come home with us.'

Daniel told him and the Birdman smiled and shook his head. 'I'll be warm enough by the fire,' he said. 'I shall stay here and Prince will stay with me to keep me company, won't you, Prince? Maybe later when it gets light I'll take the boat out. I want to be sure they've gone – got to be sure they don't come back. You take those two children of mine home before they catch cold.' And as we were leaving, he called out without turning round. 'It's over now, children. The curse of Samson is redeemed, finished. All will be well now, I promise you. You'll see.'

So we left him there in the glow of the fire with Prince sitting beside him. As we went we saw the gulls settling on the beach all around him and from nowhere his one-legged kittiwake flew up and landed on his shoulder.

No one ever saw the Birdman again. They found his sou'wester washed up on Hell Bay some days later, but his boat was never found. I have always thought that he knew he might not be coming back because otherwise he would never have left Prince behind on the beach, and because of the remnants of a shell message we found the next morning in the sand beside the dog. The shells were scattered but we could still make out the letters 'Z.W.'.

12   THE END OF IT ALL

I HAD NEVER SEEN THE CHURCH SO FULL AS IT WAS
that next Sunday morning, not even at Christmas. It was a
service, the Vicar said, not just for one but for two fine
men of Bryher who had given their lives for us all. I did
not hear much of what he said. He had that kind of
droning, dreary voice that is impossible to listen to for
very long. I remember sitting in the front pew with
Mother on one side of me and Daniel on the other, and
feeling very important and not nearly as sad as I knew I
should be. I prayed though, or I tried to; but it came out as
a thought rather than a prayer in the end. I was thinking
how good it would be if Father and the Birdman were to
meet up in Heaven, and I wondered what they would say
about me. Daniel sat hunched up in a stiff collar beside
me, his hair unnaturally slicked down. On the way home
afterwards we walked along together. Daniel was angry.

'They still don't trust him,' he said. 'After all he's done for them, they still don't believe him. Father told me to keep off Samson. Says he wants to be sure the curse is finished. He says only time will tell. He's still scared, Gracie. They're all scared, except Aunty Mildred. She's not scared of anything. Only one way to prove it to them, Gracie. We'll have to go and fetch that horn back. If they see that they'll have to believe everything then, won't they? Even Father, even Big Tim.'

But for two weeks after the memorial service the winter gales came and lashed the islands and not a boat could move out of Bryher. It was too dangerous even to cross the sheltered channel to Tresco. That meant there was no school and I was grateful for that. We had brought Prince back to live with us in Southill Cottage, and those horrible goats came too, much to my disgust. Mother said someone had to look after them. I wanted Daniel to look after them, but Daniel's father would not have any animals near his house, and so I found myself milking them twice a day. We had to leave the Birdman's hens and Friend up on Heathy Hill, not because we wanted to but because we could not catch them. Each day during the gales Daniel and I went up there to feed them, hoping to be able to catch them and bring them home; but they were always too wily for us, even when they were hungry.

Then one morning we woke up and the wind had died; the tamarisk tree outside my window was still at last. I lay there beside Mother hoping the sea would be too restless after the storm for us to go to school that day. I did think it was strange when the church bell began to ring, for by my reckoning it was a Monday morning; but I was quite content to believe that I was wrong and that I had another day without school. So I lay back on my pillow and was almost asleep again when Mother sat up suddenly.

'It's not Sunday,' she said. 'The church bell's ringing and it's not Sunday.'

'You sure it isn't Sunday?' I asked. 'It could be, couldn't it?'

'It's Monday, Gracie,' Mother said, 'and a fine day by the look of it, and you're going to school. Out of bed with you.'

'Then why are they ringing the bell if it's Monday?' I asked.

'No idea, but whatever it is it can wait until after breakfast.' Mother climbed out of bed. 'Come on now, Gracie, hurry else you'll miss the school boat.' She looked across the bed at me. 'And just so you won't miss that boat I'll walk you down to the quay; we can find out then why they're ringing that bell.'

Prince came with us sniffing every gateway as they passed, his tail constantly circling, and all the while as we walked up the path the bell kept ringing and ringing. Daniel was not waiting for me as he usually was and every house as we passed seemed to be empty, the front doors flung open wide and left there. The bell had stopped ringing by the time we reached Aunty Mildred's house. We were just passing her gate when we first heard the crowd. As we rounded the bend we saw the quay below us was full of people. You could not see the quay for the crowd. The school boat was there but no one was getting into it. There was another boat beside it, one that often came from St Mary's. Everyone was laughing and clapping and cheering. And then one of them, a man in blue it was, was hoisted on their shoulders and they began to march in a great calvalcade up the path towards us. Prince sat down as he often did when he needed time to consider things.

'Who's that, Gracie?' Mother said, her eyes squinting into the sun. 'What's all the fuss about?'

Daniel was haring up the path towards us and shouting at us as he came. 'That'll show them, Gracie, that'll show them. Now they'll have to believe us. It's over, just like he promised. The curse of Samson is over. Can't you see who it is, Gracie, can't you see?'

And now I could see. Mother saw too, but she could not believe her eyes. As they set my father down on his feet again one of them handed him a stick and the crowd fell silent around him. He looked at Mother, then took off his sailor's cap. 'Bit late for breakfast, am I, Clemmie?' Mother stared at him. 'Well don't look at me like that. It's me, Clemmie, honest it is. They tell me I'm supposed to be dead and drowned, but I'm not. Didn't they tell you I was coming? No, by the look on your face I don't think they can have done. What do I have to do to prove it to you? Here, take my hand, Clemmie, feel that. It's me isn't it? Tell me it's me or I'll begin to doubt it myself. I had my ship sunk from under me, Clemmie – torpedoed off Gallipoli she was, went down in two minutes. There was no one else left alive in the water except me. I hung on to a bit of a lifeboat for a whole day and night and then a fishing boat picked me up. You can't believe it, can you? Well neither could I, I can tell you. I'm a lucky fellow, Clemmie. I don't deserve to be here, but I am. I've got sick leave. Knocked my leg about a bit when I fell in the water, but I won't be needing this old stick for too long.' Father looked down at me. 'Ride home, Gracie?' he said. 'Just off to school, were you? Well Mr Wellbeloved will have to do without you for a day, won't he? Hop up,' he said crouching down, and I jumped up onto his shoulders. 'Coming, Clemmie?' he said and took her hand. 'I could eat a horse.'

That same afternoon every boat on Bryher set out over a sun-dancing sea for Samson. No one stayed behind, not even Big Tim. Mind you, I did notice he was the last one to set foot on Samson when we got there.

They marvelled at the horn above the fireplace in the cottage – and everyone wanted to touch it just to be sure it was not made of wood. We roamed the island from end to end. The great black rabbits were everywhere and Prince chased them ineffectually all afternoon. He rampaged over the island like a wild thing and I found him stretched out on the bed in the Birdman's cottage, his tongue lolling out of his mouth and dripping.

'He's thirsty,' I said. 'Needs a drink.'

'There'll be water in the well now,' said Daniel. 'I know there will be; there has to be.' And we ran down the hillside together, Prince bounding along after us. Sure enough the well was full, full to the brim. We all three lay down on the ground, put our faces in it and drank together.

Everyone drank from the well on Samson that day as if it were the elixir of life, and after that no one ever doubted the Birdman's story, not in my hearing anyway.

*   *   *

If you ever do go to the Isles of Scilly, go over to Samson and look round for yourself. The old ruined cottages are still there, a mound of limpet shells outside each one; and you'll find the well full of water. No one lives there, so you'll have only the terns and the black rabbits for company. You'll be quite alone.

THE GHOST OF GRANIA O'MALLEY

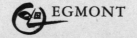 EGMONT

CONTENTS

1 SMILEY

JESSIE WAS ALWAYS FINDING BONES IN THE GREAT
bog-oak field where they dug the peat for the winter fires.
It was here too that her father found most of the wood he
needed for his wood sculptures, his 'creatures' as she
called them. She was forever going off there alone,
mooching around, bottom in the air looking for her bones.
She had a whole collection of them, but she never tired of
looking for more. Mostly they were just sheep bones –
skulls, jawbones, legbones, vertebrae. She had shrews'
skulls too, birds' skulls, all sorts of skulls. But there was
one skull she found that was unlike any other, because it
was a human skull. She was quite sure of it.

She never said a word to anyone. She kept it with the
rest of her collection in the ruined cottage at the bottom of
the bog-oak field. No one but herself ever went near the
place. She called him Smiley because he would keep

grinning at her. She put Smiley in pride of place in a niche in the cottage wall; and from time to time she'd go and talk to him and tell him her troubles – which were many. Smiley would listen, stare back at her and say nothing, which was what she wanted.

But as time passed, Jessie began to feel more and more uneasy about Smiley. So one day, in confession, she told Father Gerald about her skull, partly because she'd been worrying herself about it, and partly because at the time she could think of no other sins to confess. If she told him she had done nothing wrong, nothing bad enough to confess, he just wouldn't believe her. She'd tried that before. So she blurted it out about Smiley, told him everything; but she could tell from the tone of his voice that he just thought this was another of Jessie Parsons' little white lies.

'Bones should be buried in hallowed ground and left undisturbed, Jessie,' he said sonorously. 'Then the souls of the departed can rest in peace.'

So, one dark night with the owl hooting at her from high up in the ruined abbey, she dug a small hole under the abbey walls, said goodbye to Smiley in a whisper, laid him carefully in the wet earth and covered him up. She felt a lot better afterwards; and although she did miss him for a while, she felt pleased with herself that she'd done the right thing.

Some time later Father Gerald had asked after the skull and she'd shown him one of her many sheep's skulls. He'd laughed. 'It's as I thought, Jessie Parsons, that's never a human being. Do you not know a sheep's skull when you see one?' He'd counted the teeth carefully. 'I'd say that's a six-year-old ewe, by the teeth in her.'

Jessie went and put flowers on the unmarked grave just once. 'I hope you're feeling better now, Smiley,' she said. 'I'll leave you be, so's you can rest in peace, like Father Gerald says.' So she did, and as the weeks and months passed, she thought of Smiley less and less.

All this happened a year or more before the rest of it began.

2 THE BIG HILL

THERE HAD TO BE MIST OR JESSIE WOULD NOT EVEN try it. If she failed, and so far she had always failed, she wanted no one else to know of it, especially her mother and father. She'd lost count of how many times she'd lied to them about the Big Hill, about how she had made it all the way to the top. They mustn't see her. No one must see her. If she was going to fail again, then she would fail alone and unseen.

Old Mister Barney might see her, and probably often did, as she passed his shack at the bottom of the Big Hill, but he'd be the only one; and besides, he wouldn't tell anyone. Mister Barney kept himself to himself and minded his own business. He hardly ever spoke to a soul. Jessie was ten and he had spoken to her maybe half a dozen times in her entire life. He would wave at her through the window sometimes, but she was as sure as she could be that he would never spy on her. He just wasn't like that. There was smoke coming from his chimney and one of the chickens stood one-legged in the porch; but today, as Jessie walked across the clearing outside his shack, there was no sign of Mister Barney.

The mist cut the hill off halfway up and dwarfed it, but Jessie knew what was waiting for her up there, how high it really was, how hard it was going to be, and was daunted by it all over again. Mole, her mother's black donkey, nudged her from behind. Mole would go with her. He went everywhere with her. More than once it had been Mole who had spoilt it, nudging her off balance at just the wrong moment.

There was a lot that annoyed her about her 'lousy palsy', as she often called it. But it was balance that was the real problem. Once she'd fallen over, it took so much of her energy to get up again that there was little left for the Big Hill itself. If she could just keep her rhythm going – one and two, one and two, one and two – if she could just keep on lurching, and not fall over, she knew that one day, some day, she'd have strength enough to reach the top of the Big Hill, and then she'd never have to lie about it again.

Mole rubbed his nose up against her back. 'All right, Mole,' said Jessie, clutching the donkey's neck to steady herself. 'I'm going. I'm going. It's all very well for you. You've got four good legs. I've only got two, and they won't exactly do what I tell them, will they?' She looked up at the Big Hill and took a deep breath. 'I'm telling you, Mole, today's the day. I can feel it inside me.' The donkey glanced at her and snorted. Jessie laughed. 'Race you to the top, big ears.'

She started well enough, leaning forward into the hill, willing her fumbling feet forward. She knew every rut and tussock of the track ahead – she'd sat down hard enough on most of them. Mole walked alongside her, browsing in the bracken. After a while he trotted on ahead, all tippy-toed, and disappeared into the mist. 'Clever clogs!' Jessie called after him, but then she tried all she could to put him out of her mind. She knew she had to concentrate. The path was wet from the mist, and slippery. One false step and she'd be on her bottom and that would be that – again.

She could hear Mole snorting somewhere up ahead. As like as not, he'd be at the waterfall by now. Jessie had reached the waterfall just once, the week before – it was as high as she'd ever gone on her own. That time, too, her legs had let her down. They wouldn't manage the stones and she'd tripped and fallen. She'd tried crawling, but she wasn't any better at crawling than she was at walking. She'd crawled on through the water, become too cold and had had to give up. Today would be different. Today she would not let herself give up. Today she would reach the top, no matter what. Today she would prove to Mrs Burke, to Marion Murphy, and to everyone else at school that she could climb the Big Hill just like they could.

She could see Mole up ahead of her now, drinking in the pool below the waterfall. Jessie's legs ached. She wanted so much to stop, but she knew that she mustn't, that rhythm was everything. She passed Mole and laughed out loud at him. 'Haven't you read the one about the hare and the tortoise?' she cried. 'See you at the top.' This was the spot where she'd come to grief the week before, the part of the track she most dreaded. The track rose steeply beside the waterfall, curling away out of sight and around the back of the hill. Every stone was loose here and until she reached the waterfall, *if* she reached the waterfall, the track would be more like a stream, the stones under her feet more like stepping stones. From now on she would have to be careful, very careful.

She was standing now on the very rock where she'd tripped last time. She punched the air with triumph and staggered on, on and up. She was in unknown territory now. Only on her father's back had she ever gone beyond this point and that was a long time ago when she was small. She felt her legs weakening all the while. She fought them, forcing them on. She breathed in deep, drawing what strength she could from the air, and that was when the mist filled her lungs. She coughed and had to go on coughing. Still she tried to go on.

She felt herself falling and knew she could do nothing about it. She threw her arm out to save herself and was relieved to see she was falling into the water. She would be wet, but at least she wasn't going to hurt herself. But she hadn't accounted for the stone just beneath the surface of the water. She never even felt the cold of the stream as it covered her face. There was an explosion of pain inside her head and a ringing in her ears that seemed as if it would never end. Then the world darkened suddenly around her. She tried to see through it, but she couldn't. She tried to breathe, but she couldn't.

She was dreaming of her father's 'creature' sculptures. They were all in the cottage and Smiley was telling them a story and they were laughing, cackling like witches. She woke suddenly. She was sitting propped up, her back against a boulder. Mole was grazing some way off, his tail whisking. Jessie's head throbbed and she put her hand to it. There was a lump under her fingers, and it was sticky with blood. There was more blood in her ear and on her cheek too. She was soaked to the skin. She wondered for some moments where she was and how she had got there. She remembered the climb up the Big Hill, and how she had fallen; and she realised then that she had failed yet again. Tears filled her eyes and she cried out loud, her fists clenched, her eyes closed to stop the tears.

She tasted the salt of her tears and brushed them away angrily. 'I'll get there, Mrs Burke,' she shouted. 'I'll get there, you'll see.'

From nowhere came a voice, a woman's voice, but almost low enough to be a man's. 'Course you will, Jessie,' it said. 'But not if you sit there feeling all sorry for yourself.' Jessie looked around her. There was no one there. Mole glanced at her quizzically. He had stopped chomping. For one silly moment, Jessie imagined it might have been Mole talking, but then the voice went on. 'So you've a bit of a knock on your head. Are you going to let that stop you?' Mole was browsing again, tearing at the grass. So it couldn't be him talking. 'I'm not the donkey, Jessie. And I'll tell you something else for nothing, there's no point at all in your looking for me. You'll not find me.

I'm just a voice, that's all. Don't go worrying about it.'

'Who are you?' Jessie whispered, sitting up and wiping her nose with the back of her hand.

'Is that what they teach children these days? Can you not use a handkerchief like a proper person? Have you not got a handkerchief?'

'Yes,' said Jessie, still looking all around her, but frantically now.

'Then use it, why don't you?' Jessie searched out her handkerchief and blew her nose. 'That's better now,' the voice went on. 'I've always thought that you can tell a lot about folk from the way they treat their noses. There's pickers, there's wipers – like you – there's snifflers and, worst of all, there's trumpeters. You'll not believe this, but I once knew a queen, a real queen, I'm telling you – and she was a trumpeter. Worse still, she'd blow her nose on a handkerchief and she wouldn't throw it away like you or me. She'd use it again, honest she would. She'd use the same handkerchief twice. Can you believe such a thing? And herself a queen! I told her straight out. I said: "There's no surer way to catch a cold and die than to use the same handkerchief twice." She was no one's fool, that queen. Oh no, she listened to me. She must have, because she lived on and into a ripe old age, just like me. She died sitting up. Did you know that?'

Chuckling now, the voice seemed to be coming closer all the time. 'That queen, she wouldn't lie down for anyone, not even death. A lady after my own heart she was. English, mind, but she couldn't help that now, could she? Listen, Jessie, are you just going to sit there or are you going to get up on your feet and climb the Big Hill, like you said you would?'

'Who are you?' Jessie asked again. She was hoping against hope that maybe she was still asleep and dreaming it all. But she *was* bleeding and there *was* real blood on her fingers, on her head. So the voice had to be real too – unless she was going mad. That thought, that she might be going mad, frightened Jessie above everything else.

'It doesn't matter who I am,' said the voice, and it came from right beside her now, 'except that this is my hill you're walking on. I've been watching you these last weeks, we all have, the boys and me. They didn't think you'd make it, but I did. I was sure of it, so sure of it that I've a wager on it – five gold doubloons. And, Jessie, if there's one thing I hate losing, it's money. And here you are, sitting there like a pudding, crying your eyes out and wiping your nose with the back of your hand. I'm ashamed of you, Jessie.'

'I'm sorry,' said Jessie. 'I didn't mean to . . .'

'So you should be. I tell you what.' The voice was whispering in her ear. 'I'll make it worth your while. I'll leave a little something for you at the top of the hill. But if you want my little something, then you'll have to go up there and fetch it for yourself. How about it?'

Jessie was still thinking about what she should do when she felt strong arms under her shoulders, lifting her on to her feet and then holding her for a moment until she had steadied herself on her legs. Then someone tapped her bottom. 'On your way, girl.' And Jessie found herself walking on, almost without meaning to, as if her legs were being worked by someone else. She looked behind her again and again to see if anyone was there. There was no one, only Mole ambling along, head lowered, ears back.

'Did you hear her?' Jessie whispered, as Mole came alongside. 'She's watching us, I know she is. Come on Mole, we've *got* to get to the top, we've got to.' And she lurched on up the Big Hill, rejoining the track beyond the waterfall.

The grass under her feet was spongy here; easier walking, easier falling too, she thought. She remembered how her father had galloped her on his back along this same grassy path, and how they'd fallen over and rolled down the hill together and into the bracken. She remembered too the rockstrewn gully ahead, and wondered how she was ever going to get past it. She went down on her hands and knees. It would be painful and slow, but it was the only way. There were brambles across the path that had to be pulled away, endless lacerating rocks to be negotiated. Jessie kept crawling until her wrists couldn't take it any more and she had to crawl on her elbows. That was when her knee slipped and her fingers wouldn't grasp and she slid backwards. She ended up in an ungainly heap, wedged against the rocks, knees and elbows barked and bleeding, and a vicious thorn stuck in the palm of her hand. She drew it out with her teeth and spat it on to the ground.

Mole was braying at her from somewhere further up the hill. Jessie looked up, shielding her eyes against the white of the sun that was breaking now through the mist. Mole was standing right on top of the Big Hill. He wasn't just calling her, he was taunting her. Jessie levered herself laboriously to her feet and swayed there for a moment, her head spinning. She closed her eyes, and then it all came flooding back.

April, the start of the summer term at school and they'd all of them gone, even the infants, up the Big Hill on a nature walk with Mrs Burke, her head teacher and the other bane of her life besides Marion Murphy. And Jessie had been the only one to be left behind with Miss Jefferson, the infant teacher. Miss Jefferson had insisted on holding her hand all the way to the beach, just in case, she said. They were going to find lots of interesting shells, she said, to make a shell picture. It was always shells or wild flowers with Miss Jefferson – she had her own wild flower meadow behind the school. But today it was shells.

Miss Jefferson foraged through the bladderwrack and the sea lettuce, whooping with joy every few seconds and talking nineteen to the dozen like she always did. It wasn't that Jessie didn't like her; she did. But she was forever fussing her, endlessly anxious that Jessie might fall, might be too cold, might be too tired. Jessie was used to that, used to her. It was being left behind that she really resented.

Despite all Miss Jefferson's enthusiastic encouragement she could not bring herself to care a fig about the shell picture. She wanted to be up there with them, with the others. All the while she kept her eye on the Big Hill. She could see them, a trail of children up near the summit now, Mrs Burke striding on ahead. She heard the distant cheer when they reached the top and she had to look away. Miss Jefferson understood and put her arm round her, but it was no comfort.

She had begged to be allowed to go up the Big Hill with the others, but Mrs Burke wouldn't even hear of it. 'You'd slow us down, Jessie,' she'd said. 'And besides, you know you'd never reach the top.' And then she'd laughed. 'And I'm afraid you're far too big to carry.' That was the moment Jessie had decided she would climb the Big Hill, cerebral lousy palsy or not. Somehow or other she would do it, she'd drag herself up there if necessary.

She opened her eyes. Here she was, after two months of trying, within a stone's throw of the summit. This time there'd be no stopping her. 'Here I come!' she cried. 'Here I come!' And she launched herself up the hill. Several times her legs refused to do what she told them and threatened to buckle beneath her. Time and again, she felt herself reeling. She longed just to sit down and rest; but again and again she heard the voice in her head. 'You can do it, girl, you can do it.'

Where the words came from, or who spoke them, she neither knew nor cared any more. Nothing mattered but getting to the top. She was almost there when her legs simply folded on her, and she found herself on her knees. She crawled the last metre or so over mounds of soft thrift and then collapsed. Mole came over to her and nuzzled her neck with his warm whiskery nose. She clung to Mole's mane and hauled herself up on to her feet.

There below her lay the whole of Clare Island, and all around the grey-green sea, with the island of Inishturk far to the south. And when she turned her face into the wind, there was the mainland and the islands of Clew Bay floating in the sea like distant dumplings. She was on top of the world. She lifted her hands to the sky and laughed out loud and into the wind, the tears running down her face. Mole looked on, each of his ears turning independently. Jessie's legs collapsed and she sat down with a sudden jolt that knocked the breath out of her for a moment, and stunned her into sanity.

Only then did she begin to reflect on all that had happened to her on the Big Hill that morning. There could be no doubt that she had made it to the top, unless of course she was still in the middle of some wonderful dream. But the more she thought about it, the more she began to doubt her memory of the climb, the fall in the stream, the disembodied voice that had spoken to her, the arms that had helped her to her feet, the words in her head that had urged her on to the top. It could all have been some extraordinary hallucination. That would make sense of it. But then, what about the bump on her head? And there was something else she couldn't understand. Someone must have rescued her from the stream. But who? Maybe it was all the bump on the head, maybe that was why she was hearing voices. And maybe that was why her memory was deceiving her. She had to be sure, really sure. She had to test it.

'Hello?' she ventured softly. 'Are you still there? I did it, didn't I? I won your bet for you. Are you there?' There was no one, nothing, except a solitary humming bumble-bee, a pair of gulls wheeling overhead and Mole munching nearby. Jessie went on, 'Are you anyone? Are you someone? Are you just a bump on the head or what? Are you real? Say something, please.' But no one said anything. Something rustled behind her. Jessie swung round and saw a rabbit scuttling away into the bracken, white tail bobbing. She noticed there were rabbit droppings all over the summit. She flicked at one of them and it bounced off the side of a rock, a giant granite rock shaped by the wind and weather into a perfect bowl, and in the bowl was a pool of shining water fed by a spring from above it.

Jessie hadn't been thirsty until now. She crawled over, grasped the lip of the rock and hauled herself up. She put her mouth into the water like Mole did and drank deep. Water had never been so welcome to her as it was that morning on the summit of the Big Hill. She was wiping her mouth when she saw something glinting at the bottom of the pool. It looked like a large ring, brass maybe, like one of the curtain rings they had at home in the sitting room. She reached down into the water and picked it out.

'I am a woman of my word.' The same voice, from behind her somewhere. 'Didn't I say I'd leave a little something for you?' In her exhaustion, in her triumph, Jessie had quite forgotten all about the promised 'little something'. She backed herself up against the rock. 'Don't be alarmed, Jessie, I'll not hurt you. I've never hurt a single soul that didn't deserve it. You did a fine thing today, Jessie, a fine thing; and what's better still, you won me my wager. I'm five gold doubloons richer, not that I've a lot to spend it on, mind. None of us have, but that's by the by. None of the boys thought you could do it, but I did. And I like to be right. It's a family failing of ours. "Her mother's an O'Malley," I told them. "So Jessie's half an O'Malley. She'll do it, just watch." And we did watch and you did do it. The earring's yours, girl. To be honest with you I've not a lot of use for such things these days. Look after it, won't you?'

When Jessie spoke at last, her voice was more of a whisper than she had intended it to be. 'Where are you? Can't I see you? You can't be just a voice.' But there was no reply. She tried again and again, until she knew that whoever had been there either didn't want to answer or had gone away. 'Thanks for the earring,' Jessie called out. 'I won't lose it, I promise.'

It should have sounded silly talking to no one like she was, but somehow it didn't. Talking to Mole was silly and she knew it, but there was no one else and she had to talk to someone. 'See what she gave me, Mole? It's an earring. It's because I climbed the Big Hill and she won her bet.' The donkey lifted his upper lip, showed his yellow teeth and sniffed suspiciously at the ring in the flat of Jessie's hand. He decided it wasn't worth eating.

Jessie looked back down the Big Hill. It was a very long way back down again. She had never given a single thought as to how she would get down if ever she got to the top, probably because in her heart of hearts she had never really believed she *would* get to the top. She knew well enough that, for her, climbing down the stairs at home was always a more difficult proposition than climbing up. She'd never manage it, not all the way to the bottom. It was impossible. Then she had an idea, an obvious idea, but a good one. Mole would take her down. She would use the rock as a mounting block, lie over Mole's back and hitch a ride all the way back home. Easy.

It did not prove as easy as she had imagined. First of all, Mole wouldn't come to the rock and had to be dragged there by his mane. Then he wouldn't stand still, not at first. Mole wasn't at all used to being ridden and shifted nervously under Jessie's weight; but eventually he seemed to get the idea and walked away, taking Jessie down the Big Hill and all the way back home, Jessie clinging on like a limpet, desperate not to slide off. She waited until Mole was grazing the grass on the lawn in amongst her father's 'creatures', and then just dropped off. It was a fairly painless landing. That was where her father found her when he came back from the sheep field a short time later.

'Didn't you see me, Dad?' she said.

He stared at her in horror. 'There's blood all over you, Jess,' he said, running over to her. 'What have you been up to?'

'I did it, Dad. I climbed the Big Hill! Mole brought me back, but I did the rest all on my own.'

'I thought you'd climbed it already,' said her father. In her excitement, Jessie had even forgotten her own lies.

'I did,' she said, recovering quickly, 'I did, but I did it again, faster this time.'

Her father carried her inside and sat her down in the kitchen. 'What do you want to go and do a crazy thing like that for?' he said, dabbing her grazed knees with wet cotton wool. It should have stung, but it didn't. 'Your mother will kill me, letting you go off like that. Don't you say a word about it when she gets back, you hear me? And just look at the lump on your head!'

Jessie clutched the earring tight in her fist. The sheepdog was sniffing at it. 'Get off, Panda,' she said, pushing him away. Panda gazed up at her out of his two white eyes and rested his wet chin on her knee. He'd been rolling in something nasty again. 'When's Mum back?' Jessie went on.

'This evening, if the weather holds,' said her father, pressing a cool tea towel on her head. 'Here, hold that. It'll get the swelling down. He's arrived. Your cousin, Jack. Your mum rang from the airport at Shannon.'

'What's he like?' Jessie said. Panda was trying to lick his way into her fist. She pushed him away again.

'Quiet, doesn't say very much. Make a change from you, won't it?'

'All summer!' Jessie protested. 'Why does he have to come all summer?'

'Because he's a relation, your Uncle Sean's son, your cousin.'

'But I've never even met Uncle Sean.' Her father lifted up her arm to examine her elbow. She pulled away. 'I'll wash it myself,' she snapped.

'What's the matter, Jess?' he asked, crouching down beside her.

'I wish he didn't have to come, Dad,' she said. 'I like it like it is, with just the three of us.'

'Me too,' said her father. 'But we'll be three again after he's gone, won't we? Now get upstairs and wash that elbow of yours. We don't want it going poisonous on us. Your mum'll have fifty fits.'

Jessie had already thought where she would hide the earring before she even reached her room. The goldfish bowl. She'd hide it in the stones at the bottom of Barry's bowl. Barry went mad while she was doing it. He always hated her putting her hand in his bowl. 'Look after it for me, Barry,' she said, and the goldfish mouthed at her from under his wispy weed and then turned his tail on her. 'Please yourself then,' she said. All the while, Panda was on her bed and watching her intently. 'Secret,' she said, putting her finger to her lips. 'No one must ever know, just you and me and Barry. He's not telling anyone and neither are you, are you? You stink, Panda, you know that?'

3 THE FACE IN THE MIRROR

CLATTERBANG WOULDN'T START. SHE NEVER DID when there was mist about, and there was often mist about. Clatterbang was a rusty old black taxicab that had seen better days on the streets of London and Belfast, but she was perfect for the island – when she worked. You could carry up to six sheep in the back, or twelve bales of hay, or a 'creature' sculpture. But today it was just Jessie, with Panda curled up beside her on the back seat. Her father had his head under the bonnet, and said something that he would never have dared say if her mother had been home. He tried whatever he was trying again and suddenly the engine started. He slammed the bonnet down and jumped in.

'We'll be late,' he said. 'Hold tight.' They bumped and rattled down the farm track, out on to the road, past the abbey ruins and along the coast road towards the quay.

They weren't late. The ferry was just tying up. Her father stopped the car and turned to her. 'Once more, Jess, how'd you get the bump?'

'I fell over.'

'Where?'

'In the garden.'

'Good. And you stick to that story, no matter what, understand?'

They could see her mother now, tying her scarf over her head. She was standing at the end of the quay, and beside her was a tall boy, almost as tall as she was, with a white baseball hat on, sideways. He was gazing around him, hands thrust deep into his pockets. 'Will you look at that beanpole of a boy!' said Jessie's father, opening the car door. 'I'll give her a hand with those bags. You wait here.' And he was gone.

Jessie got out of the car and tottered along after him as fast as she could, which wasn't fast at all. Her legs were still tired from the climb up the Big Hill. She glanced up at the Big Hill, but it was no longer there. The mist had cut off its top again. She thought then of the voice and heard it again in her head. The more she thought about it, the more she believed it must be the first sign of madness. Maybe she had cerebal palsy of the brain as well as the body. Or maybe it was the voice of a saint she had heard. She hoped it was that. She'd heard the stories of St Patrick talking to folk as they climbed up Crough Patrick just over the water on the mainland. If it could happen there, it could happen here. It wasn't impossible. But then she thought that the voice hadn't sounded at all like a saint, not Jessie's idea of a saint anyway.

They were all three coming towards her now, her father carrying the bags, her mother striding out ahead, almost running as she reached her. 'What do you mean, she fell over?' she said. Then she was crouching down in front of her and holding her by the shoulders. 'Are you all right, Jess?'

'Fine, Mum.'

'What happened?'

'I just tripped, that's all.'

'Where?'

'In the garden.' Jessie didn't dare look up in case she caught her father's eye. Her mother was examining the lump on her head. 'One week,' she went on, 'I go away one week. Have you seen the doctor?'

'No.'

'Dizzy?'

'No.'

Then the boy was standing there. He had a silver brace on his teeth – more brace than teeth, Jessie thought.

'This is your cousin Jack,' said her mother, smiling now. 'All the way from Long Island, New York, America, to Clare Island, County Mayo, Ireland, isn't that right, Jack?' The boy was staring at her, and frowning at the same time. It was a normal reaction, when people saw her first. It was the way she stood, a little lopsided, as if she was disjointed somehow.

'Hi,' said the boy. He was still scrutinising her. 'How are you?'

'Fine,' said Jessie. 'Why wouldn't I be?'

'She's not fine at all,' said her mother, and she smoothed Jessie's hair out of her face. 'She's a terrible lump on her head.' Panda jumped up at Jack, and the boy backed away in alarm.

'He won't hurt you,' said Jessie. 'Only a sheepdog, not a wolf, y'know.' Jack laughed, a little nervously, Jessie thought.

'We've got bigger ones back home,' he said, recovering himself. 'We've got wolfhounds, Irish wolfhounds, three of them.'

'Well, one's good enough for us,' Jessie said. 'He's called Panda.'

'On account of his eyes, I guess,' said Jack.

'Not necessarily,' said Jessie, unwilling to hide her irritation.

'We'll be home in a few minutes, Jack,' said Jessie's father. 'Nowhere's far on Clare Island. Four miles end to end.' He put the bags down, and flexed his fingers. 'You can walk the whole island in a couple of hours. I've got Clatterbang down the end of the quay, by the castle there.'

Jessie felt the boy watching her walk. She looked up quickly to catch him at it. She was right. He *was* watching. 'You play American football?' she asked. It was just something to say.

'Some.'

'I've seen it on the telly. You any good at it?'

'Not that good.'

'Makes two of us then, doesn't it?' she said. She smiled at him and got a ghost of a smile back. Perhaps she liked him a little better now than she had at first, but she still wasn't sure of him. She eyed him warily as he walked along beside her in his spongy trainers, shoulders hunched. His hair was cut close. It was so close and so fair she could see every contour of his head, and he had more freckles on him than Jessie had ever seen on anyone. He was thin too, so that his blue jeans and his New York Yankees pinstripe sweatshirt hung loose on him. He was pointing up at the castle now. 'Who lives up there?' he said. 'Looks kind of old.'

'It is. No one lives there, not any more.'

Jessie's father had stopped by the car and was opening the door. 'Jeez, that's some car,' Jack said, running his hand along the bonnet. 'Diesel, right? Three-litre engine? Old, I guess.'

'It goes,' Jessie snapped. 'And that's all a car's got to do, isn't it?' Now she had quite definitely made up her mind. She did not like this boy. She would not like this boy, she wouldn't ever like this boy. This was going to be the longest month of her life. Her mother was giving her one of her pointed looks.

'You two cousins getting on, are you?' she said.

'Perfect,' said Jessie, and she got in the car and slammed the door, leaving Jack to walk round the other side.

Clatterbang spluttered a few times and then started up reluctantly. No one spoke until they were well along the coast road.

'Miss me?' said Jessie's mother.

'Missed you,' her father replied. 'We both did, didn't we, Jess?' He turned to her. 'And how was Dublin?'

'Don't ask.' She spoke so quietly that Jessie could hardly hear.

On the back seat, cousin Jack and cousin Jessie sat side by side in silence. Panda looked first at one and then the other. At supper, Jack hardly touched a thing. He chewed on a piece of bread and said it wasn't the same as the bread 'back home'. The water, he said, tasted 'kind of funny' and he screwed up his nose when Jessie's father offered him some of his home-made sheep's cheese.

'You got peanut butter?' Jack asked. 'I usually have peanut butter sandwiches and a Coke.'

'What, every meal?' Jessie's father said.

Jack nodded. 'Except breakfast. I have cornflakes for breakfast, and Coke.'

'I'll get some peanut butter in tomorrow,' Jessie's mother said, patting his arm. 'Now you'd better get yourself to bed. A good night's sleep, that's what you need. Got to be up early. School tomorrow.'

'School?'

'That's what your father said,' Jessie's mother went on. '"Treat him no different," he told me. "What Jessie does, he does." Your dad's my older brother, remember? I always did what he said when I was little – almost always anyway – and where you're concerned, what your dad says goes. So it's school for you tomorrow. Jess will be with you. You'll look after him, won't you, Jess? You need any help unpacking, Jack?' Jack shook his head. Then, without saying a word, he stood up, pushed back his chair and went out. The three of them looked at each other, the clock ticking behind them in the silence of the kitchen.

They heard Jack's bedroom door shut at the end of the passage upstairs.

'He's got his troubles,' Jessie's mother said. 'He'll be fine, he'll settle.'

'What kind of troubles?' Jessie asked.

'Never you mind,' and she tapped Jessie's plate. 'Waste not, want not. Eat. And by the way, Jess, will you tell me how come your trousers are all torn and covered in mud?'

'I told you. I fell over, I tripped,' Jessie said, suddenly busying herself with her eating so she didn't have to look up.

'In the garden,' her father added, rather too hurriedly.

'So you said, so you said.' It was quite clear she didn't believe a word of it.

Jessie's bedroom was right above the kitchen. She could always hear what was being said downstairs, even if sometimes she didn't want to. But tonight she did. She knew – everyone on the island knew – the real reason her mother had been over to the mainland. It wasn't just to fetch cousin Jack from the airport. That was just part of it. She'd been a whole week in Dublin, trying to see the bigwigs in the Dáil, the parliament, about the Big Hill.

Her mother and father rarely talked about the Big Hill in front of her, and Jessie knew why. There wasn't another thing in the world they ever argued about, just the Big Hill. They would tease one another from time to time, but they would never really argue – not in Jessie's hearing anyway. They had spats of course, like anyone. Interrupt her father when he was making one of his 'creatures' in his shed and there was always trouble. But her mother never dug her heels in, never lost her temper, except when she was defending the Big Hill.

Catherine O'Malley – her mother's name before she married – was without doubt the most beautiful woman on the island, and therefore the cause of much admiration and envy. She had a mass of shining dark hair and eyes to match. Jessie knew the story well, and she loved to think of it, often. There was hardly a man who hadn't wanted to marry her mother. She was engaged to Michael Murphy, who owned the salmon farm now and the Big Hill too, when Jimmy Parsons, this 'blow-in' from England, this foreigner, this sculptor, came to stay for a summer holiday. He set eyes on Catherine O'Malley, took her fishing one day, married her and never went away.

Everyone knew Michael Murphy was still in high dudgeon about it even all these years later. He was a squat little man and rich as Croesus – the very opposite of her father, who stood nearly two metres in his boots, and hadn't a penny to his name. He was almost always in his boots too, either out in the fields shepherding his flock or in his shed carving his beloved 'creatures' that no one ever seemed to want to buy. He didn't seem to mind too much, and Jessie didn't mind at all. They were like family to her. She had given every one of them a name, and when she was little he would tell her stories about them in the dark before she went off to sleep. Her father only took his boots off in the evenings and then his dirty toes would be sticking out of his socks, and he'd be scratching them. He wasn't perfect, but as a father he was a whole lot better than Michael Murphy would ever have been.

Jessie could picture them downstairs now as she listened to them. He'd be sitting in the rocker, Panda at his feet, and she'd be at the ironing.

'You haven't said much,' she heard him saying.

'Well, that's because there's not a lot to say.'

'You got to see the minister then, at the Dáil?'

'Yes.'

'Well?'

'Well, you'll be glad to hear that he agrees with you, you and all the others, all except old Mister Barney.'

'He said no then?'

'No, Jimmy. He said yes. He said yes to money, yes to destruction, yes to pollution. Oh, he's a real yes-man.'

'Well, you did what you could. No one could've done more, that's for sure. So if it's going to happen, best just to accept it, eh?'

'Never. Never. I'll never accept it. I was born here, remember? I grew up on that hill. I dreamed my dreams up there. The place is in my blood. And they want to send bulldozers to cut the top off my mountain, my hill, so that Michael Murphy and his kind can dig out the gold and get rich – as if they're not rich enough already. Well, they'll do it over my dead body. And I mean that.'

'Cath, for God's sake, why do you go on so? You've done what you can. Everyone respects you for it. I do, that's for sure. But this is the nineteen nineties we're living in. A hundred and fifty years ago there were over a thousand people living here on Clare, now there's barely a hundred and twenty. The way things are going, in ten years' time, there'll be half that. And why? Because there's no work here, no money. Bed and breakfast, a few tourists in the summer, sell a lobster or two, but that's it. There's nothing here for the young people to stay for. I don't like Michael Murphy any more than you do but, like him or not, at least he's brought work to the island. That gold mine will mean work for a generation or more, and money to develop the island.'

'Oh yes.' Her mother's blood was up now. 'And at what cost? We'll have streams of arsenic from the mine running down the hill, poisoning our children and our sheep – and that's what the experts said, not me. They're kicking old Mister Barney out of his shack, when the poor old man just wants to be left to finish his days in peace. And you know and I know that they won't employ islanders in the mine. They say they will, but they won't. People like that never do. They'll bring in outsiders, blow-ins.'

'I'm a blow-in, or had you forgotten?' said her father. There was a silence. 'Look, Cath,' he went on, 'in the last three years, ever since this thing started, we must have been through it a thousand times. You've made your point, you've argued your case. Your last chance was Dublin. You said so yourself, you said it was the last ditch. For goodness sake, even your own mother says you should give it up.'

'Don't you dare use my mother against me!' Her voice was sharp with anger. 'What's happened to you? You're supposed to be an artist, aren't you? A thinking man? Can you not see that it's against nature itself to cut the top off a mountain, any mountain, no matter where, just for a pot of stinking gold. All gold is fool's gold, don't you know that? You cut the top off the Big Hill, you dig out whatever's inside, and you suck out the soul of this place. There'll be nothing left. What'll it take to make you see it, Jimmy?' She cried then and Jessie could see in her mind's eye her father putting his arms round her and shushing her against his shoulder. 'I can't let them do it, Jimmy,' she wept. 'I won't.'

'I know, I know. But whatever happens, Cath, don't go hating me for what I think. I've been honest with you. I must be honest and say what I think, you know that. We've a whole life to lead here, Jess to look after, wood to sculpt and hundreds of silly sheep with their limping feet and their dirty little tails. We mustn't have this thing between us.' After that there was a lot of sniffling, and then subdued laughter.

'And talking of honesty, Jimmy Parsons.' It was her mother again, happier now, 'Jess tried the Big Hill again, didn't she? That's how she hurt herself, isn't it?'

'You can't stop her, Cath. And what's more I don't think we should. All right, so she fell over and hurt herself, but at least she tried. And if that's anyone's fault, it's yours. You were forever telling her, remember? "You can do it," you'd say. "You can do anything you want, if you want it badly enough. Forget about your lousy palsy." Well, that's just what she's doing. She's set her heart on reaching the top of the Big Hill. She's a brave little heart and I'm not about to stop her from trying.'

'How far did she get?'

'To the top, of course. Doesn't she always? You know Jessie and her capacity for wishful thinking, for telling stories. But I think maybe she got a lot further up this time. She was so happy, so pleased with herself. Wouldn't it be just about the best thing in the world if she really made it, if one day she really made it right to the top of the Big Hill?'

'There you are then, Jimmy,' said her mother, so softly Jessie could scarcely hear, 'another reason if you ever needed one, and maybe the best reason, why the Big Hill has to be saved. Call it holy, call it magic, call it what you will, but there is something about that mountain, Jimmy. I can't describe it. I've been up there hundreds of times in my life and you know something? I've never once felt alone.'

Listening in her bed, turning her gold earring over and over in her hand, the indisputable evidence that she had indeed reached the summit of the Big Hill that afternoon, Jessie was tempted to go downstairs, burst into the kitchen and tell them the whole story from beginning to end: the climb, the voice, the earring, everything. She was boiling with indignation at her parents' disbelief, at their lack of faith. Yet she knew there was no point in protesting. She had been caught out often enough before, and by both of them too. She was a good storyteller, but a bad liar because she always went too far, became too fantastical.

Yes, she could dangle the earring in their faces, but what of the rest of the story? Why should they believe her just because she'd found an earring? And were they really likely to believe she had heard a voice, and had a conversation with someone who wasn't there? She wasn't even sure she believed it herself. She looked down at the only solid evidence she had. The earring was still wet from Barry's bowl, so she dried it on her nightie. Downstairs she could hear the television was on. The Big Hill argument was over, till the next time.

She climbed out of bed and sat down in front of her mirror. She held the ring up to her ear and turned sideways to look at herself in profile. She'd try it on. She'd had her ears pierced in Galway the year before. She took out her sleepers. It hurt a little, but she persevered through all the wincing until finally there it was, swinging from her lobe, glowing yellow-gold in the light.

'Perfect,' said a voice from behind her, the same voice she'd heard up on the Big Hill. A warm shiver crawled up her back and lifted her hair on her neck. 'Pretty as a picture. It never looked half as good on me. Maybe one day I'll find you the other one for the other ear. I've got it somewhere. And by the way, who's that boy in the room next door?'

'My cousin Jack,' Jessie breathed. 'He's from America.'

'Well, now there's a thing,' came the voice again. 'America. I've been there, you know – a long while back, it's true, but I've been there. Maybe I'll tell you about it one day, when we know each other better.'

'I'm not going mad, am I?' Jessie said. 'You really are there, aren't you?' Jessie shivered. She was suddenly cold.

'Sure I am, Jessie,' said the voice, 'and you're not at all mad either, I promise you that. It's just that I want something done and I can't do it all on my own. I need help. I need a friend or two with a bit of spirit, if you see what I'm saying. In my experience, and I've had a fair bit of it in my time, you have to choose your friends very carefully.'

'But what do you need a friend for?'

'All in good time, Jessie.' The voice was fainter now. 'I'll be seeing you.'

For just a fleeting moment, there was a fading face in the mirror behind her. Jessie had the impression of a mass of dark dishevelled hair, radiant bright eyes and a ghost of a smile on the woman's face, not old exactly, not young either; somehow both at the same time. She turned around. The room was quite empty. She could feel there was no one there any more, but she knew for sure that there had been someone, and that whoever she was had gone. She had imagined none of it. She took the earring off, dropped it back into Barry's bowl and covered it over with the stones. She wiped her hand on her nightie and swung herself into bed.

From next door came a low rhythmic roar. It was some moments before Jessie worked out what it could be. Jack was snoring, just like Panda did, only louder. Suddenly the door opened and her mother stood there, silhouetted against the light.

'You awake still?'

'Yes, Mum.'

'How's the bump?'

'Fine.'

'Shall I give you a kiss goodnight?' Her mother sat down on the bed beside her and snuggled her close. 'Love you both, you know,' she whispered in her ear. 'But I'm not going to back down over the Big Hill. You understand that, don't you?'

'Course.'

She kissed her forehead and sat back up. 'And don't worry about Jack. He's a nice enough boy, you'll see. He's not had a happy time, y'know, what with his mother going off like she did, and now his dad not being well. Give him time, there's a girl.' She shivered, and looked around her. 'It's terrible cold in here,' she said. 'Have you had the window open or what?' Jessie shook her head. Her mother pulled the duvet up to her chin and stood up. 'Maybe it's a ghost then,' she laughed. 'Always cold, they say, when there's been ghosts about.'

Suddenly it occurred to Jessie that the face smiling down at her, her mother's face, was much like the face she had seen in the mirror. They smiled the same smile. They had the same hair, the same mouth even.

'You weren't in here a moment ago, were you, Mum?' she asked.

'No. Why?'

'Maybe I dreamed you,' said Jessie.

'Maybe you did. Sleep now.' And she went away, leaving Jessie alone in the dark. I *have* seen a ghost, Jessie thought. I *have* heard a ghost. I *have* felt the cold of a ghost. I should be frightened out of my skin, but I'm not. The snoring next door lulled her into a deep sleep.

Jessie and Jack were walking down the farm lane towards school the next morning, Mole following along behind.

'You snore, do you know that?' Jessie said.

'I do not.'

'How do you know? If you're asleep you can't tell, can you? I heard you.'

'Well, at least I don't talk to myself.'

Jessie knew at once what he had overheard. 'Oh that. I was just talking to a ghost, wasn't I?' She said it half to tease, but half because she longed to tell someone, and she knew he wouldn't believe her. She was right.

He looked down at her and smiled. 'Oh yeah?'

Jessie shrugged her shoulders. 'You think what you like. I'm not bothered.' The school bell was ringing. 'Sometimes I think Mrs Burke's a ghost. She sort of floats, and she's always appearing suddenly out of nowhere.'

'Who's Mrs Burke?'

'She's my teacher, your teacher now, head teacher too; real old stick. Come on, we'll be late. And she eats you if you're late.' She looked up at him and smiled. 'Don't worry, you're too skinny for her. Mrs Burke, she likes little fat things like me.' When his smile opened, the sun glinted on his silver brace.

They hurried on, passing the abbey and the church, and then turning up the school lane towards the playground. It was ominously quiet, and Jessie soon saw why. The whole school was waiting for them, staring at them through the playground fence, all silent and wide-eyed.

'He's my cousin,' Jessie announced. 'He's called Jack and he's from America. And you can all stop your gawping, so you can.'

4 JAWS

'WELCOME TO OUR LITTLE SCHOOL, JACK.' MRS
Burke took her glasses off and laid them on her open
Bible, as she always did after morning prayers. 'I did
notice,' she went on, 'that there weren't that many eyes
closed during prayers this morning. Now I know that it's a
bit like having someone from another planet, but Jack is
only from the United States of America which is just a
little way across the ocean from here, that's all. There's
hardly one of us in this room who hasn't got an uncle over
there, or an aunty or a cousin or whatever. As you see,
they have two legs like we do, two arms, a couple of eyes
and they even speak the same sort of language, don't you,
Jack?' Jack tried to smile.

'So children, we will have no more of the staring, will
we? It is not polite and not at all friendly either. Jack is
here for our last few weeks of term, and then I believe into

the summer holidays as well. So you'll see plenty of him. And we want him to have fond memories of Clare Island to take back home. So let's all of us show him just how friendly we can be, shall we?'

Liam Doherty took Mrs Burke at her word. In playtime, Liam made a beeline for Jack; and where Liam went, others soon followed. In no time at all, Jack found himself backed up against the playground fence being peppered with questions: about American football and baseball, about cowboys and cops. Liam asked if he could try on his baseball cap and Jack handed it over, a little reluctantly. It was passed around after that, but by the time the bell went for the end of playtime, he had it back again. By now he seemed to be enjoying all this new-found adulation, revelling in it almost, Jessie thought; and she was irritated by that.

Wherever he went, he seemed to be flanked by Liam Doherty and his gang. Marion Murphy seemed to have taken an instant shine to him as well, so she was never too far away either. Jessie kept her distance. Jack seemed to have forgotten that she even existed. For the rest of the day he hardly spoke to her, even at lunch-time. By the afternoon, Jessie was seething inside, and that made her written work even worse than usual.

Jessie was never much good anyway at her writing – that was why she hated doing it. Whatever she did, however hard she tried, her writing always came out all spindly and crooked. Everyone else could do it better, and faster too. Jessie's hands simply wouldn't do what her brain told them to do. And it wasn't just her hands that wouldn't obey her. It was her toes too. Whenever she tried to write, her toes would curl up under her feet and cramp themselves. She couldn't stop them. Mrs Burke came and bent over her to see how she was getting on.

'You're just going to have to try harder, aren't you, Jessie?' She'd said it often enough before, but it still hurt. 'I mean, just took at that writing. It's like a demented spider. I've told you till I'm blue in the face, hold your pencil this way, with the forefinger pressed down. You can grip it better.' How would she know what my hands can and can't do? Jessie thought. Doesn't she think I *want* to grip it better? 'Turn the page and try it again, Jessie.' Jessie sighed audibly, and with insolent intent. 'That'll be quite enough of that, Jessie Parsons. I'm not going to treat you any different from the others. It's no good you feeling sorry for yourself all your life.'

That was the moment when Jessie had finally had enough. 'I do not feel sorry for myself, Miss,' she said, so fired up now that she could not stop herself. 'And you do treat me differently. You wouldn't take me up the Big Hill with the others, would you? You said I couldn't climb it. Well, I did. I climbed the Big Hill. I climbed it all by myself.'

'You did what?'

'I climbed it,' Jessie insisted.

Mrs Burke's furious frown lightened to a half-mocking smile. 'I don't think so, Jessie. I think what you mean to say is that you climbed it in your head. You always did have a powerful imagination. But what you mustn't do – and I've told you this before – is to confuse the one with the other, fact with fiction. Perhaps your father helped you up, gave you a piggyback, was that it?'

'I did it on my own,' Jessie said, her eyes fixed on Mrs Burke, the defiance quite undisguised, quite fearless.

'Jessie Parsons.' Mrs Burke looked down at her severely and arranged a wisp of grey hair behind her ear. 'What you are telling me is an untruth, a lie, and if I teach you just one thing before you leave this school it will be to tell the truth.' The class were all silent now, all watching. Mrs Burke went on, her voice thin with menace, 'You did *not* climb the Big Hill, and I won't have you say that you did. I won't have you use your disability as a weapon against the world, as an excuse for lying. You will write out fifty times, and neat, mind: "I did not climb the Big Hill." Is that quite clear and understood? You have one week. I'll not hear another word about it.'

There were lots of words about it, mostly from Marion Murphy, all of them disbelieving, most of them mocking. Jessie endured them all – it was the best way. Jack kept out of it and said nothing, until they were walking home together after school.

'Did you?' he asked suddenly.

'Did I what?'

'Did you climb that hill like you said?'

'If I say I did, I did,' Jessie snapped.

'All the way to the top?'

'Yes, and with these two legs,' Jessie said acidly. 'They're the only ones I've got.' They didn't speak for a moment or two.

'I brought my rollerblades,' said Jack.

'So?'

'You want to try?'

Jessie smiled for the first time that day. 'All right,' she said, and they walked on for a while before she asked what she had been wanting to ask ever since she first saw him. 'What do you have all that steel in your mouth for?'

'Keeps my teeth straight,' Jack replied.

'I've got calipers. You know what calipers are?' Jack didn't. 'Same as your thing, only for legs,' Jessie explained. 'I don't like them, so I don't put them on, unless I have to. You know what Liam Doherty called you?'

'No.'

'Jaws,' she said, and he flashed his teeth at her and laughed.

The rollerblading was not a great success, not for Jessie anyway. They used the road at the end of the farm lane. It was tarmac, and smooth enough in places; but there were always a lot of pot-holes and bumps in the way, and, worst of all, sheep droppings. Then there were sheep themselves and Mole, loitering with intent, somehow always in the way. For days and days she practised with Jack, but no matter how hard she tried, the only way she could ever stay upright was by hanging on to him. Whenever she let go, she simply fell over. In the end she was forced just to sit on the bank and watch him whizzing along the road, gliding and weaving with consummate ease. It was not doing much for Jessie's self-esteem, and anyway she had her lines to do. Mrs Burke had given her a week. The week was almost up and she hadn't even started yet. She left him to it.

Later that evening, she was still at the kitchen table writing her lines when she heard the tractor coming up the lane. Her mother came in, kicking off her boots, and washed her hands at the sink.

'Homework?' she said.

'Lines,' Jessie replied, curling her arm round to hide what she was writing.

'Why? What did you do?'

'Nothing. Just my writing wasn't good enough, that's all.' And she said no more about it.

'How many have you got to do?'

'Fifty.'

'That's nothing at all. It was always at least a hundred when I was at school.' Jessie felt like having a good rant about Mrs Burke, but there was no point. It wasn't only Mrs Burke who thought she was lying about the Big Hill, was it? Everyone did, even her own mother and father. They might pretend to believe her, to make her feel better, but they didn't. Besides, Jessie had learnt a long time ago that neither of them would hear a thing against Mrs Burke. So any troubles at school, she always kept to herself.

'Where's Jack?' her mother asked.

'Upstairs with his walkman. He's got two walkmen and three Gameboys. Are they made of money or what?'

'Your Uncle Sean's worked very hard for what he's got, Jess. That's maybe what's made him ill.'

'What's the matter with him?'

'He's ill, very ill. Let's just leave it at that, shall we?'

'Will he get better?'

'Yes,' she said quietly. 'God willing.' She put her arms round Jessie's neck and hugged her. 'You remember we've got to go out tonight, don't you? Island Meeting.'

'It'll be about the Big Hill again, I suppose,' Jessie sighed, and her mother moved away. 'Doesn't anybody talk about anything else around here?'

'Don't you care what happens to it, Jess?' said her mother, sitting down across the table from her.

'Of course I do, but why does everyone always have to shout about it? You and Dad, you go on and on. You never agree. No one ever agrees about it.'

'Sometimes, Jess, you've got to shout, else people just won't listen.' She leaned towards her and lifted her chin so that Jessie had to look into her eyes. 'And there's some things that are so important,' she said.

'Not that important,' Jessie replied. 'I don't like it when you and Dad shout; and besides, I don't know what the fuss is all about. The mining people, they've said they'll fix it afterwards, haven't they?'

'There's some things you just can't fix, Jess,' said her mother. 'It's like an egg. You cut the top off an egg, but you can't put it back on again, can you?'

'Well, I'm not getting into your silly arguments,' Jessie shouted, throwing down her pencil. The tears came into her eyes. 'You see? As soon as you start talking about it, we start shouting.'

Jack was standing at the door, pale and distraught. He looked from one to the other.

'It's gone,' he said. 'I looked all over. I've lost it.'

'What is it, Jack?' Jessie's mother went over to him.

'My lucky arrowhead. It was in my coat pocket, and now it's gone.'

'We'll find it, Jack,' said Jessie's mother. 'Don't worry. It's got to be somewhere, hasn't it?'

'I never go anywhere without it,' said Jack. 'It brings me luck.' And Jessie saw then that his eyes were red with crying. 'If I don't find it, my luck's gone for good. I know it is.'

'We'll find it,' said Jessie's mother. 'It'll turn up, you'll see. Now, how about some nice soda bread and honey. You like honey? We've got the best honey in all of Ireland. Will you try some?'

Jack did like the honey, just so long as it was spread on top of peanut butter. It was about the first thing he had liked in all the time he'd been with them. Jessie looked on in awe as he ate four whole slices and then washed it all down with Coke. He seemed a lot happier after that. They turned Jack's room inside out looking for his arrowhead, searched through every drawer, through every pocket. It was nowhere. They went up and down the road where they had been rollerblading. Nothing. Then it came on to rain and they had to go in.

'Tomorrow,' said Jessie's mother. 'We'll look again tomorrow. I've got to get ready for the meeting.'

That evening, Jack and Jessie were left on their own, with peanut butter and honey sandwiches for their supper. Jessie didn't like to admit it, but she'd taken quite a liking to them. She was eating them at the same time as she did her lines. The television was on in the corner. It was football again, or 'soccer', as Jack insisted on calling it. Jessie was suddenly aware that Jack was looking over her shoulder. 'You left a word out,' he said, pointing. 'It says, "I *did* climb the Big Hill." '

'I told you, I did,' said Jessie.

'I know, but Mrs Burke said . . .'

'I don't care what Mrs Burke said. I've done lines for her before, hundreds of them. She won't read it anyway – she never does – and I'm not going to write it when it's not true. I climbed that hill and I'm not saying I didn't, not for her, not for anyone.'

Jack grinned broadly. 'My dad would say you've got guts.'

'Are you very rich?' Jessie asked.

Jack looked at her for a moment. 'Yeah,' he said. 'I guess you could say we've got pretty much everything you'd want. Two houses, one on Long Island and a farm up in Vermont. Two yachts, three cars. Rich enough, I guess.'

'Three cars? What d'you want three cars for?'

'Well, maybe two, and the VW Beetle I work on. I love engines.'

'Your father, Uncle Sean, how come he's got so much money?'

Jack shrugged. 'I don't know. He just makes it. Like he says, he makes money make money. Doesn't tell me a lot about it. He's great. He takes me places – hunting, skiing, all that. Just the two of us.'

'What about your mum?' She knew she shouldn't have asked it, and she was relieved when Jack didn't seem upset.

'I don't see her any more,' he said quietly. 'Dad says it's best that way. Guess he's right too. They were always at each other's throats, shouting and stuff.' She wanted to ask him about how ill Uncle Sean was, but she didn't know how to. 'All that shouting about the Big Hill, a few nights back,' Jack went on, 'what was that all about?'

'You heard it?'

'And Marion Murphy at school. She kept going on about it, too.'

'She would be,' said Jessie. 'It's the lousy gold mine. You've got those who want it and you've got those who don't – not many now – in fact, just Mum and old Mister Barney. Marion's dad, Mr Murphy – he's the one that got it all going – well, he owns the Big Hill, and he's told everyone it'll mean lots of jobs and lots of money for the island. He's persuaded just about everyone now, even my dad. Tonight it's the final meeting, the last vote. Mum knows she'll lose, but she still won't give in. She says it's wrong. Dad says it's right. That's why they were shouting.'

'There was a lot of that back home,' said Jack, 'shouting I mean, Mom at Dad, Dad at Mom. And after that, they wouldn't even talk. Then Mom just left.' He was looking at her steadily, almost as if it were a warning.

Jessie was up in bed, and still thinking about what Jack had said, when she heard Clatterbang pull up outside. Panda was scrabbling at the door to get in, and then he was charging around downstairs like a wild thing. She heard a tap running in the kitchen and the kettle going on.

Her father was doing the talking. 'Well, maybe they won't find enough gold to make it worth their while.'

'But the damage will be done by then, won't it?' came the reply. 'Either way, they've still got to take the top off the hill to find out. But anyway, that's hardly the point is it? You voted against me, in public, and for everyone to see. Only Mister Barney stood up for the hill, Mister Barney and me. And what did that Michael Murphy say? That Mister Barney was objecting out of self-interest, just because he was going to have to move house, and how the mining company had laid on such a wonderful house for him to move into. "A minor inconvenience," he called it. Poor dear Mister Barney. And did you speak up for him? No. Did you speak up for me? No. I feel like you stabbed me in the heart, Jimmy. That's what I feel.'

Jessie pulled the duvet up over her head and clamped a pillow round her ears. She wanted to hear no more. She didn't want to think about it, but she couldn't help herself. She was wondering what would happen to her if they split up like Jack's mother and father had, about which of them she would be left with. She'd have more fun with her father. He could at least forget about her lousy palsy and treat her straight. She loved him for that. But then he never cuddled her that much. Her mother did. When she was in real trouble, it was always to her mother that she went. She'd cry up against her softness and her mother would smooth her hair, and Jessie loved her for that. She was crying now and trying not to because she didn't want them to hear. She heard a knock and her door opening. She pushed back her duvet. Jack was standing in the doorway.

'I was thinking,' he said slowly. 'You're going to get in real trouble about those lines.' He came further into the room. 'Something the matter?'

'No.'

'Well, I was thinking. If Mrs Burke does read those lines and you get in more trouble, then maybe you could prove it to her, and to all the kids in school.'

'How do you mean?'

'How'd it be if I got some of the guys, Liam Doherty and the others, and we all went up the Big Hill with you, and then we told Mrs Burke? She'd have to believe us, right? How about it? Would you do it?'

'Course I would.' Jessie spoke without really thinking. It seemed to her this was like a challenge, that maybe Jack didn't believe her either. But when she did think about it, she immediately began to regret it. Just because she had climbed the Big Hill once, it didn't mean she could do it again.

'Anyway,' she said, 'if she doesn't read them, and she won't, then I won't have to do it, will I?' She just hoped she was right.

'Your mom lost her vote?' Jack went on.

She nodded. 'See you,' he said, and then he went out.

Jessie couldn't sleep that night, and it wasn't just the owl outside. Her head swarmed with endless puzzlements and debates and anxieties. Was Jack right about the shouting?

Would it just get worse until they split up? Should she put in the one word in her lines that would make life easier at school tomorrow? If she did, and Mrs Burke did read them, then at least she wouldn't have to climb the Big Hill again. And what would happen if she tried to climb the Big Hill in front of everyone, and then failed? She'd never live it down. Marion Murphy wouldn't let her. And that was another thing. Marion Murphy was hovering around Jack a lot too close, and she didn't like it. She didn't like it one bit.

She got out of bed and went to watch Barry for a while. He was asleep at the bottom of his bowl, just breathing, nothing else. It was as much to wake him up as anything that she put her hand in and fished around in the stones for the earring. She took it out and shook it dry. And what of the voice she had heard on the Big Hill? Was it real or imagined? What of the face in the mirror and the earring in her hand? What *was* going on? Her feet were getting cold, so she hid the earring deep in the stones again, said goodnight to Barry, and went back to bed.

The moon lit her room and the shadows from the tree danced across the ceiling above her head. 'Are you there?' she whispered. 'Can you hear me?' The owl answered from the abbey tower. 'Bog off,' she said. 'I wasn't talking to you.'

But as she drifted into sleep at last, watching the moving shadows, she fancied they were not shadows any more, but waves. Dipping through the waves came a galley and on the prow of the galley stood a woman, her hair flying out in the wind, her cloak whipping about her shoulders, a flag fluttering over her head, a flag with a red pig emblazoned on it. Then the woman was looking down at her from the ceiling and smiling at her. 'It's late, Jessie,' she was saying. 'Just you go to sleep now, and let tomorrow take care of itself. It always does.'

6 THE GHOST OF
GRANIA O'MALLEY

TRUE ENOUGH, TOMORROW DID TAKE CARE OF itself. Mrs Burke remembered the week was up and asked for the lines. As expected and hoped for, she gave them no more than a cursory glance and dropped them into her waste-paper bin. 'No more of your nonsense now, Jessie,' she said, and that was that. Jessie looked across at Jack and smiled her relief. So she wouldn't have to prove it, she wouldn't have to climb the Big Hill again after all. For Jessie, school that day was one long sigh of relief.

Jack's rollerblades made him, without any question, the most popular person the school had ever known. Jessie sat on her place on the wall and watched him, her legs swinging. She felt real pride that Jack was a cousin of hers. She was less pleased when Marion contrived to have more turns than anyone else, and somehow she always seemed to need Jack to help her up when she fell over.

Miss Jefferson had a try too, and she was quite good. Jack showed her what to do and stood back. She wobbled just once across the playground, and everyone cheered and clapped, even Mrs Burke. It seemed to set her in a good mood for the rest of the day.

That afternoon they all did a comparative study of Clare Island, County Mayo, Ireland, and Long Island, New York, U.S.A. – the one barely four miles long, the other over a hundred; the one you could only get to by ferry, the other with a road and rail link to and from New York; the one inhabited until four hundred years before by Red Indians (Jack said they were called 'Native Americans', not 'Indians'), and the other the last stronghold of the Irish-Gaelic tribes against the Normans and the English.

Then Liam Doherty was asked to stand up and explain the rules of Gaelic football, and Jack had to say how American football was different. Jessie was bored by all this, for there seemed to her to be very little difference between the two. The goalposts were about the same shape and, to her, it was just a lot of people running around kicking a ball and shouting, and not very interesting at all. The Americans wore funny helmets and dressed up like mutant giants and the Irish didn't – for her that was the only difference. Liam was becoming a little edgy because people weren't as interested in what he was saying – mostly because they knew it already – as they were in what Jack was saying.

Mrs Burke finished off the whole day by telling them all what both Irish and American had in common, Clare Islanders and Long Islanders. 'The main thing is,' she said, 'that we speak the same language, and that's good, because it means we can understand one another better. We are both free countries and democracies, and we've that to be thankful for. Do you know what a democracy is?' No one answered. 'Well, it means that we Irish vote for what we want; and so do you Americans, don't you, Jack?'

'I guess,' said Jack.

'Take for instance, last night,' Mrs Burke went on, 'when we had our Island Meeting. A perfect example of democracy in action. Almost everyone was for the gold mine, and just two were against. So like it or not, the gold mine is coming. No one can stop it now. That's the power of democracy for you.'

Jessie could not leave it like that. She had to speak up, she had to defend her mother. Her anger made her suddenly brave. She put her hand up.

'Yes, Jessie?' said Mrs Burke.

'My mother says that voting is all very well, Miss, but just because a thing is popular, she says that doesn't make it right. She doesn't think the gold mine is right, and neither does old Mister Barney.'

Mrs Burke glowered at her for a moment over the top of her glasses and then looked up at the school clock. 'I think that'll be all for today,' she said. 'Tidy your tables, children.'

They were in the playground at the end of school, shrugging on coats when the skirmishing began. It was Marion Murphy that started it all. She sauntered up to

Jessie with that lipcurl of a smile on her face, the smile that Jessie always knew meant trouble. She was a head taller than Jessie and big all over, a great round face and a mouth to match.

'Your mum,' she said, 'is she mad in the head, or what? My mum says that your mum just likes the men to look at her – that's why she gets up and talks like she does. A bit of tart, my mum says. Married a lousy blow-in too.'

'You've a filthy mouth on you, Marion Murphy,' Jessie said, fixing her with her most contemptuous and withering stare. But the sneer on Marion's face was still there, so Jessie had to go on, 'My mum's got a perfect right to say what she thinks about the Big Hill – and besides, she's right and the rest of you's wrong. You *shouldn't* go cutting the tops off mountains just for a lump of gold, and they *will* poison the water like she says, and there *won't* be work for everyone either, and they *won't* put it all back as good as new when they've finished, like your daft daddy says. It's all lies. And if the men look at my mum, that's because she's beautiful, and if they don't look at your mum, that's because she's an ugly old cow.'

She had gone too far. She knew it, but she just could not rein herself in. She was trembling with fury, and with fear too. She was probably safe enough from physical attack – there were some advantages to being the way she was. And anyway, Marion was all mouth – she hoped. There was a crowd closing in round them now, almost the whole school. Jessie was glad to find Jack there beside her.

Marion's face was scarlet. 'Cripple!' she screamed at her. 'You're just a cripple, you know that, just a cripple.

My mum says you shouldn't be allowed in the same school with us. They should send you away so's no one's got to look at you.'

Jessie had never liked Marion, and she knew Marion had never liked her, but she'd never said such a thing before. No one had. They might have thought it. Jessie had often caught sight of a side-glance here, a lowering of the eyes there, and she knew what they meant well enough, but it had never been spoken out loud before. It was suddenly out in the open, and the shock of it took her breath away. She was stunned to silence. Jack spoke up.

'We're going home,' he said, taking her elbow. The crowd parted for them and seemed a little disappointed it had come to no more than harsh words.

'I hate her, I really hate her,' Jessie said much later, as they walked away past the abbey ruins. The post van came down the hill past them. Mrs O'Leary, postlady and pubkeeper, waved at them cheerily.

'What's a blow-in?' Jack asked. 'Marion said your pa was a blow-in.'

'Someone like you – foreigner, English, Irish, no matter what. If you weren't born here, you're a blow-in.'

'So?' said Jack. 'Back home, that would make just about everyone a blow-in. Well, maybe not the Native Americans, but even they probably blew in from somewhere, I guess.' They walked on for a while in silence.

'D'you find your lucky arrowhead yet?' Jessie asked.

Jack shook his head. 'Maybe it wasn't that lucky anyway,' he said. He stopped suddenly. 'Hey, listen. You want to take me up this hill of yours?' he asked. 'You want to take me up the Big Hill?' It took Jessie by surprise.

'What, now?'

'Why not? You've done it before, haven't you?' he said. 'I'll tell the guys afterwards. How about it?'

'I don't want you to tell them,' she said. 'I don't care if they believe me or not. Don't care if no one believes me.'

'I believe you,' Jack said. 'I just want to go up there, OK? I've got to find out what all the fuss is about, that's all.'

'OK,' said Jessie, but she meant more than that. She meant: 'Thanks, thanks for believing in me.' She gave him a smile to tell him so, and then immediately began to worry whether she would be able to make it to the top again. She had no choice but to try. There was no way out of it.

They had to go past the end of the farm lane to get to the Big Hill. Mole was grazing the grass verge and followed them. By the time they reached the grassy clearing by Mister Barney's shack, Panda was there too, bounding away into the bracken after rabbits, his tail whirling. Jessie was counting out her rhythm in her head: one and two, one and two, one and two. She hadn't the breath to talk. Having Jack alongside made it easier in one way, but more difficult in another. It was easier because she knew he'd be there to help her if she tumbled, but more difficult because she knew he'd never believe her ever again if she failed to reach the top.

When they got to the stream across the path, Jack sat down on a rock for a breather, wiping the sweat from his face. 'We're only halfway up,' she said, tottering on past him, 'so we're neither up nor down. What's keeping you?' Seeing him sitting there exhausted, made her feel good, very good; but she felt even better still when she reached the gulley beyond the waterfall, and could see the summit up there ahead of her. But then, without warning, she sat down with a bump and Jack was crouching beside her.

'You OK?'

'I need a hand up, that's all.' He helped her up and steadied her. 'I'm fine,' she said. 'Fine.' From now on it simply did not occur to her that she might not reach the top. She sat down only once more, more awkwardly this time, and fell sideways into the undergrowth. Jack hauled her on to her feet again and freed her from a bramble that was caught in her hair.

'Almost there,' he said; and they were too. They were calling out the rhythm together now: 'One and two, one and two, one and two.' A last scramble over rocks on hands and knees, and then they were stretched out on a great soft cushion of pink thrift at the summit, their eyes closed against the sun. After a while Jessie propped herself up on her elbows. Jack was standing on the highest rock and gazing out to sea.

'Your mom's right, Jess,' he said. No one ever called her Jess, except her mother and father, but Jessie found she didn't mind at all. In fact, she liked it. 'They shouldn't do it,' he went on. 'They shouldn't go cutting the top off. I don't care how much gold there is inside here. I never saw anything like this place. It's really special, you know that? If we let them knock it down, then no one's ever going to stand here like I am and look at this. All you get from gold is money. Money sure makes you rich, but rich doesn't make you happy. This makes you happy.'

'You on Mum's side then?'

'I guess I am. What about you?'

Jessie was looking around her. Jack was right. It *was* special. It *was* beautiful. It was the *perfect* place. 'I don't think I ever really made up my mind about it until now,' she said, 'until right now. But yes, I am on Mum's side, and not just because of what Marion said either. Mum's right. She's been right all along.' She tried to get up, but found it difficult. He came over and helped her to her feet. 'Anyway,' Jessie said, 'it doesn't matter any more. It's too late, it's all decided.'

The sunlight danced over the rock pool and seemed to be inviting them to drink. Jack was there before she was. He cupped his hands under the spring, caught the water and drank it. Jessie tried it the same way too, but could not keep her fingers tight enough together to hold the water. So she knelt down and put her mouth to the surface of the pool, as she had the last time she was up there. She drank long and deep, her eyes closed until she'd had enough. She wiped her mouth and watched the reflected clouds moving across the pool. She was remembering the earring and how she had found it there before. And then she knew she wasn't remembering it at all, she was looking directly at it. It was there, right in front of her eyes, lying at the bottom of the pool. It was like an echo in her mind, this feeling of having been somewhere before and then the same thing happening, in exactly the same place and in exactly the same way, like a dream, only clearer, more real. She reached down into the water, shattering the clouds, but Jack's hand was quicker than hers.

'Jeez, what's this?' he said, dangling the earring in front of her eyes.

'What does it look like?' a voice spoke from behind them, a voice Jessie recognised at once. 'You'll be needing the pair, I thought.' They turned. She was the woman from the mirror. She was the woman from Jessie's dream. And she was here and now and barefoot on the rock, her hair all about her face.

'Well, have you no manners at all?' she said. 'You're gawping at me like a pair of gasping salmon. Look around you. It's just like you said, Jack. Isn't this the most perfect place in the entire world? My mountain this, my hill. I fought for it, we all did. We spilled good red Irish blood for it, and I'll not let them do it. I won't. But I'll need help.' And then to Jack: 'That was a fine speech you made. Did you mean it?' Jack nodded, backing away now and taking Jessie with him.

'Now where do you think you're going to?' She sprang down off the rock, lithe like a tiger, a sword hanging from her broad leather belt. She was about Jessie's mother's age, a little older perhaps and certainly stronger. There was a wild and weather-beaten look about her. 'Would I hurt you? Would I? Haven't I just given you my own earrings? Gold they are, Spanish gold. I filched them myself from the wreck of the *Santa Felicia*, a great Armada galleon that washed itself up on our rocks – a while ago now. And there's a whole lot more where they came from, my life's winnings you might say – or what's left of them anyway.'

She drew her sword and flourished it at the sea. 'These are my waters. You sail in my waters and you pay your dues. I took from anyone who came by, English, Spanish, Portuguese – all the same to me, all perfectly fair and square and above board. But if they didn't pay, well then, I took what was mine. Wouldn't you? A poor pirate's got to earn her crust somehow. How else is she to live into her old age? Tell me that if you will.'

Jessie sat down because she had to, because her legs wanted her to. It could not be what Jessie was thinking, because what she was thinking was impossible; but then maybe she had to believe the impossible might just be possible after all. The woman now striding towards her said she was a pirate, that the Big Hill was her mountain. It could be no one else. It had to be . . . but then it couldn't be. She had been buried in the abbey hundreds of years ago. Jessie had seen the gravestone. They had read about her at school, the Pirate Queen of Clare Island. Mrs O'Leary's pub down by the quay was named after her.

Jessie screwed up all her courage, and then spoke. 'You're not . . . you're not Grania O'Malley, are you?'

'And who else would I be?' she said.

6 GONE FISHING

THEY WERE ALONE AGAIN ON THE HILL. IT WAS AS IF time had stood still, and they had just rejoined it. For some moments they simply stood and stared at each other. Then Jack looked down at his hand. 'It's gone. I had it. I had the earring,' he whispered. 'I found it in the pool, didn't I?' Jessie nodded. 'And she *was* here, wasn't she? I wasn't dreaming it?' He didn't wait for an answer. 'Let's get out of here,' he said.

Mole wouldn't be caught, so Jack had to give Jessie a piggyback all the way down the hill. They reached the bottom in time to help Jessie's father drive the sheep along the road into the barn. They would be shearing the next day, he said, and it felt like rain. The fleeces had to be dry, so it was best to keep the sheep in overnight.

That evening the thunder rolled in from the sea and clattered around the island, and the rain fell hard and straight in huge drops that drummed incessantly on the tin roof of the kitchen. Inside, there was an unnatural silence over the supper table. Jessie's mother and father weren't speaking. She looked from one to the other willing them to talk, but neither did. It was just as Jack had said, first the shouting, then the silences.

Jack ate his peanut butter sandwiches ravenously and scarcely looked up. He seemed all wrapped up inside himself. Jessie longed to talk to him about everything that had happened up on the Big Hill, but there was never an opportunity to be alone together. He went up to bed early, and Jessie was about to follow him upstairs when her father asked her to help him check the sheep. 'Two pairs of eyes are always better than one,' he said.

The sheep filled the barn from wall to wall. Every one of them was lying down, except for one in the corner. 'I thought as much. She's lambing. She shouldn't be, but she is. That old ram must have got out again,' he said. 'She's only young. I think she'll need a hand. Do you want to do it?' Jessie had never told her father that she didn't like doing it. It was all the slime and the blood; and worst of all, the possibility that the lamb might be dead. She pretended. She had always pretended, and she pretended again now. Her father knelt down, holding the sheep on her side. Jessie found the feet inside and felt for the head. The lamb was alive. She tugged and her hands slipped. The little black feet were sucked back inside. She tried again. The lamb came out at the third pull and lay there, steaming and exhausted, on the ground. They sat watching the ewe for a while as she licked over her lamb, her eyes wary.

'Something the matter with Jack, is there?' her father asked suddenly.

'Not as far as I know. He can't find his lucky arrow-head, that's all.'

She had never before found it difficult to talk to her father, but then she'd never before wanted to ask him about such a thing. She wanted to ask him outright: 'Are you and Mum going to split up?' Then it occurred to her that maybe just by asking, just to speak of it, might make it more likely to happen.

'Come on, Jess,' he said, 'what's up?'

Luckily, there was something else troubling her, something she was longing to talk about to someone.

'I think I've seen a ghost, Dad.'

He looked down at her and laughed. 'Have you been at my whisky, Jess?'

'Course not.'

'You're serious, aren't you?'

'I've seen her in my mirror, Dad, and I heard her up on the Big Hill. Then today, this afternoon, I saw her. I really saw her. Honest, up at the top of the Big Hill.'

'At the top of the Big Hill, you say,' said her father, getting to his feet and brushing himself down. 'Now there's a thing.' He smiled down at her and helped her. 'D'you know, Jess, you go on like this and you'll make a writer one day. All the best writers don't know where the truth begins or where it ends. They're not liars at all, they're just dreamers. Nothing wrong with dreaming.' He pulled some straw out of her hair and let it fall to the ground. 'And by the by, don't you worry about your mother and me. It's the Big Hill. It's only the Big Hill that's between us. Once the mining's begun and there's nothing more to be done about it, then we'll be fine, you'll see.' Jessie felt a surge of relief coursing through her and warming her like sunshine. It didn't matter that he hadn't believed her ghost story. It didn't matter at all.

'Your hands are disgusting,' he said, and she wriggled her fingers in his face and giggled.

The weekend was spent shearing the sheep, all four of them together in the barn: her father pouring sweat as he bent over the sheep, her mother and Jack rolling the fleeces into bundles and sweeping up, while Jessie opened and shut the gate and drove the sheep into the shearing pen. Jack took to the shepherding as if he had been doing it all his life. Through it all, Jessie's mother and father scarcely spoke. Liam called in on Sunday morning after Mass. Marion Murphy had found a baseball bat, he said. Her father had brought it back from Miami on one of his trips. She'd lend it if she could play too. 'You could teach us,' said Liam. 'I've got a tennis ball. Five o'clock at the field. Will you come?'

Jessie went with him that evening, not because she had the slightest interest in baseball, but because at last she'd have a chance to talk to Jack about Grania O'Malley. All they had been able to do since they had met her was to exchange conspiratorial glances. They sauntered along the farm lane, side-stepping the puddles, Mole following along behind. Jack did all the talking.

'Jess, I've been thinking. About her, I mean, about what happened up there. Here's what I remember, or what I think I remember. We got to the top, right? We found the earring in the pool. I had it in my hand. Then out of nowhere comes this weird lady, kind of like a gypsy. She said she was a pirate, right? And she had a sword. She kept telling us all about the gold she'd taken off some ship, a Spanish ship, wasn't it? And her hair was black and curling down to her shoulders. I mean, I can see her like she was here right now. I didn't make this up, did I? You saw her too, right?' Jessie tried to answer, but Jack wouldn't let her.

'Now, we've got two choices. Either the whole thing was some fantastic dream, and we just dreamed the same dream – or it really happened. I don't reckon two people *can* dream the same dream. So, it happened, and if it happened, then we really met a ghost up there. Right? But there's something I can't figure out. It seemed like she knew you somehow, like she'd given you an earring before.'

'That's because she did,' said Jessie. 'I've seen her before. She came to my room. And she talked to me, on the Big Hill, the day you came. That's when I found the first earring. In the same pool. I keep it in Barry's bowl. But I didn't know who she was.'

'Something O'Malley, wasn't it?' said Jack.

'*Grania* O'Malley,' she said and Jack looked at her blankly. 'Don't you know who she is? She's in the history books. She was a terrible woman, a sort of pirate queen. She'd slit your throat as soon as look at you. Mrs Burke says she was a wicked scarlet woman. She had as many husbands as she had children, and sometimes they weren't husbands at all. But what I don't understand is the earring, the second earring. If she really was there, if it wasn't a dream, then where's the second earring? You had it in your hand.'

Then Liam and the others came along on their bikes and walked with them down towards the field. There could be no more talk of Grania O'Malley's ghost or the missing earring.

Baseball was like rounders, Jessie thought, except you wound yourself up into a frenzy before you threw the ball, the bat was a lot longer and, for some reason she didn't quite understand, the batter always got to wear Jack's baseball hat. She kept her distance. It wasn't the kind of game she could play very well. When they picked sides, she would be the last to be chosen and she always hated that. And besides, she didn't want to encounter Marion Murphy again. She'd sit it out.

Watching from the seat under the tree, with Mole grazing around her feet, Jessie could think of nothing else except the ghost on the Big Hill. Even when her legs cramped up with the cold and she had to rub the life back into them, she hardly felt the accustomed pain. There was still this niggling doubt in her mind. One way or another she had to know for sure. Perhaps the ghost was close by somewhere, watching, listening, just invisible, that's all. 'You're there, aren't you?' She said it aloud. 'Grania O'Malley, can you hear me? If you can hear me, let me see you, *please*.' The ball came rolling towards her feet, chased by Marion.

'Talking to yourself again?' said Marion, bending down to pick it up.

'No, I'm not,' she replied. Marion gave her a puzzled look, threw the ball in and ran off.

With each day that passed, and with no sign of the ghost, no reappearance, and no second earring, the two began to believe that they must have had some kind of joint hallucination. They went over it again and again, and both clearly remembered every little detail – or they thought they did. Jessie showed Jack the evidence of her first meeting with Grania O'Malley. Time after time she took the earring out of its hiding place in Barry's bowl and showed it to him, and each time Jack was even more sure it was the same as the one he'd had in his hand that afternoon on the Big Hill, quite sure, he said. She showed him the mirror where she'd seen the head of the ghost all those weeks before, and he sat in front of it just as she had, holding the earring in his hand, and looked deep into the mirror. 'And she was right behind you?' he said.

'Not all of her, just her head. But it was the same woman. It was Grania O'Malley. Honest it was.'

'But if we saw her like we think we did,' Jack went on, 'then where's the other earring?' That was always the problem they came back to. There *was* no second earring, and until there was a second earring, then there was room for doubt. They searched everywhere, everywhere they had looked for Jack's lucky arrowhead, and elsewhere too. But they found neither the second earring nor the lucky arrowhead.

Their shared doubts and fears threw them more and more together in school, as well as out of school too. In school, all the playground talk was of the controversy still raging over the Big Hill. Anyone who said a word against the gold mine was branded at once as some kind of traitor. So no one spoke up against the mine, except Jessie; and the more she found herself standing up for the preservation of the Big Hill, the surer she was of her cause. And being alone against the others only made her more defiant, more determined. Jack was her sole ally, but a silent one. He rarely left her side, and was, Jessie thought, the main reason anyone listened to her without shouting her down.

Jack was still new enough to fascinate. Baseball had become all the rage – every evening down on the field. Anyone who was anyone had by now acquired a baseball hat of sorts. He had a quiet way with him that everyone liked and respected. Marion Murphy, and she wasn't alone, still hung around him all she could. Jessie overheard her one rainy playtime when they were cooped up inside. 'I can't understand it,' Marion was saying. 'He's Jessie's cousin, and I fancy him rotten.'

It was Marion too who did most to stoke up the furore about the Big Hill. She would do all she could to provoke frequent and often nasty confrontations with Jessie. She'd catch her alone in the playground with her back to the fence so she couldn't get away, and she'd start yelling at her, nose to nose. Jack would intervene, always just in time. 'Getting mad won't help,' he'd say. 'Let's just cool it.'

And Marion would back off, just like that. He had a way with Marion that no one else had.

But Jack couldn't be with Jessie all the time. It was the end of school one afternoon, and it was hot. Jessie was tired. Her legs had been hurting all day, and she just wanted to go home. Suddenly they were all around her, Marion Murphy and her pack. They were on about the Big Hill again and how Jessie's mother was the only one against it. She felt battered and bruised by their angry, scathing looks and their vicious words. She just wanted to run. But there was no way out. Suddenly, inexplicably, she felt a new power, a new courage rising within her, a new kind of strength; and she knew as she spoke, that the words that came out were not hers. She had become the face in the mirror, the voice on the Big Hill. She knew it was Grania O'Malley talking through her, she was quite sure of it. Where else could she have found the nerve? The words flowed out fluently, without her even having to think about them.

'Will you let me speak or not?' She waited till they were quiet, and then went on. 'Let's say you get your share of the gold – which you won't – what will you do with it? You can't eat it, you can't drink it.'

'Get rich, stupid!' Marion Murphy shouted into her face, and they all roared their support.

'Oh yes?' Jessie was quite undaunted. 'And meanwhile, they'll have torn a great hole in the Big Hill with their machines, so none of us will ever be able to stand up there again and look out to the Islands in Clew Bay. You'd like that, would you? Oh, and of course Mister Barney's in the way, isn't he? So we'll just kick him out and move him on. No problem. And the water in the wells will all be poisoned. But who cares? It won't matter, will it, because we'll all of us be eating off solid gold plates, and that'll make us as happy as pie, won't it? That hill has been there, Marion Murphy, since the beginning of time. Didn't St Patrick himself pray on it? Didn't Grania O'Malley keep watch on it against the English?'

Before the words came out, Jessie had never even known that St Patrick had prayed on the Big Hill, nor that Grania O'Malley had kept watch on it. Her speech silenced them, but only for a few moments. Then Marion was railing again. 'Don't listen to her. It's a lot of bull. Stuff St Patrick. Stuff Grania O'Malley. It'll be jobs for everyone, money for everyone – that's what my dad says. And anyway, it doesn't matter what you say, or your stupid mum says, 'cos she can't stop it now and neither can you. They're coming. The bulldozers are coming. What are you going to do, ask them nicely to stop?'

There was no way out for Jessie. She was in too deep to back away now. 'I'll lie down in front of them,' Jess said quietly. 'You see if I don't.' They all scoffed at her, hurled a few more insults, and at last went away and left her in peace.

She told Jack about it afterwards, when they were alone. 'You wouldn't really do it though, would you?' he said.

'If I have to. If I have to, I will. Now I've said it, I've got to, haven't I?'

'Then we'll do it together,' he said firmly.

'Honest?'

'We're family, right?'

It was that evening that Jessie and her mother found the newborn lamb dead beside the ruined cottage in the bog-oak field, the ewe still nuzzling it. The lamb was covered in black flies. 'Poor thing,' said her mother, waving the flies away. 'Born at the wrong time and in the wrong place. Bit like me, I think.' They dug a hole in the corner of the field, laid the lamb out and covered it up. Jessie looked away. She saw tears in her mother's eyes, but she said nothing. 'I saw Liam's mum. She told me about school,' said her mother, as they walked away.

'What about it?'

'About you, about Marion Murphy, about lying down in front of the machines when they come.'

'Jack says he'll do it with me,' said Jessie.

'Did he now? Well, he's a fine boy. I like him more every day, and so does your dad, but no one's going to lie down in front of anything. No one's going to get hurt. I'll find a way without that. I'm not going to give up, that's for sure.' They walked on in silence for a while. 'I'm so proud of you, Jess, you know that?' she said. 'So pleased you're on my side.'

'What about Dad?'

'Oh, he'll come round.' She smiled and put her arm round Jessie's shoulders. 'Give him time.'

'Only if you talk to him, Mum,' said Jessie. 'You've got to talk. Jack's mum and dad – he says it all started with shouting first of all, and then no one talked. And she just went off.'

'Listen, Jess, I'm not leaving. And your dad's not leaving either. He's dug his heels in over this, and so have I, that's all. We're both just doing what we think is right. I don't love him any the less, I promise. What he doesn't seem to understand just yet, is that I'm right. He still thinks he is. I have to persuade him that he's wrong, and that's never easy with anyone. I can promise you this though, Jess: there'll be no blood on the carpet when it's over. Believe me?'

Jessie said she did, but there was still an aching worry inside her that would not go away.

Jack came back at dusk, happy as a sandboy. He'd spent half the day with his head and hands deep inside Clatterbang's engine, and the rest of the time he'd been coaching the 'Pirates' – that was what the Clare Island baseball team now grandly called themselves. He was full of smiles as he threw himself breathless on to the sofa. 'The guys want some gloves and a real ball. I'm going to get Dad to send them over. They want Yankee caps like mine, too. What do you think? Can I call home?'

When he came back into the room some minutes later, all the light had gone from his eyes. He barely touched his peanut butter sandwiches. Jessie found herself talking nineteen to the dozen, just to cover up the silence round the table. In the end she ran out of things to say, so she asked Jack about the phone call.

'Is your dad sending them then, the gloves and things?' Jack nodded, but he didn't even look up.

At last her father spoke up. 'I tell you what, how would you two like to come fishing tomorrow? Bit too much of a swell for the boat. We'll try the rocks. There's mackerel about and bass. Have you ever done any fishing, Jack?'

'Some.'

'That's settled then. After school tomorrow. I'll pick you up.'

All through school the next day, Jack hardly spoke to anyone. In playtime, in spite of all Marion's begging and badgering, he left Marion and Liam and the Pirates to their training, and went to sit by himself on the wall. Jessie joined him.

'You all right?' Jessie asked.

'My Dad's sick, really sick,' Jack said quietly. 'He sounded really bad on the phone. He's going to have surgery. It's because I lost my arrowhead. I know it.'

'What's he got?' Jessie asked.

'Something's wrong with his heart. He said he needs a new valve.'

'That's nothing,' said Jessie. 'My gran had that, and she's fine now, honest.'

'You sure?' Jack said, the life in his voice again.

'Course I am.'

Just before the end of playtime, Marion Murphy came over to them, swinging her baseball bat. As usual she had her whole pack with her. 'You changed your mind yet, Jessie Parsons?' she demanded. Jessie shook her head. 'Well, we've all decided. We're not speaking to you till you do, not a word. None of us.'

Jack jumped down off the wall and put himself between them and Jessie. 'Why don't you guys get lost!'

he shouted. No one had ever heard him like this before. 'Why don't you just leave her alone?' And he pushed through them and walked away. But Marion was as good as her word. No one spoke to Jessie. They'd just look at her and smile amongst themselves. It was the longest school day she'd ever lived through.

Her father met them in Clatterbang at the school gates and drove them across the island to Portlea. He was prattling on about the last bass he'd caught off the rocks at Portlea. 'Ten pounds it was, and not a word of a lie,' he said. He looked at them in the rearview mirror. 'Not the happiest pair I've ever seen,' he said. 'What's going on?'

'Nothing,' said Jessie.

'Well, you could have fooled me,' said her father. 'Whatever it is, the fishing will help. A great healer is fishing. You haven't quarrelled, have you?'

'No,' said Jessie firmly. But she said no more.

Her father was right about the fishing. There was the heart-stopping clamber down the rocks clutching her father's hand. There was the wind and spray on her face, and the great grey sea heaving in towards her. All her troubles were soon forgotten. And Jack was his old self again. Jessie's father fixed up a rod and line for him and helped him with his first cast. He didn't need any more help than that. Jessie watched him. Each cast was more expert than the one before. He knew what he was doing. Jessie always loved this place. She couldn't hold a rod, not to fish with; but she didn't mind. She was happy enough just watching them both, and listening to them wittering on about engines and turbos, pistons and filters and suchlike. And when she tired of that, there were the cormorants and shags to look at, standing like black sentinels on their rock below her, wings outspread and drying in the sun; and there were the gulls too, and the fulmars and the terns swooping and screaming overhead.

A mist was creeping in over the sea and Jessie wondered if there was any real difference between clouds and mist. She was already cold, and her legs ached, but she didn't mind. She was just thinking about Grania O'Malley again when she heard her father curse loudly.

'Lousy reel's jammed again,' he said. 'It's never been any good. And there's fish about too, I can smell them. Listen, can you two look after yourselves for a while? I'll just pop back home for my old one. Old-fashioned it may be, but at least it never lets me down, not like this beggar. You stay where you are, Jess, and you too, Jack, y'hear me? No climbing down. There's a wicked-looking swell out there today. Stay put. I shan't be long.' And he took his rod and was gone, up over the rocks to the cliff path. Jessie heard Clatterbang starting up.

'Hear that?' Jack called out. 'Starts better already. I'm a genius with engines, a real genius.'

'Any luck with the fish, genius?' she called back. Jack never answered. He just reeled in and cast again. In her armchair of rock, Jessie was too far away from him to talk properly. They had hardly said a word to each other since the incident in the playground. She wanted to talk. So she left her rock and sidled towards him on her bottom, until she was sitting right beside him and looking down into a cauldron of surging sea. 'I don't care, you know,' she said. 'I don't care if they never speak to me ever again. I don't care. They can stuff themselves.'

That was the moment the fish caught on and Jack shouted, 'I've got one! I've got one!' He braced his legs and began to reel in furiously. Then he slipped. His legs went from under him and he was sliding past her towards the edge.

Instinctively, Jessie reached out for him. For a fleeting moment she had hold of his jeans, just long enough for Jack to cling on to a rock and stop his slide. But then Jessie herself was slipping, rolling over and over and over, trying to find something to clutch at, anything. But there was nothing, no way she could stop herself. She caught a glimpse of Jack throwing himself full-stretch on the rock to save her. Then she was over the edge and falling through the air. The sea smothered her before she could scream. The water came into her mouth and into her ears and she was sinking deeper and deeper and could do nothing about it.

She looked up. There was light up above her, light she knew she had to reach if she was to live, but her legs wouldn't kick and her flailing arms seemed incapable of helping her. She had often thought about how drowning would be, when she was out in her father's boat or crossing over from the mainland on the ferry. And now she was drowning. This was how it was. Her eyes were stinging, so she closed them. She closed her mouth too, so she wouldn't swallow any more seawater. But she had to breathe – she couldn't help herself. She gasped and the seawater came in again and she began to choke.

Then something was holding her down. She fought, but the grip tightened about her waist and would not let go. Her head broke water, and suddenly there was air, wonderful air to breathe. She was spluttering and coughing. Someone was shouting at her. It was Jack and he was holding her. 'It's me! It's me! Hang on, just hang on to me. You'll be OK.' His face was near hers. 'Can you swim?' She shook her head. 'Just try to keep your mouth closed. Someone'll see us. We'll be OK. We'll be fine.'

Jessie looked beyond him. The shore was already a long way off and they were being carried away from it all the time. She looked the other way. Whenever they came up to the top of a wave she could see the bank of mist rolling over the sea towards them. One more wave and the mist would swallow them and then no one would ever see them.

'We've got to keep floating,' Jack cried. 'Just hang on.' The cold had numbed her legs already and she knew her arms couldn't hold on much longer. And then the mist came over their heads and shrouded them completely. Jack was crying out for help, screaming. She tried herself, but could only manage a whimper. It was hopeless.

From out of the mist came the unreal sound of oars dipping in rhythm, of men's muffled voices calling over the sea. Jack cried out again and the rowing stopped almost at once. They heard the sea slapping the sides of a boat, and then they saw it. It loomed out of the mist, riding the waves, its rearing prow ploughing through the sea towards them. There were arms pointing, heads leaning out, and then an oar to cling to. Rough hands reached for them, hauled them in over the side and they lay on the bottom of the boat gasping like landed fish. The faces that looked down at them were unshaven and weathered. One of them wore a black eyepatch. None of them was smiling.

7 ROCKFLEET

BY THE TIME THE MIST LEFT THEM, THEY WERE OUT of the swell of the open ocean and in amongst the sheltered islands of Clew Bay. The boat moved faster through the water now, the men rowing more evenly, their strokes longer, deeper. Jessie and Jack sat shivering side by side, covered in a huge cloak of skins. There were fifteen men rowing on each side, and the boat – which was more like a great open galley – must have been longer than the Clare Island ferry, thirty yards or more, with a pointed prow and her raised stern covered in by a canvas roof. There was a tall mast for a sail, but no sail was set. The men at the oars cast hard, searching looks in their direction. They had the least hospitable faces Jessie had ever seen.

'Who are they?' Jack whispered through chattering teeth. It was the first time either of them had dared talk.

'I don't know,' Jessie said. She thought for a moment of jumping overboard and escaping, but knew at once that she couldn't do it. She hadn't the strength even to stand up, let alone swim; and besides, she'd had quite enough of swimming for one day. Completely exhausted by now, Jessie drifted into sleep against Jack's shoulder.

She was woken suddenly by a splash and a barked command. She heard an anchor chain running out. They shipped the oars and the galley was gliding silently through still water before grinding to a halt in the shingle. Jessie looked up. Now she knew exactly where she was. Above the prow of the galley, stark against the sky stood a castle, Rockfleet Castle. It rose sheer from the rocks, a tall stone tower with ramparts round the top and slits for windows. She had often been past it in the car on her way to Gran's house on the mainland, and had stopped to look more than once; but the door had always been locked and they could never get in. She remembered her father pointing out the stone drain where the lavatory emptied out into the sea, and her mother saying it must have been a bit draughty, and her father laughing; but that was all she could remember about it.

The men were leaping out over the sides now and splashing ashore through the shallows. They were dressed peculiarly, in long baggy breeches, in rough shirts that were too big for them, and most had some kind of jerkin made out of leather or canvas. All of them carried swords at their sides.

Jessie found herself picked up and dropped unceremoniously overboard into the arms of one of the sailors who grinned down at her toothily out of his gnarled face – the kind of man who slits throats, she thought. Then he was carrying her up the beach, over the rocks and in through the castle door. She was in a small low-ceilinged room. From the shadows all around, grizzled faces stared at them, eyes glowing in the dark. Many were bearded, and most wore woollen caps pulled down to their ears. And then came a voice from somewhere above them and it was a voice both of them recognised at once, the voice of Grania O'Malley. 'Will you bring them up here to the fire, boys, and fast. They'll die of the cold.'

Jack was ushered on ahead up the narrow, winding stone stairs. Jessie still had to cling tight to her sailor, leaning her head inwards to avoid bumping it against the walls. The stairs brought them out into another room about the same size, but lighter. Here the floor was covered in rushes and there were tables set for eating. But there was no one there. Then they were climbing more winding stairs until at last Jessie was set down on her feet in front of a great crackling fire. Jack was beside her. Her hand crept into his and gripped it. He squeezed back. It was some reassurance, some comfort. Again, there seemed at first to be no one else in the room. Then one of the shadows moved and became Grania O'Malley. The yellow of the flames lit her face as she came towards them. She was dangling something from her little finger, something that glittered and glowed, like gold. It *was* gold. It was the earring.

'I think you dropped this on the Big Hill, remember?

Here, let me put it on for you, so's you won't forget it again.' Jessie's face was so cold that she could scarcely feel the fingers that touched her. 'Don't lose it now, will you?'

It was some time before Jessie could find her voice to speak. 'Are you really her?'

'If you mean, am I Grania O'Malley?' she said with a smile, 'then I am, indeed. Granuaille, Grany – they call me all sorts. The English call me Grace, but I'm always O'Malley even to them, and that's the bit that counts, isn't it, Jess? Your mother's an O'Malley, am I right? So, you and me, we're O'Malleys both. So's half the island, and you too, Jack.' She leaned towards them, hands on hips. 'It was my boys who fished you out of the sea and brought you home. Good boys all of them – well, maybe not good exactly – but fine pirates all the same, the best. We've been keeping an eye on you, so we have. If I couldn't be there myself, then I'd always have the boys looking out for you. Just as well too, wasn't it? Now come over by the fire, why don't you, and dry yourselves out. We'll fetch you some hot soup. You'd like that, wouldn't you?' Jessie hoped Jack wouldn't insist on a peanut butter sandwich and a Coke. He didn't.

What was in the soup neither of them knew nor cared. It was some kind of thick broth and it warmed them from the inside; and there was bread to wipe around the bowl when they had finished, coarse bread that you had to chew, full of grain and grit. But they didn't mind. Grania O'Malley smoked a pipe and studied them from her chair while they ate. Jessie could just about feel her hands again now, but she was still numb from the waist down.

'Should I rub your legs for you like your mother does?' Grania O'Malley asked. 'Would you like that?' How does she know about that? Jessie thought. And how does she always seem to know what I'm thinking, what I'm feeling? 'I told you, Jessie, we've been keeping a watchful eye on you. Call me your guardian pirate, if you will. I've been in school with you, I've met your Mrs Burke, your Miss Jefferson too. I've been in church with you, with Father Gerald. I've been in your room – but I think you know that already, don't you? I was out in the sheep shed when you were shearing the sheep. And I was with you up on the Big Hill, wasn't I? You see, Jess, I've a debt to pay you. Pirate I may be, but I always pay my debts.'

'I don't understand,' said Jessie.

'Well, of course you wouldn't. Why should you? But what if I tell you that I was the skull you found? That's right. I am Smiley. You kept me and talked to me, remember? You told me your troubles. I got to know you inside out, Jess. And then, out of the kindness of your heart, you buried me back where I belonged. That was a fine and a good thing you did for me. It made me feel needed again; and whenever Grania O'Malley feels needed, she comes back, and where she goes, her boys go too. So we've come back for a while, not to haunt you, but maybe to help you out a little. That was the idea in the beginning anyway. But as it turns out, I think I'll be needing you as much as you'll be needing me. Now will I rub some life into your legs or won't I?'

She set aside her pipe and held her hands to the fire for a few moments. Then she knelt down beside Jessie, and began kneading, slapping and rubbing, until Jessie's legs began to tingle back to life. Grania O'Malley looked up at Jack and blew into her hands before she began again. 'See that chest over there, Jack? Have a look, why don't you?' Jack got up and walked across the room. He lifted the lid on the chest under the window. It was heavy and needed both hands.

'Gold!' he whispered. 'It's all gold!'

Grania O'Malley frowned. 'Not that chest. There's my whole life's winnings in there. Get out of it, out of it! I meant the other one, over there by the flag in the corner, the little one. Do you see that flag, Jack?'

Jack held it out to look. A red pig was striding across a black background under a small rearing horse, red too; and the whole thing was decorated with crossbows in each corner, and at the bottom was a ship just like the galley they had come in.

'I tell you, Jack, in its time that red pig put the fear of God into every sailor that set eyes on it,' said Grania O'Malley. Jack let the flag fall and was fumbling now with the lock on the smaller chest. 'That's the one,' she said. 'You'll find in there all the really precious things I ever had,' she said. 'I have a book of poems by Sir Philip Sidney, signed by the man himself. He turned a lovely phrase, and he was a lovely man too. It wasn't his fault he was an Englishman.' Jack had the chest open by now and was reaching in.

'Where d'you get this?' he said, and he was holding up in his two hands the shell of a strange prehistoric-looking brown crab with a tail like a sting-ray. 'That's a horseshoe crab,' Jack went on. 'We've got them back home, on the beach, thousands of them.'

'And that's just where I found it,' said Grania O'Malley. 'Course I couldn't swear it was from the same beach, but not so far from what you call Long Island these days. Oh, I know where you're from, Jack. I've been listening in, remember?'

'You've been to America?' said Jack.

'Isn't he the clever one now? And how else would I have such a thing? Of course I have. The boys and me, we all went there together. So we had a bit of luck. When all's said and done, life's nothing but a gamble. You need a bit of luck. We had a map, from a Portuguese privateer that needed teaching some manners. Well, the fellow was sneaking into Galway Harbour, and without so much as a by-your-leave. He should have paid his dues like everyone else. We weren't going to have it, were we? We took everything he had. He didn't have much; but he did have a map of the east coast of the Americas.' She turned to Jessie. 'Is your legs any better now?'

'A little,' said Jessie.

'Got to get you warm,' she said, flexing her fingers. 'You too, Jack. Come here, closer to the fire.' And she beckoned him over. 'You're an American, so I suppose you've got a right to know. I'm going to tell you something no one else in the living world knows, not even Mister Barney – and over the years I've told him plenty. Good fellow is Mister Barney, good company. But first we've got to get that chill out of you. Come closer, boy.' And she sat Jack down with his back to the flames.

'That's better.' And she started on Jessie's legs again, talking as she rubbed.

'There's not much I like about being a ghost, I can tell you, but at least I don't feel the cold any more like I used to. Five castles I had, and each as cold as the other. Worst of all was that draughty place on Clare down by the quay. Rockfleet was the best, but this too was a bitter cold place to live through the winters. Not like America, where the sun warmed you through to your bones. I tell you, it's a place I'd have stayed, given half a chance. We were there first too, before the Hollanders, and before the infernal English. You don't believe me, do you? Well, no one believed me then, not even my own miserable husband. But I was there, I tell you. I was there.'

She spoke low now, and in earnest. 'There was trouble at home, there was always trouble, but this time it wasn't something I could fight my way out of, or talk my way out of. The English were hounding me and the Scots were raiding down from the North, and my husband was nothing but trouble. I took the Portuguese map, I took my son and I left. We had one galley, thirty good boys and all the food and water we needed, and we went westwards, towards the setting sun. Three months at sea, hardly a drop of water left and the boys weren't at all happy with me. Then I got lucky. We sighted land. America.'

She pointed to the flag. 'That was the very same flag I took with me. I planted it at the top of the dunes. The place was a paradise. Fruit, fresh water, game, fish, all you wanted. How we lived! We were going to stay for ever. None of us wanted to come home. But then one morning, it all went wrong. My little boy, called Tibbott he was, went off along the beach looking for his crabs, just like that one. He had dozens of them already, but he had to have just one more, didn't he? He disappeared, vanished into thin air. We looked everywhere. Nothing. The next morning we woke up and there were Indians all around us – hundreds of them and they weren't at all friendly. They shot an arrow at me, missed me by a whisker. Landed in the sand right by my foot. And there was my little Tibbott, taken as hostage. The boys wanted to fight it out, but there's a time to fight and a time to talk. This was a time to talk. It was a simple deal. I could have my son back if we left and didn't come back. We none of us spoke the language of course, but we got the gist of it. They let us take all the food and water we needed, the flag and one crab shell for my son, and the arrow that nearly killed me. Not a lot to show for it. So there y'are. Now you know what no one else knows, that the Irish were first in America.'

She sat back and smiled at them. 'I *owned* America. It was mine and I lost it. And then I managed to lose it a second time, didn't I?'

'How?' Jessie asked, and by now she had quite forgotten that she was talking to a ghost.

'It was that son of mine, that Tibbott, the one who went collecting crabs in America. I deserved better. He was maybe twenty by now and wild in the head. He got himself shut up in prison by the English – well, that wasn't difficult, it happened to a lot of people. I spent a year or two behind bars myself, and it was no fun at all, I'm telling you. They'd have hanged him given half a chance, but I wasn't going to let that happen. A mother hen has to look after her chicks, doesn't she? So the boys and me, we sailed for England, up the Thames to Greenwich to see the English queen, Queen Elizabeth herself. I sent ahead and told her I was coming, that I wanted to see her. I was polite about it mind. Always best to be polite if you want to get what you want. I said to her, I said: "I want my son out of your jail. He's done nothing wrong." Which wasn't strictly true.

'And she says to me, she says: "What's in it for me?"

'And I replied quick as you like, "How would you like America?" So it wasn't mine to give, but she wasn't to know that. "It's mine," I told her, "It's Irish."

' "Indeed?" she said, all smiling and hoity-toity. Anyway, to cut a long story short, she took America for the English, and I had my son back – so I hadn't lost anything I hadn't lost already and I'd got what I wanted out of it. Happy as a lark I was. Only, as I was leaving, she says to me: "You're a bit of a pirate, aren't you?"

' "Sometimes," I replied.

' "So am I," she said. "But don't tell anyone. And listen, Grania O'Malley, if you're going to pirate from now on, then do it quietly so's no one notices, then we shan't have cause to disagree." I tell you, that queen was a woman after my own heart.'

She threw a log on to the fire and nudged it in with her bare foot. 'Well, there you have it, my life story in a crab shell. But that's all done with and a long time ago. These last centuries, the boys and me, well, we've been sort of waiting around. You don't like to interfere once you're dead, but there's times when you just can't sit by and watch. There's times when you're needed. And in recent years I've not liked what I've been seeing, what I've been hearing. Dead or not, these are my lands, my sea. All my life I defended them as best I could. Sometimes we won, sometimes we lost. And I never minded the losing, because I always knew we'd win in the end. Invasions and occupations, they come and they go – the Normans, the English, the Scots. They've all come and they've all gone. We've had the famine, we've had the plague. There was nothing a poor ghost could do but watch and weep. But the Big Hill on Clare, once they do that you can't put it right afterwards. There are some things time won't heal. I'm with your mother, Jess, and with you. One way or another, the thing has to be stopped.'

'But no one listens, do they, Jack?' said Jessie. 'Mum's told them and told them, but they don't listen. It's the gold. They're all greedy for the gold.'

'And you can hardly blame them, can you?' said Grania O'Malley. 'After all, they're only human, aren't they? It's a natural enough thing to be greedy – not good maybe, but natural. I was quite keen on the gold myself at one time. I never knew a pirate that wasn't. Now listen, me and the boys, we've been pondering this for some time now, and we've all agreed that the treasure in the big chest over there is not a lot of use to us any more. I mean, all we do is gamble with it, and we can do that with the pebbles from the beach just as well. I'll not pretend they're at all pleased with the idea of parting with it, but they know as well as I do, that it's in a good cause. And besides, they do what they're told – mostly.'

A gleam came into her eye. 'I've been waiting for just the right moment, and this is it. When you're all dried off again, the boys will row you home to Clare and drop you off, not that far from where they found you. There's a cave there – Piper's Hole, we used to call it. I've hidden in there a dozen times when the English came looking for me. It's maybe the deepest cave on the whole island and you can only get at it from the sea. It'll be just perfect. And guess what you'll find at the very back of the cave, undiscovered for close on four hundred years? The lost treasure of Grania O'Malley. Are you beginning to catch my drift?'

She got up and walked over to the chest under the window. She lifted the lid. 'This treasure came from the *Santa Felicia*, one of the great galleons of the Spanish Armada, driven on to the rocks in the worst gale I ever saw. We rescued most of the crew, and the treasure, and the captain too – Don Pedro. He was a sick man, so I nursed him like a good Christian woman should. He was handsome too, eyes so dark you could drown in them – but then that's another story.' She seemed suddenly sad. 'Another story for another day maybe. Let's just say that, ever since, we've been keeping Don Pedro's treasure for a rainy day, and now the rainy day has come. There's more gold in this chest than they'll ever find inside the Big Hill. It'll be you that finds it, so by rights it'll be you that decides what's to be done with it. All you have to do is to tell them that you're happy for everybody on the island to share the treasure, providing they leave the Big Hill alone. How would that be now?'

'That's cool,' said Jack, a broad grin on his face, 'that's real cool.'

'That's what I thought too,' said Grania O'Malley.

'Can I look?' Jessie asked. Her legs were stiff with cold, and walking wasn't easy, but she had to get up and look. The chest was filled to the very top with gold cups, gold plates, gold doubloons, and gold chains. There were crosses that sparkled with emeralds and rubies, there were rings and pearls and bracelets and necklaces, and heaven knows what else.

'Is this where my earring came from?' she asked.

'Both of them,' said Grania O'Malley.

Jessie dug her hand in, cupped a handful of coins and let them run out through her fingers. 'It'll work,' she said. 'It'll really work. Once they see this, once they touch it they'll forget all about the gold on the Big Hill, they're bound to.' They looked up together as they heard a helicopter flying low overhead. 'They'll be out searching for us,' said Jessie. 'My mum and dad, they'll be worried sick.'

'They won't have to be worried for much longer,' said Grania O'Malley. Jack ran to the window. The helicopter was heading out over the islands of Clew Bay, out towards Clare. 'We'll get you home soon enough,' said Grania O'Malley. 'We'll wait just a little for the high tide to float the galley off the beach and then we'll be on our way.' She was gone down the stairs and they were left alone.

Jack stared down into the chest. 'I do not believe this,'

he said. 'I just do not believe this.' Jessie draped a necklace around his neck and filled his hands with coins.

'Believe it now?' she said.

There were raised voices downstairs, and then they heard Grania O'Malley shouting above the others. 'Will you be still and just listen! Did I ever let you down, did I?'

'Yes,' said one of the pirates.

'Well, maybe I did, but not often. And we always shared and shared alike, the good times and the bad? And we all agreed, didn't we? The treasure has to go, so we can save the Big Hill.' There were still rumblings of discontent. 'Tell me this, will you?' she went on. 'Being a rich ghost, does it make any one of us happier? Well, does it?' There was a long silence. 'Brendan, Donal, upstairs with you, and get that chest down. And be nice to those children while you're at it. Try smiling, for God's sake. It won't hurt. There's nothing I hate worse than a bunch of sulking pirates.'

The two pirates that came up the stairs shortly after did try to smile at them, but not very successfully. They looked longingly into the chest for a moment, before they closed the lid and carried it away downstairs. It wasn't long after that Grania O'Malley came for them, took them back down the winding stone stairs, and led them out of Rockfleet Castle and into the bright light of day. Both she and Jack took a hand each and helped Jessie down over the rocks towards the waiting galley.

High in the stern, with Grania O'Malley sitting on the treasure chest beside them, they went one last time through the plan to be sure they all understood, but it was difficult for Jack and Jessie to concentrate. There were two helicopters buzzing about overhead. The lifeboat was out looking, and the ferry too. It looked as if every boat on the island was at sea. As they came out into the open ocean, out of the shelter of Clew Bay, the ferry passed within hailing distance, the deck lined with searchers – Michael Murphy was there, Father Gerald too, and Mrs O'Leary from the pub. Some of them had binoculars trained right on them. But none of them seemed to be able to see them at all. The galley raced on, dipping into the wash the ferry had left behind, the spray showering everyone on board.

'You'd think they'd look where they were going,' laughed Grania O'Malley, wiping her face. 'Now have you been hearing me, you two? They only have my treasure if they leave off the mining on the Big Hill. Are we clear? It'll work a treat, you see if it won't.'

As they neared the shore, Grania O'Malley took the tiller herself and navigated the galley in through the surging seas. She waited for the right wave, gave the word, and then they surfed the crest of it through a narrow opening in the reef and into the calmer waters of a hidden inlet. Half the pirates shipped their oars now and scrambled forward, leaping into the sea and wading waist-high towards the shore. Heaving on the ropes, they hauled the galley in. They unloaded the treasure chest first, and with the greatest care. Then came the children's turn to be handed over the side. They were carried – a lot less carefully, Jessie thought – out of the shallows, up the shingle, and dumped on the beach beside the chest.

'We'll be off then,' said Grania O'Malley, 'before we all

change our minds.' The crew looked their last at the chest, like dogs that have had their favourite bones taken away. Grania O'Malley bent down and patted the chest. 'Parting is such sweet sorrow,' she said wistfully, and then she smiled at them. 'Shakespeare. Now there's a fellow I'd like to have met. Maybe I will one day. But there's a lot of things I never did that I should have done, and many more things I did that I should not have done. Maybe that's why I'm doing this. Who knows?'

She ruffled Jack's hair; and then stood, hands on her hips, looking down at Jessie. 'Well, do I get a kiss, or don't I?' Jessie did not hesitate. She reached up, put her arms round Grania O'Malley's neck, kissed her on the cheek and hugged her. 'I'll know it if you need me,' said Grania O'Malley, 'and not a word to a soul about me and the boys. Promise? They'd not believe you anyway.'

She turned and strode out through the shallows towards the galley. The last they saw of her, she was standing on the prow of the galley, just as Jessie had seen her in her dream. She waved, and the galley simply vanished. They were left standing alone on the beach, the treasure chest beside them, the retreating surf hissing over the shingle.

The chest was unbelievably heavy. At first they wondered if they could shift it at all. But they knew they had to. They didn't want anyone to see it until the time was right, until they were ready. It had to be hidden. One heave at a time they dragged the chest up the beach and into the dark depths of the cave until they could drag it no further.

They were still sitting on it, trying to get their breath back, when they heard voices from high above them on the clifftop. 'Shall we answer?' Jessie said.

But Jack had noticed something. 'Not with your earring on,' he said. Jessie clapped her hand to her ear. She had forgotten all about it. She took it off quickly, and slipped it into the pocket of her jeans.

'Ready,' she said.

'Let's go,' said Jack, and they walked out of the cave and began to shout. 'Down here! Down here!'

Even as they shouted, their voices were drowned by the sudden thunderous din of a helicopter overhead. It hovered for some moments over the cliffs, swooped out to sea, dipped and turned back towards them. There was a man leaning out and waving, and then he was being lowered towards them. The down-draught blew Jessie on to her bottom and she stayed sitting where she was on the wet pebbles as the man landed and ran over towards her. He crouched down beside them. 'Nothing more to worry about,' he said. 'You'll be fine now, just fine. Bit cold, are you?'

'A bit,' said Jack.

'We'll get you back soon enough,' said the man. 'Ladies first, eh? I'll be back for you in a minute.' He put his hand on Jack's shoulder. 'Just stay where you are. Won't be long.'

He snapped Jessie into the dangling harness and up they went, turning and swirling in the air together. Strong arms grabbed her and hauled her into the helicopter. She was strapped in at once and smothered in blankets. It seemed no time at all before Jack was beside her in the helicopter, and they were skimming low over the fields, over the quay, over the abbey ruins and the school; and there was the farm below them, and the house, and the 'creatures' in the garden. Jessie found Jack's hand, squeezed it hard and got a squeeze back in reply.

As they landed in the field, the sheep scattering in all directions, they saw Jessie's mother and father come running out of the house and Panda too, his hair flattened along his back, barking at the helicopter. Mole was scampering away in amongst the sheep as fast as his legs could carry him. The hugging seemed to go on for ever, two at a time, and then all four of them together. Jessie thought they'd never let go. The helicopter rotors slowed at last to a whine and then stopped. There was quiet again, except for Mole braying his indignation, and Panda still barking at this extraterrestrial invasion.

There was a hot bath, hot chocolate and peanut butter sandwiches, and all the time the questions. Jessie answered them – that's what they had both agreed. She kept as close to the truth as possible. She had slipped on the rocks and fallen into the sea. Jack had dived in after her and saved her. They were a long time in the sea, and so cold, and then they'd been swept into this inlet and had found shelter in a a cave. Jack had tried to climb the cliff but he couldn't, so they just waited there in a cave. She kept it simple, and if they asked more, she said she couldn't remember.

Dr Brady was helicoptered over from the mainland to examine them. He said they were remarkably well, considering the ordeal they had been through. There were more questions. They stuck to their story and everybody seemed to believe them. There were cups of tea for the helicopter crew in the kitchen; and then the entire island, it seemed, came visiting. Even Marion Murphy came – and that was the first time she'd ever set foot in Jessie's house – but of course she turned out to be a lot more interested in Jack than she was in Jessie.

There were more tears, more hugs, and still more questions. Through it all, Jessie could think only of how she was going to tell her mother and father about the plan to save the Big Hill without mentioning Grania O'Malley. It wasn't going to be easy.

She waited until everyone had gone and caught Jack's eye across the sitting-room. The time had come. She was still wondering how she was going to make it sound at all convincing when her father helped her. 'I still can't think how you managed it, Jack,' he was saying. 'The current against you, tide against you. And how come no one spotted you sooner? I tell you, it's a miracle, a miracle.'

'We were inside the cave a long time,' said Jessie, seizing her moment. 'I expect that's why no one saw us. It's deep, like a long tunnel and we just went in to get out of the wind, didn't we, Jack?' Jack nodded, but he didn't say anything. He clearly wasn't going to be much help. 'And then Jack went off exploring. That's when he found it.' They were looking at her, expecting more. There was no stopping now. 'We thought we should tell you first, didn't we, Jack? I mean it's ours, because we found it, and we've decided what to do with it, haven't we?'

'With what?' said Jessie's mother, completely bewildered by now. 'What on earth are you talking about, Jess?'

And that was when, quite unexpectedly, Jack spoke up. 'Treasure. Gold. I found a whole chest of it at the back of the cave. Jess says it's Grania O'Malley's treasure, whoever she is.'

Jessie's mother and father looked at each other for a moment. 'Let's get this straight, Jack,' said her father. 'You were in the cave and you found a chest full of gold, is that what you're trying to tell us?'

'Yes, sir,' Jack replied. 'Right at the back of the cave, like I said. Pretty dark in there too, but you could see just about enough.' Jessie did her best to keep her smile inside herself.

Her father laughed, a nervous laugh. 'Are you kidding, or what?' he said.

'I can prove it too,' said Jessie triumphantly, 'I brought some of it back.'

'You've got some of the treasure, some of the gold? You've got it here?'

'Upstairs. In my jeans pocket. I'll fetch it.'

She found all her clothes where she'd left them, in a heap on the bathroom floor. The earring fell out as she picked up the jeans. Barry panicked when her hand came into his bowl and circled manically until Jessie had retrieved the other earring from under the stones. 'Not yours, you know,' she whispered. They were still silent in the kitchen when she came downstairs again. She beamed at Jack and opened her hand. Her mother took them from her one by one, and held them up to the light.

'They're beautiful,' she whispered. 'Just beautiful.'

'I pinched them,' Jessie said. 'I pinched them from the treasure chest. There's a whole lot of stuff like this, chains and crosses and plates – all sorts. And it's all gold, isn't it, Jack?'

Jessie's father was on his feet. 'And it's still there?' he said. 'Still in Piper's Hole?' Jessie nodded. 'I'll have to take the boat, and I'll need a torch.'

'I'm coming too,' said her mother, putting on her coat. 'You two stay here, stay in the warm.'

When they were quite sure they had gone, the two of them looked at each other, smiled and then burst out laughing. They laughed until it hurt, out of joy, out of relief. Suddenly Jack stopped laughing and grabbed her arm.

'Jess, I just hope Grania O'Malley hasn't changed her mind and come back and taken it away. Some of those pirate guys weren't at all happy about giving it away, you know, and neither was she.'

'You can trust her,' said Jessie, and she was quite sure of it; but the longer they waited the less sure of it she became.

It was nearly two hours later, and dark outside, when they heard Panda barking and Clatterbang come rattling up the lane. They ran outside. Jessie's mother and father were struggling to carry the chest between them across the yard. Jack ran to help, while Jessie held the door back for them. They heaved it up on to the kitchen table. Her father leaned on the table, shaking his head.

'You were right,' said her mother breathlessly.

'Have you seen inside?' Jessie asked.

'It's the real thing,' said her father. 'It's real treasure. I can't believe it. I just cannot believe it.'

'And it's ours,' said Jessie. 'All ours!'

8 MISTER BARNEY

BY THE TIME THEY HAD FINISHED EMPTYING THE chest, the kitchen was glowing with gold, the dresser festooned with gold chains, the shelves lined with gold goblets and gold beakers. From every knob and every cup hook dangled a jewelled necklace. The table-top was almost invisible, covered as it was with doubloons and crosses, and gold plates piled high with glittering jewels. And in the centre, in pride of place, stood a great golden ewer with a fish's mouth for a spout. They sat down and simply gazed around them. Jessie put her earrings on and looked down at herself in one of the golden plates. For a long time no one spoke a word.

'Will someone please pinch me?' said Jessie's father at last. 'This afternoon I thought for certain you were both of you dead and drowned and gone for ever – and here you are sitting in front of me all alive again. And now all this.'

'The lost treasure of Grania O'Malley,' breathed Jessie's mother. 'You're right, Jess. It has to be. It's old Mister Barney's story come true.'

'What do you mean?' Jessie asked, trying not to sound too interested.

Her mother sat back in her chair, quite unable to take her eyes off the treasure. 'And we all thought the old man was cracked in the head, his mind all to pieces. But he wasn't at all, was he?'

'For goodness' sake, Cath,' said Jessie's father, 'Mister Barney's stories are just stories. There's not a word of truth in any of them, everyone knows that. You'll frighten her silly.'

But Jessie's mother went on: 'I was about your age, Jess, when it happened. Mister Barney was already old, but he'd still cut more peat in a day than any man on the island. Us kids, we'd go up to his place to help him stack it sometimes, and afterwards he'd give us a drink of water and we'd sit down and he'd tell us all sorts of tales. I've forgotten a lot of them, but not this one. He told us how one day he'd been up on the Big Hill and he'd met the ghost of Grania O'Malley. He said how she'd got talking about her pirating days and how she'd fallen in love with some Spanish captain or admiral – I can't remember. Anyway, this Spanish captain was blown round the top of Ireland in his galleon – part of the Spanish Armada and all that – and was wrecked on the rocks. Everyone on Clare wanted to kill the lot of them, him and his crew. But she wouldn't let them do it – it seems she'd taken a bit of a fancy to him. She said there was no need to go killing

251

anyone when they could have all the treasure they liked anyway. More Christian that way, that's what she told Mister Barney. So she saved her Spanish captain and his crew, and kept the gold. Everyone was happy.'

'Oh, come on,' Jessie's father interrupted. 'You can't seriously believe all that stuff.'

Jessie's mother gave him a long and withering look. 'As I was saying,' she said, 'she looked after the treasure herself and the captain and his crew stayed for a while. He was ill and she nursed him back to life. She told Mister Barney that it was the only time in her whole life she ever met a man she could be truly happy with. But then there was some quarrel, and the captain – I think he was called Don . . . Don Pedro, that's it, Don Pedro – anyway, he was wounded, and on his deathbed he made her promise she would take his crew safely back to Spain. So she did, but she kept his treasure of course. She hid it away because she didn't want the marauding English to find it. And then later, when she was older, she still kept it hidden – keeping it for a rainy day, that's what she told Mister Barney.

'Of course, we none of us believed him, not really. We wanted to, mind. I remember a few of us went digging for treasure afterwards, but we never found anything, so we soon gave up. Old Mister Barney didn't though. You'd see him out there with his metal detector, and in all weathers too, looking for Grania O'Malley's lost treasure. The older we got, the more we laughed at him. He found bits and pieces, a coin or two, not much. But then his hips gave up on him, poor old fellow, and so now he can hardly get about at all.'

Jessie's father was about to interrupt again. But she wouldn't have it. 'I'm not saying he isn't strange, Jimmy. I'm not saying it isn't an unlikely story, but will you just look at all this treasure! The story fits. And it's no good just saying he's crazy in the head. You heard him the other night arguing to save the Big Hill. You've seen his place. Packed to the gunwales with history books, isn't it? He's no fool. He's no idiot. The man knows more about this island than anyone else alive. I tell you, he's a walking encyclopaedia.'

Jessie listened, spellbound. She thought that maybe this was the moment to tell the whole story as it had really happened, confess that they had lied about finding the treasure in the cave, that they too had met Grania O'Malley just as old Mister Barney had. But then she thought again. Hadn't Grania O'Malley herself made them promise not to say a word? Hadn't she said that no one would believe them anyway? She was right. They'd just say she was making it up; and besides, Jessie hardly believed it herself. It was all too utterly fantastical.

Her father was snorting. 'Baloney,' he said. 'All a lot of baloney. I thought it was baloney before and I still do. He's mad as a hatter – it's a known fact. There's some things that just aren't possible. Ghosts is one of them.'

'Is that so?' said Jessie's mother acidly. 'Will you look at the coins on the table. Spanish doubloons, aren't they? I've seen others just like them, and you have too. If they are Spanish, then like as not they're from an Armada ship. It's a known fact that at least one of the Armada galleons was wrecked off Clare Island. For God's sake, don't people come here every summer and go diving on the wreck? Hardly surprising they haven't found much, is it? It's all been hidden away in Piper's Hole, for hundreds of years. You remember there was that cannon dragged up last year in the fishing nets? That was off the Armada galleon, wasn't it? You can't deny it. And everyone knows too, who's got any knowledge of it, that Grania O'Malley ruled in these waters at the time of the Spanish Armada. Now tell me, who else could all this belong to, if not to her?'

They were arguing again, and Jessie wanted to stop it. 'It doesn't matter whose treasure it was, Mum,' she said. 'It's ours now, Jack's and mine, and we've already decided what we're going to do with it, haven't we, Jack?' Jack smiled at her, but a little anxiously. That was when Jessie lost her nerve. Panic gripped her and her mind seemed to stall. She just couldn't think straight. 'You tell them, Jack,' she said, in desperation.

For some moments Jack looked down at his hands and said nothing. 'Well,' he began, 'we were in the cave, Jess and me, and we were figuring out what we'd do with all this treasure – you know, how we'd spend it. I said I'd like an old Studebaker or a Bugatti, remember, Jess? And you said you'd rather have a pair of new legs, right?'

Jessie could not believe her ears. He was brilliant.

Jack went on: 'Just talk, just dreaming, that's all we were doing. See, we didn't reckon we were going to get out of there. The tide was coming up real fast, almost into the cave, and we had nowhere else to go. We thought we were going to drown. So we made ourselves a promise.'

'What sort of a promise?' asked Jessie's mother.

'Not a promise, I guess, more like a deal,' Jack said. 'That's it, more a kind of deal. We said that if we got out of there alive, then we'd give all the treasure away, we wouldn't keep it for ourselves. We'd share it with the islanders. It was Jess's idea. She said that if everyone on the island had a fair share – and it looked like there was more than enough treasure to go round – then they wouldn't need to cut the top off the Big Hill, because they'd have all the gold they ever wanted. It seemed like a great idea to me. So we both promised that's what we'd do if we survived, and we did survive.' He looked straight at Jessie's mother, cool as a cucumber. 'She thought you'd like that. Isn't that right, Jess?'

Jessie was dumbfounded. Jack was a better liar than she could ever be. Her mother was holding her hands out to her, her eyes full of tears. 'Come here, Jess,' she said. 'I want to cuddle you the biggest cuddle you've ever been cuddled.' Sat on her mother's lap, Jessie was happy enough to let herself be cuddled. 'Well,' said her mother, sniffing back the tears. 'What do you think of this daughter of ours, Jimmy? Isn't that the most wonderful idea you've ever heard of in all your life? And you can't argue with it, can you? It's true enough. Jess and Jack found it, all of it, so it's theirs by right. And if they found it, then they should decide what happens to it.'

But Jessie's father was not looking at all enthusiastic. Whenever he was worried, he always sat with his hands together as if he was saying his prayers, thumbs under his chin, fingertips touching the tip of his nose. 'I'm not sure,' he mumbled. 'I'm not sure at all.'

'Well, of course you're not,' Jessie's mother said, her voice rising at once. 'That's because like the rest of the idiots on this island, you've set your heart on that stupid, iniquitous gold mine.'

'That's not fair and it's not true,' Jessie's father replied.

'Well, what then?'

'Look, it's just that I think we all need to think about this. It's not that simple. I mean, for a start, just because you find something, it doesn't mean it's yours. There's laws about these things. And even if it is yours, to share it out fairly you'd have to sell it and divide the money. How else are you going to share it all out? I mean, we don't know how much these things are worth, do we? You'll need an expert in treasure trove. Who's to say what that ewer, for example, is worth compared to that necklace or that beaker?' No one answered him, not for some time.

'Old Mister Barney,' Jessie's mother said suddenly, her eyes lighting up. 'You remember when those divers found that cannon last year? It was Mister Barney they fetched down to the beach, wasn't it? He dated it for them, and he told them all about it. Well, we'll do the same thing. We'll get Mister Barney down here, have him look at it all and tell us how much each piece is worth. He'll tell us what's what.'

Jessie's father took his hands from his mouth and nodded slowly. 'You're putting an awful lot of faith in that old man. But all right, I'll go tomorrow and bring Mister Barney back here, if he'll come. I don't know if he will though. He doesn't come out much these days, only when he has to.'

'You'll tell him what we've got here, Jimmy,' Jessie's mother said. 'And I'm telling you, he'll come, lickety-split. No problem.'

At that moment, there was a loud and insistent knocking on the front door and Panda was barking his head off.

'Only me, Mrs Parsons!' It was Mrs Burke. Never had the kitchen been cleared so quickly. With Panda careering round their legs, they scoured the kitchen for the last necklace or plate or beaker, slammed the chest shut, dragged it into the pantry and closed the door. 'Is anyone at home?' Mrs Burke was knocking again, louder this time. Jack was wiggling his earlobe at her frantically. Jessie took a moment or two to realise she was still wearing her earrings. She snatched them off and slipped them into her dressing-gown pocket. They were ready for Mrs Burke.

By the time Jessie's mother brought her into the kitchen, they were all sitting round the table and Jack was dealing a pack of cards. Panda was whining at the door of the larder and scrabbling at it. Jessie hauled her away. 'Always at the food, he is,' she said, by way of explanation.

'Well,' Mrs Burke beamed about her, 'aren't we the famous ones! Helicopters, lifeboats, whatever next? I've been over on the mainland all day – head teachers' conference, you know – and I missed all the excitement. Everyone's talking about it. It was on the radio. I just had to come and see for myself how you were.' Jessie was outraged. How could she be so sickly sweet and concerned in front of her parents, and such an old dragon back at school?

'That was kind of you, Mrs Burke,' said Jessie's mother, her eyes darting everywhere, looking for any stray treasure. 'As you can see they're fine, aren't you, children? Jessie fell in and Jack pulled her out. Saved her life, so he did. And now he's teaching us blackjack, aren't you, Jack?' She giggled at that, but nervously.

Mrs Burke clapped her hands in delight. 'My, my, a real hero,' she cried. And then, all at once, her face creased into a puzzled frown. She was pointing at the pantry door. Everyone turned and looked. A gold necklace was dangling from the handle, a long chain of delicate gold links interwoven with flowers of white enamel.

'What a lovely, lovely thing,' breathed Mrs Burke. 'Yours?' Jessie's mother nodded. 'Gold, is it?'

'Wouldn't that be nice now!' laughed Jessie's mother. 'Of course not. I got it in Galway, last time I was over. Just a bit of tinsel, but I like it.'

At that Mrs Burke seemed immediately to lose interest and turned to Jessie's father. 'Mind you,' she went on, 'there'll be those, I've no doubt, who will be wondering what the two of them were doing left all alone out on the rocks like that.' Ah, thought Jessie, that's more like the Mrs Burke I know and love. And she was delighted to see that both her father and mother were looking daggers at Mrs Burke.

Mrs Burke cleared her throat in the silence. 'Well, I just thought I'd call in,' she chimed. 'Will I be seeing the children at school tomorrow?'

'I expect so,' said Jessie's mother, hustling her to the door. 'If they've recovered well enough.'

They heard the door close. Jessie's mother came back into the room, leaned back against the kitchen door and closed her eyes. 'I know I shouldn't say it, seeing as she's Jess's teacher and all, but sometimes I could really strangle that woman, Miss Tittletattle that she is.'

Jessie was running the white enamelled necklace through her fingers. She tried it round her neck. 'Do you think she knew?' she said.

Jessie's mother shook her head and laughed. 'Course not. She'll be in every shop in Galway looking for one just like it. Now take that gorgeous thing off before someone else walks in. Come on, Jimmy, we'd better hide this lot away, and quick. And you two can get yourselves to bed.'

Tired as she was, Jessie did not want the day to end. She took her earrings out of her dressing-gown pocket, put them on and sat in front of her mirror. She smiled at what she saw. She looked like a real woman for the first time, like her mother, like Grania O'Malley. The dramatic events of the day kept churning around in her mind, the fishing from the rocks, the tumble into the sea, the rescue, the pirates, Grania O'Malley, the treasure, the helicopter, the plan to save the Big Hill. It was as if she was inside some wild and wonderful dream. Yet at the same time, she knew for sure it was no dream, that in the room next door was the boy who really had saved her life. He had saved her life! In all the excitement she had forgotten that. She had never even thanked him.

Jessie did not want to be heard. Walking quietly was never easy for her, so she crawled along the passage and tapped lightly on Jack's door. 'Jack?' she whispered. 'Are you still awake?'

'I guess so,' came the reply. She reached up and opened the door. The light was still on. He was sitting up in his bed, propped against his pillows. 'You can't sleep either?' he said, as she got to her feet. 'I was just thinking about that horseshoe crab shell she had,' he went on, 'that maybe all those years ago she landed right on my beach on Long Island, that maybe I've walked on the same sand she did. That'd be amazing, wouldn't it?' Jessie sat down on the end of the bed. 'I've got this teacher back home, Mrs Cody. She's really up on history, you know, Christopher Columbus, the Pilgrims, the Revolution, the Civil War, all that stuff. Soon as I get back, I'm going to tell her she's gotten it all wrong – everyone has. The first person to land in America – on Long Island, anyway – wasn't Dutch or British at all. She was Irish, an Irish pirate called Grania O'Malley. Mrs Cody'll be real excited – she's Irish herself. Real excited. But then, I guess maybe she won't believe me. She'll just think I'm nuts.'

'But we're not nuts, are we?' Jessie asked. 'It really did happen, all of it, didn't it?'

'Sure it did, Jess,' he said. 'Kind of makes you wonder. I mean, if all of this really happened, and it did, then almost anything can happen, right? Maybe when I get back home, Dad won't be sick any more, even without my lucky arrowhead. No use just hoping. I guess you've just got to believe.' Jessie didn't know what to say. 'You know something else, Jess?' he went on. 'You're really lucky. Your mom and dad, even when they get mad at each other, you know they're just saying what they have to say. They don't want to hurt each other.'

'You think so?' said Jessie.

He smiled broadly now. 'And we fooled them real good, didn't we?'

'I don't know about Dad,' said Jessie. 'I think he knows something's going on, but he doesn't know what. And even if we told him, he wouldn't believe us, would he? No one would.'

'What wouldn't I believe?' The door was open and her father came into the room. 'What are you two cooking up?' he said.

'Nothing,' said Jessie.

'You still got those earrings on? Off with them, you little pirate. They belong downstairs with the rest. You'll be going to school in them next.' Jessie wanted to protest, to tell him the earrings were really hers and not part of the treasure at all, but she knew there was no point, not unless she told her father everything. Too many lies had already been told for that. She took them off and dropped them reluctantly into his hand.

'Where are you going to hide the chest?' Jessie asked.

'You bury treasure, don't you?' her father said. 'Your mum's outside now. We're digging a hole behind the hen-house. It'll be safe enough there, don't you worry. Now, to bed with you.'

Jessie was back in her room and sitting on the edge of her bed before she remembered she still hadn't thanked Jack for saving her life. She would have to do it tomorrow.

It was a long night and she couldn't sleep a wink. Her

body wanted to drift away, but her mind simply would not let it. She could see Grania O'Malley's face so clearly in her head that she felt quite sure she must be there with her in the room. And then there was still the cloud of doubt that hung over their plan to save the Big Hill. Her father was right, to share the treasure out fairly amongst everyone, it would have to be sold. But what if old Mister Barney said it wasn't worth that much anyway? And worse still, what if he said it wasn't theirs to sell? What if? What if? She said her prayers over and over again, something she hadn't done for a long time; and it was in the middle of one of her long begging prayers, for God to make everything turn out all right, that she finally went off to sleep.

In school the next day she could not stop herself from yawning. She yawned when Mrs Burke had the two of them up in front of the whole school and thanked God for their rescue. Everyone seemed to have forgotten about not speaking to her, even Marion Murphy. When all the children gathered round them at playtime and bombarded them with endless questions about their adventure, she still had to yawn. It was good to feel popular. She wasn't as popular as Jack, she knew that; but not a word was mentioned about the Big Hill. Everyone seemed to have forgotten all about that too.

Jessie basked in it all, but the yawns kept coming and there was nothing she could do about it. Even when the newspapers and the radio and television people turned up and asked what it had been like and told them both to smile into the camera, she still had to stifle a yawn. It should all have been so exciting, but somehow it just wasn't. All she enjoyed of the day was the secret she and Jack shared, the true story of what had really happened, the story that no one else in the world would ever know – except Grania O'Malley and her pirates.

Only on the way back home after school did she manage at last to talk to Jack alone. 'Mrs Burke said we'll be on telly tonight,' she said. But Jack did not look at all happy about it.

'What's the matter?' she asked.

'Nothing much, just something Liam said.'

'What?'

'The diggers. His dad told him. They'll be over here by the weekend. We haven't got much time.'

'I wonder if Mister Barney's been yet?' said Jessie.

When they got home, Jessie's mother was singing in the kitchen, and that was something Jessie hadn't heard for a long time. 'We're going to be on the telly,' Jessie told her.

'I know, Jess,' she said, hugging her tight and then taking off her coat. 'Everyone knows. It's all over the island. Front page in *The Irish Times* tomorrow. I've had the newspapers on the phone, photographers in and out all day.' She kissed them both. 'I could eat the two of you, so I could. I could eat you, I'm so proud of you,' she said.

'Mum,' Jessie had to tell her, 'have you heard about the diggers coming?'

'I heard,' she said, and then she went on, 'but we're not finished yet. I was thinking, Jess. I've been thinking all day. There could be another way of doing this, a quicker way, and without selling the treasure at all. We could take the whole lot round to Michael Murphy, here and now, and make him an offer he couldn't refuse. We could buy the Big Hill off him. Then it would be your hill, our hill. We could stop the diggers in their tracks. One look and he'd jump at it, I know he would. Your father thinks it's all wishful thinking. He's wrong. I know he's wrong. What d'you think?'

'It could work,' cried Jessie, seeing the sense of it at once. 'It could really work.'

'Has Mister Barney come over?' Jack asked.

'In the sitting room,' she lowered her voice. 'He's been here for an hour or more.'

'Well, what does he say?' said Jessie.

'Nothing, not yet. He just looks at everything through his magnifying glass, mutters to himself and that's that. You go in. I'll bring the tea in a moment.'

Mister Barney was sitting in the big armchair by the fireside, the open treasure chest on the floor beside him. He looked up as the children came in. Jessie had not seen him this close for some time. He seemed all skin and bone, somehow lost inside his great dirty coat. It was difficult not to stare at the raised veins in his hands.

'Jessie, isn't it?' he said. 'Haven't I seen you going up and down the Big Hill like a yo-yo?' He beckoned Jack closer to him and held out his hand to be shaken. 'And you must be the American boy.' He was looking Jack up and down. 'What do they feed you on over there? You should put some weight on you. Like a giraffe, you are. It was you that found all this, was it, and in Piper's Hole?'

'Both of us, sir,' said Jack.

'It is real, Mister Barney, isn't it?' Jessie asked. 'Real gold? Real Spanish treasure?' Mister Barney leaned forward, picked out a doubloon from the chest and examined it through a magnifying glass. 'I'll tell you all you need to know soon enough, Jessie, soon enough. Won't be long. Patience now.' He rubbed his hands and blew in them. 'What's next, Jimmy?'

Jessie's father dipped into the chest and brought out a gold cross encrusted with dark green stones. He laid it carefully on the table in front of Mister Barney who picked it up with loving care and peered at it long and hard. He grunted and set it aside. 'Next,' he said.

So it went on all through tea, all of them sitting in expectant silence and watching old Mister Barney for any sign of excitement or disappointment. There was none. When the chest was empty at last, he sat back and wiped his eyes with his handkerchief. 'I could do with a little glass of water, Cath,' he whispered. Jessie's mother hurried to the kitchen and fetched him one. Old Mister Barney sipped it slowly. 'That's lovely,' he said. 'Well, you'll be wanting to know what I think, I suppose.' He sipped again, agonisingly slowly. 'What I think is what I know for a fact. Now, do you want to hear the glad news first, or the sad news?'

'Glad,' said Jessie at once.

Mister Barney smiled at her. 'The same sweet thing your mother was at your age.' He turned to Jessie's mother. 'Do you remember, Cath, all those stories I used to tell you when you were little? Do you remember I told you once about Grania O'Malley's treasure? Well, there's not a doubt about it. You're looking at it. All my life I've been looking for this. This is off the *Santa Felicia*, the great Armada galleon wrecked in a gale off Clare in 1588. She told me she'd hidden it, but she never said where and I never dared ask her. I told you I'd met up with her ghost, didn't I?'

He smiled gently at Jessie's mother. 'I bet you thought I was cuckoo, didn't you? Drunk maybe. Well, I don't blame you. But it wasn't the drink. I've never drunk a drop of anything that wasn't water. I'm telling you now that I met her ghost – that's a plain and simple fact. She was a friend to me when I needed one, a real friend. And d'you know what a real friend is? A listener. And she was quite a talker too. I'm telling you now that this is the treasure of Grania O'Malley herself.'

'But is it worth a lot of money?' Jessie asked. 'We need to know how much.' Mister Barney seemed reluctant to reply. Either that or he hadn't heard properly.

'Mister Barney,' said Jessie's father, annunciating each word carefully, 'you remember I told you. Jessie and Jack, they found it. It's theirs. They want to share this treasure amongst everyone on this island so that then no one will need to cut the top off the Big Hill for the gold. To do that we've got to sell it.'

'I hear you,' said Mister Barney, and he reached out and patted Jessie's hand. 'I understand. That's a fine and noble thought, Jessie; and I could tell you the date of every piece, weigh it, tell you the worth of it too. But it wouldn't do you any good, I'm afraid, not you, not me, nor the Big Hill up there. And believe me, there's nothing I want more than to save that hill. It's come too late, Jessie. Now, if you'd found all this a few months back, then we'd have a chance. But your mother tells me the bulldozers will be over any time now to start their digging.'

'What are you saying, Mister Barney?' Jessie's mother asked.

'What I'm saying, Cath,' Mister Barney went on, 'is the sad news. You can't share it out, like Jessie wanted. And you can't use it to buy the Big Hill off Mr Murphy either, like you wanted, even if he'd sell it. You see, it's the law of the land that's in your way. If you find treasure like this, any treasure, you have to tell the Garda. You have to tell the authorities. I've looked into this for myself and I know it's right. You have to tell them and then they tell Dublin, and someone from the government comes and takes it away. They don't let you keep stuff like this. It's too important. It doesn't matter who finds it, it belongs to the nation, to the people. As soon as they hear about all this, and they would – you couldn't hardly keep it a secret, could you now? – they'll be coming for it, to take it away. They might pay you some compensation later, but it would be too late for the Big Hill. So you see, it isn't yours to share out. You want to save the Big Hill, then I'm afraid you'll have to find another way to do it. You'll have to find yourself another miracle.'

9 THE DIGGERS ARE COMING

MISTER BARNEY STAYED LATE INTO THE EVENING, the treasure spread out all round him. In all that time he scarcely stopped talking. It was as if he was trying to make up for all the years of silent solitude in his shack on the Big Hill. He pored over the treasure like a man obsessed, obsessed not with greed but with sheer joy at the discovery of it all. Every piece was a marvel to him. Again and again he revelled in the fact that he had at last been proved right about the lost treasure of Grania O'Malley.

'I tell you,' he said, 'it's terrible hard to believe in yourself when no one else does. That's why I like to hide myself away up on the Big Hill, out of sight of their mocking eyes. I don't care to be laughed at. And do you know another thing? I remember meeting Grania O'Malley up on the Big Hill. Clear as day I remember it, but in these last years, I've become more muddled in my head, and I'd begun to wonder myself if it was just my own imaginings I was remembering, and that maybe she was nothing more than that.'

He ran his hands lovingly around the gold plate on his lap. 'Now I know for sure that I really did meet her, and that what she told me was the truth. I have the proof of it, don't I?' He waggled a crooked finger at the children. 'I spend my whole life, searching the island end to end for this treasure, and I find nothing but a few miserable bits and pieces. You two go fishing, and find it without even looking for it!'

He laughed as he shook his head. 'Life's a pig sometimes, but then I suppose you'll not be needing me to tell you that, will you? Take the Big Hill. It's not fair what they're going to do and it's not right. They'll be moving me out of my place just because I'm in the way of their infernal diggers. They're going to cut the top off the Big Hill. It'll happen for sure now, and there's nothing more can be done about it. Still, now I've seen this, now I've touched it, I suppose I can't complain.'

He looked up at them, his eyes full of sadness. 'I've tried to tell them that it's not right, but no one listens. They're all too young. The whole world is too young. Maybe you have to be old before you understand that what happens tomorrow isn't what counts, it's what happens in a hundred years' time – there's an awful lot of tomorrows in a hundred years. But the trouble is you don't know that till you've lived them. I've lived them.'

Jessie tried to listen, but she was tired by now and she had other things to be thinking about. She sat on the carpet, her chin resting on her mother's knee. Every now and again she would catch Jack's eye, and she'd know he was wondering exactly what she was wondering. Is Grania O'Malley in the room with us? Has she heard what we've heard, that her plan to save the Big Hill isn't going to work? What will she do now? What will we do now?

'What'll you do now?' Mister Barney asked, echoing her thoughts.

'I'm not sure,' said Jessie's father. 'I think maybe we'd all better sleep on it. And I think we'd best not say anything to anyone for the moment, Mister Barney – about the treasure, I mean.'

'And who would I talk to now, all alone up there in my house?' Mister Barney replied. 'I can tell my chickens, can't I? I'll have to tell someone at home, I'll be bursting with it.'

'Chickens are fine,' said Jessie's mother.

As he left, Mister Barney put his arms round Jessie's mother and hugged her. 'I'm sorry, Cath, so sorry,' he said. 'Maybe there's still a way to stop them. There has to be.'

'I hope so,' Jessie's mother replied. But Jessie could hear in her voice that she no longer had any hope left inside her. Jessie felt just the same.

While her father took Mister Barney back home, the three of them loaded the treasure back into the chest. Jessie thought of rescuing her earrings, but there just wasn't the opportunity, not with her mother there. They used a wheelbarrow to carry the treasure chest across the yard, and then they lowered it again into its hole behind the chicken shed. It was as they were burying it that her mother suddenly burst into tears and ran indoors. Jessie thought about going after her, but decided she would want to be alone. It was a still night, the sky full of stars, and the moon was riding through the clouds on the Big Hill.

Without warning, Jack called out into the night: 'Grania O'Malley, you're up there somewhere, aren't you? We've got a problem down here. The treasure's no good. The diggers will be here by the weekend, and we can't share the treasure like you thought. Unless you come up with something, and something really good, we're going to lose the Big Hill. I guess you've been watching, so you know how bad things are. Are you going to help us, or what?' The sea breathed softly in the distance and the abbey owl screeched once. The chickens shifted on their perches in the shed. But there was no answer from Grania O'Malley.

'Please,' Jessie begged, looking up into the sky. 'Please help us.'

'Think she's really listening?' Jack asked.

'She'd better be,' said Jessie. 'She'd just better be.'

Later, they were all round the kitchen table in their night things, sipping hot chocolate, except Jack who had his Coke as usual. 'You know what we forgot?' said Jessie's father. 'I just remembered. You were going to be on the telly, weren't you? I wonder if it's too late.'

He reached over and switched on the television. An advertisement was showing. Dozens of huge yellow diggers were working in a dusty quarry. A siren sounded and they all backed away from the quarry face, except for one. The driver was biting into a chocolate bar. He didn't seem to have heard the siren – either that, or he didn't care about it. There was a huge explosion above him. He wasn't bothered, he just went on with his chewing. The avalanche of rocks tumbled down towards him, and then suddenly froze in mid-air. He looked up, smiled, backed away in his own time, chewing and smiling smugly. Once he was out of the way, the avalanche thundered down, only just missing him. No one dared look at Jessie's mother. Then it was the local news. A smiling, simpering face came on.

'Good evening. Drama yesterday on Clare Island. Helicopters were called in, and the Westport lifeboat was launched when two children went missing. Ten-year-old Jessie Parsons, who suffers from cerebral palsy, was fishing off the rocks with her cousin . . .' And the report rambled on over aerial longshots of Clare Island. '. . . both are fit and well after their ordeal. So, everyone's smiling on Clare Island tonight.'

And there they were on television, the two of them, outside the school, Jessie lurching along beside Jack. Jessie got up and switched it off herself. 'Well, I'm *not* happy,' she stormed. 'And do they have to tell everyone about my lousy palsy? Do they?'

Upstairs she threw herself on the bed and hit the pillows again and again until the tears finally stopped. She felt the bed sag beside her, and then a warm tongue was licking her ear. Panda was panting in her face, tongue lolling and dripping.

It wasn't too long before her mother came up, as Jessie

had hoped she would. 'You and me,' she said, 'we're a couple of old misery guts, aren't we?' And Jessie couldn't disagree. 'Still,' her mother went on, 'tomorrow can only be better, eh?'

But tomorrow wasn't any better. After morning prayers. Mrs Burke played the video tape of the television news bulletin in front of the whole school. Jessie didn't look. She tried to bear it as best she could, as everyone pointed at the screen, shrieking with delight when they recognised anyone or anything. Jessie spent most of that day looking out of the classroom window. She hoped, and she believed, that Grania O'Malley would appear from nowhere, that same smile on her face, the smile that would tell Jessie everything would turn out fine after all, that somehow another way had been found to save the Big Hill. But hope and belief often gave way to doubt, and doubt to despair.

At afternoon playtime she wandered away from the others, away from Jack who was still surrounded by infants clamouring for their hero's autograph. She found herself a hidden corner round the back by the kitchens, where she sat and waited on a dustbin for Grania O'Malley to come to her, or speak to her, anything. When she didn't come and she didn't come, Jessie began calling for her, softly, so that her voice wouldn't carry to the playground. She was still sitting on the dustbin and still calling for her, when she turned round and saw Marion Murphy staring at her.

'Who are you talking to?' Marion demanded.

'No one.'

'You were.'

'I was not.' Now there were more of them, half a dozen more.

'Well, anyway,' Marion's lip was curling ominously, and Jessie knew there was worse to come. 'You know where we're going? We're all going down to the quay after school. You coming?'

'What for?'

'The diggers are coming in, that's what for. You were going to lie down in front of them, remember?' They were closing in all around her. There was no way out. There was nowhere to run to. 'Well?' Marion said, thrusting her face into hers. 'Well?'

Jessie stared back at her and hoped they wouldn't notice the tears welling into her eyes. Suddenly Marion staggered backwards and fell, taking all the others with her, all together, like ninepins.

'You pushed me!' Marion screamed at her. 'She pushed me. The little cow pushed me!' Jessie sat on her dustbin and laughed out loud. She could not help herself. It was the sight of them all sprawled on the ground, their mouths gaping in astonishment. It was quite wonderful. Of course she knew at once who had done the pushing, and that meant she was there. Grania O'Malley was there, her or one of her pirates, it didn't matter. Either way, she knew without a shadow of a doubt that they had heard her. They knew what had happened about the treasure. And if they knew that, then they knew the diggers were coming. Somehow they would stop them, somehow they could still save the Big Hill. Jack was there now, Liam beside him. Marion was clutching her elbow and crying, still accusing. She was appealing to Jack. 'She pushed me! She pushed me! I'm telling Mrs Burke.'

'She pushed all of you?' Jack asked. Jessie was smiling at him from her dustbin, and he understood from her smile just what had happened.

Marion was scrambling to her feet now. 'That's it. You've asked for it, Jessie Parsons. You've done it now. If the diggers don't flatten you, then I will. You've asked for it!' And when she ran off, the others followed, promising as they went all manner of dire and terrible retribution. But Jessie didn't mind any more. Jessie knew now that Grania O'Malley was there, that no matter what, she would protect her. There was nothing to be afraid of. Liam and his friends were still gawping at her in disbelief when the school bell rang. She smiled at them.

'Bell's going,' she said nonchalantly, and she slipped down off her dustbin and tottered past them. 'Better not be late.' She felt so good, so triumphant.

When they got home after school, Jessie's mother wasn't there. There was no sign of anyone. Even Panda was missing. They were looking for the peanut butter to make up their sandwiches when they heard Clatterbang coming up the track, Panda chasing alongside, yapping at the tyres. Jessie went to the door. 'Where's the peanut butter?' she called out. Her mother and father had been talking to each other earnestly over the top of the car. Now they stopped, both of them looking at her. There was bad news. Jessie could see that much – and she could also see neither of them wanted to break it to her.

'We've just been up to see Mister Barney,' said Jessie's father.

'What's the matter with him?' Jessie asked. Jack was there too now.

'Nothing. He's fine.' Her father slammed the door and came walking round the front of Clatterbang towards them. 'He's fine, but he was the only one who could have known about the treasure – besides the four of us, that is. And even then, he couldn't have known where we'd hidden it.' The children looked from one to the other.

'It's gone,' said Jessie's mother. 'The treasure's gone.'

Jack ran across the yard towards the chicken shed, and Jessie followed as fast as she could. She found him staring down into an empty hole. 'I just can't understand it,' her mother was saying. 'I thought maybe one of us might possibly have mentioned to Mister Barney where we were hiding it, but we didn't. He didn't know anything about it. But we had to ask, just to be sure.'

'I told you, Cath,' said Jessie's father. 'Someone must have seen you burying it last night.'

'But it was dark, you know it was.' Jessie's mother was near to tears. 'Why do you keep trying to blame it on me?' The two children said nothing. They knew very well who had taken it.

'I didn't mean it like that,' Jessie's father said. 'But it has gone, hasn't it? That means someone's stolen it, someone on this island. It wasn't us, was it? And it certainly wasn't old Mister Barney. I told you there was no point in going up there. How could he possibly have moved a thing like that all by himself? There's only one answer. Someone must have seen us fetching it back in the boat from Piper's Hole. They must have spied on us, and then later on, watched us bury it. But who? Who?'

Jessie tried not to look across at Jack, but she could not stop herself. It was the barest flicker of a smile, but her father noticed it. 'You don't seem very upset, Jess,' her father said.

Jessie shrugged her shoulders. 'Of course I am, but what can we do? If it's gone, it's gone. And besides it's no use to us any more, is it? Jack and me, we only wanted it so's we could share it out and save the Big Hill.' She turned to her mother. 'The diggers have come, Mum. Marion Murphy said.'

'I know,' said her mother quietly. 'I know.'

'There's four of them,' said Jessie's father. 'Down by the quay. They start work Monday.'

Jessie's mother walked away towards the house, talking as she went. 'You know, I'm beginning to wonder about all this. I'm really beginning to wonder. When we were kids, and Mister Barney told us he'd seen Grania O'Malley's ghost, we never believed him. When he said she'd hidden her treasure on the island, we never believed him. He spent his life looking for it, and we laughed at him. Then Grania O'Malley's treasure turns up, out of the blue.'

'So?' Jessie's father said, following her into the kitchen.

'You still don't see it, do you? If he was telling the truth about the treasure, and it seems he was, then it follows he was telling the truth about the ghost. And today, when we find the treasure's been dug up and taken away, what did he tell us? Grania O'Malley's come back for it, he says, because she knows it's no use to us any more. Well, if that's true, and let's just pretend it might be true, then it fits, don't you see. The whole thing fits. The children were *meant* somehow to find the treasure, and the treasure was *meant* to save the Big Hill. It was all her idea. Do you understand what I'm telling you, Jimmy? And now she knows it can't be done, because she's heard all about how it's not ours to share, how you can't just give treasure away when you find it. So she came to take it back.'

They were in the kitchen now, and she turned to face Jessie's father. 'I know it sounds mad, I know it does. But that's the gist of what Mister Barney said, isn't it? Well, I don't laugh at old Mister Barney, not any more. And there's something else you haven't thought of. No one has thieved anything on this island in my lifetime – maybe the odd sheep does go missing from time to time, but that's all. We leave the doors unlocked, don't we? The keys in the car, don't we? Does anything ever get taken? Think about it. I didn't dig that treasure up. You didn't, the children didn't, Panda didn't. If Mister Barney says it was the ghost of Grania O'Malley that dug it up, then you know what? I believe him. And if that makes me cracked in the head, then maybe I am.' And with that, she opened the drawer and took out the bread knife. 'I'll make you your sandwiches, Jack. And, Jess, why don't you help your father fill in that hole before a chicken breaks a leg?'

It was a weekend when time itself seemed to stand still. There was a calm and a quiet over the island, only a breath of wind off the sea. Even the owl in the abbey stopped calling at night. They dipped the sheep on Saturday morning, and through it all, Jessie's mother never said a word. She scarcely looked up. After it was over, Jack said he was off down to the quay. He wanted to see the diggers for himself, he said, and besides, the quay was on the way to the field and he was expected for a game of baseball with Liam and Marion and the others. It would be too far for Jessie to walk, if they had to hurry. 'Then you can push me in the wheelbarrow,' said Jessie. She did not like the idea of being left behind one little bit. Jack didn't argue. He laid some straw in the bottom of the squeaky wheelbarrow, and off they went, Mole and Panda tagging along behind.

When they reached the quay, there was a great crowd standing round the diggers. Everyone seemed to be there: Father Gerald, Mrs Burke, Miss Jefferson, Michael Murphy, and dozens of others that Jessie had never seen before. The pub was overflowing into the street with people. Jack and Jessie left the wheelbarrow, made their way through the crowd and gazed up in awe at the gigantic bulk of the machines. Just the tyres were as high as Jack could reach. Painted on each of their yellow sides was one word, in huge black letters: 'Earthbuster'. Jessie saw them suddenly as living creatures, as monsters sleeping in the sun, but only for the moment. Once woken, they would rampage across her island and swallow up the Big Hill.

Marion Murphy was being lifted up on to a digger by a man in orange overalls. There were a dozen others dressed the same. Jessie soon worked out these must be the digger drivers, or maybe they were mechanics. They were swigging pints and rolling cigarettes as they folled up against their diggers. Swaggerers, Jessie thought, swaggerers every one of them. But the islanders were swarming around them and around their machines in open admiration. Marion had clambered on to the top of the digger by now, and stood there posing triumphantly, arms upraised, while her father took photo after photo of her. Jessie stared stonily up at her until she caught her eye. I'd give a lot, an awful lot, Jessie thought, for Grania O'Malley to push her off that digger. 'I hate you, Marion Murphy.' Jessie tried to say it with her eyes, and must have succeeded because Marion looked away at once and posed again, more nervously now, an uneasy smile on her face.

'Let's go, Jack,' said Jessie. 'I've had enough.' But Jack wasn't there. She went looking for him, and found him at last round the front of a digger with one of the orange-overalled drivers who appeared to be showing Jack over the engine. She tugged at his coat, but he didn't seem to grasp how impatient she was to leave, nor how annoyed she was becoming.

'You see this, Jess? This guy says it's got to be about the biggest earthmover in the world. This is some powerful machine. Makes my Volkswagen at home look like a tricycle. How many horsepower, d'you say, sir?'

'Over five hundred,' said the driver, wiping his hands

on an oily rag. He had ginger hair, Jessie noticed, a ginger that almost matched the colour of his overalls. 'Four-wheel drive, fuel injection. Thirty tons of power. Do anything you want, this will. Move mountains if you want it to.' He heaved with laughter at that, and then Jack was laughing with him and asking more questions about the engine. Jessie had had enough. She glared at them both and walked off.

Later, with Jack pushing her in the wheelbarrow along the road towards the field, Jessie was still bridling at what she saw as Jack's betrayal. He had been fraternising with the enemy, and she was furious with him. It was a long and silent walk. 'Something on your mind?' Jack said at last.

Jessie let fly. 'Don't you ever think of anything but engines?'

'Hey, I was just talking to the guy. What are you so mad at me for?'

'If you don't know, then I'm not saying.' And they relapsed into a simmering silence that lasted until they reached the field.

Liam and the others were already practising. As usual, Liam and Jack were the captains and they picked the teams; and as usual Marion managed to get herself picked for Jack's team. Jessie went off on her own and sat down under the tree. It was the first real argument she'd had with Jack, but it was entirely his fault and she wasn't going to make it up, not ever. She could see too, that he was really angry. He was winding himself up and pitching with real venom. No one stood a chance. They ducked and dodged and protested, but Jack just kept pitching. They hardly managed to hit a ball at all. And when it came to his turn with the bat, he belted the ball right over the fence and into the potato field beyond. He ran six home runs before they found the ball; and when they told him that wasn't fair, he said that he knew the rules better than they did.

Even after the game was over, she could see he was still furious. 'You coming or what?' he snapped at her. All the way home in the wheelbarrow she sat with her back to him, arms folded, lips pursed.

The evening was worse still. After supper, her mother sat staring into space. Jessie went and sat on her lap to console her and to be consoled. Jack phoned home, and then just took himself off to bed without even saying goodnight to anyone.

'Is something the matter with Jack?' her father asked.

'He's just sulking,' Jessie said.

'*He's* sulking!' Her father smiled wryly.

'Only one more day before they start.' Her mother spoke as if she were speaking to herself. 'One more day for the Big Hill.' And she looked up at Jessie's father. 'You know, somehow I always thought something would happen to stop it. First, I thought I could do it by talking to people, explaining, persuading. I couldn't. Then I thought that the people in Dublin must have more sense. They didn't. But even then, I still had faith. I don't know why, but I still believed it could be stopped. Then when the children brought us the treasure, I thought for sure that we'd win, that the Big Hill was reprieved. Just another false hope. And now I cling to anything, even Mister Barney's ghost. I know it's silly, Jimmy, I know it's nonsense. But there's nothing else left, except prayer maybe. Am I going to pray in Mass tomorrow! I'm going to pray like I've never prayed before.'

'I'll pray with you,' said Jessie's father.

'You don't come to Mass,' she replied tartly.

'I can still pray, can't I?' he said. 'And I've a lot more faith in prayers than I have in ghosts, that's for sure.' He went on, 'Everywhere I went today, I kept looking at people, and thinking: was it you? Was it you that stole the treasure? Even Father Gerald, honestly. I'm telling you, one of them must have stolen it.'

Jessie lay in her bed that night and listened to Jack snoring in the next room. Every snore she heard made her angrier still. She made up her mind that she wouldn't speak to him the whole of the rest of his time on the island. Hadn't he laughed with that digger driver, and about the digger being able to move mountains too? He'd laughed! She felt so angry, and so lonely at the same time.

She longed to climb into her parents' bed and snuggle up to them and tell them the whole story of Grania O'Malley. She would tell her mother there and then not to worry, that Grania O'Malley would never stand by and watch the diggers move in on the Big Hill. But she just couldn't bring herself to do it. Even if her mother believed her – and maybe she would now – her father most certainly would not. And what if she did tell her story, and then Grania O'Malley didn't come back and save the Big

Hill. What then? Where would that leave her? No, better to wait and see how things turned out.

The snoring stopped next door. She heard Jack's bed creaking, his door opening, and then footsteps coming along the passage outside her door. 'Jess?' He was whispering through the door. Pride would not let her answer. She pretended she hadn't heard. 'Jess?' The tiptoeing steps moved along the passage and then there was silence.

She wished at once that she had answered, but it was too late. Through her window she saw the full moon sitting on top of the Big Hill, too bright to look at, and anyway, she thought, you mustn't look at the full moon through glass. It makes you mad. She closed her eyes.

'Oh talk to me, Grania O'Malley, please,' she whispered. 'Please, please. Just let me know you're there.' Barry surfaced and splashed in his bowl. She said her proper prayers, closing her eyes tight shut. 'You've got to stop them, God. You've got to save the Big Hill. Please.' And she went on praying, until sleep overcame her.

Jack wasn't there when Jessie came down late for breakfast the next morning. Her father said he had gone off to play baseball with Liam. Jessie sat through Mass but could not concentrate. Either she was still fuming inside about Jack's treachery or she was watching the swallow high up in the roof, swooping down over the heads of the congregation and up to the rafters by the door, searching for a way out but never finding it. Her mother's knuckles were white under her forehead as she prayed. Jessie prayed to Jesus and to Grania O'Malley at the same time. She felt a little guilty about doing that in church, but she thought that Jesus wouldn't mind, that he'd forgive her just this once. As Father Gerald had so often said: 'Jesus understands, Jesus forgives. All you have to do is ask.' So she asked for forgiveness, and went on praying to both of them.

They were all standing and chatting outside the church door after Mass when Liam came racing down the hill on his bike, scooted to a stop, threw it down and came running up the church path waving his arms and shouting, 'It's sabotage! Sabotage! Someone's fixed the diggers.'

Father Gerald took him by the shoulders and calmed him down. 'What are you saying Liam? What do you mean?'

'Someone's fixed them. They won't work, Father. They won't start. None of them will.' Jessie and her mother looked at each other, a sudden bright hope in their eyes. Jessie felt a cheer of joy bursting to get out, but she held it inside her until she was alone with her mother in Clatterbang, and rattling along the road towards the quay, in convoy with everyone else.

'It's the ghost!' cried her mother. 'It's the ghost of Grania O'Malley, like Mister Barney told us. It's Grania O'Malley.' And the tears were running down her cheeks. 'Well, don't look at me like that, Jess. It *has* to be her, it *has* to be.'

'I know, Mum!' Jessie laughed above the clatter. 'I know!' And Clatterbang coughed loudly and backfired.

Jack was there with everyone else on the quayside. The digger drivers in orange overalls were gathered in a huddle and talking to the Garda. There was a Garda boat moored out in the harbour. People were still coming from all over the island, in Land-Rovers, on motorbikes, on foot. Mrs O'Leary was standing in the road outside her pub, still in her fluffy slippers. Father Gerald hadn't even taken his surplice off and it was flapping about him in the breeze. The whole place was a buzz of excitement. It was Mrs O'Leary who came over towards them as they got out of Clatterbang. 'Someone's fixed them, Cath,' she said. 'They don't know what's the matter with them. They just won't work, not any of them.'

'Well, it wasn't me, if that's what you're thinking,' said Jessie's mother, laughing. 'I wish it was, but it wasn't. But I think there'll be a few here who'll think it was.' And it was true. Several people were glaring at them, Michael Murphy amongst them. They walked away from Mrs O'Leary over towards Jack. 'If I told them who it really was,' Jessie's mother whispered to her, 'they'd not believe me, not in a million years.'

Jack had seen them now. He was sauntering over to join them, hands deep in his jeans pockets, baseball bat tucked under his arm. 'Hi,' he said, and he was grinning happily at Jessie. 'Never seen anyone half as mad as those digger guys,' he said. 'I'm going home. You coming, Jess?'

Jessie walked alongside him for some way, until they had left the houses well behind them, until she was quite sure no one could overhear them. Then she tugged at his arm and stopped him. 'It was *her*, wasn't it? She came!'

'Maybe, maybe not,' said Jack cryptically, and he wandered on. She tottered after him, dragging him to a stop again.

'What do you mean?'

He was laughing now. 'It wasn't my idea,' he said. 'It was your dad's. He doesn't believe in ghosts, not like us. He came to me and he said, did I know how to gum up the digger engines? I told him I could, anyone could, but first you got to find out a few things. So I went and asked that digger guy to show me his engine. You were there, right? Found out all I needed to know. Then, last night, your dad and me went and did it. I tried to wake you, but you were asleep. All you have to do is take off the distributor heads, and then pour a whole lot of sugar in the gas tank, and presto, nothing works. Told you, when it comes to engines and stuff, I can fix – or gum up – just about anything.'

'You did it?'

'I told you, me and your pa.'

'So it wasn't the ghost. It wasn't Grania O'Malley.'

'I guess not,' said Jack, and then, 'are we friends again?'

'I could hug you,' Jessie said. 'I could really hug you.'

'OK by me,' he said. And so she did. She felt like skipping all the way home, but she couldn't. She laughed instead, prattling on and on about how it served them right, about how she couldn't wait to tell her mother what had really happened. Jack said very little until they were nearly home. Mole came trotting down the road to meet them. Jack ran his hand along his back as he walked along beside him.

'It won't stop them, Jess, you know that,' he said, trying to break it to her as gently as he could.

'What do you mean?'

'Well, it'll maybe stop them for a day or two, but they'll soon fix it again. They've got to take them all apart and clean out the sugar – blocks the fuel injection. But once they clean them out, they can start them up again. We haven't won the battle or anything, Jess. We just put it off for a while, that's all.'

10 THE LAST STAND

THE DIGGER ENGINES HAD TO BE STRIPPED DOWN, cleaned and reassembled. Jack went down to the quay after school each day to watch the mechanics at work. There were rumours, he said with a wicked smile on his face, that some 'bits' had mysteriously gone missing. But in the end, as Jack had predicted, their jubilation was to be short-lived. The missing parts were being helicoptered in from the mainland. The diggers would soon be on the move again.

The children were in school on the Wednesday morning when it happened and, much to Mrs Burke's annoyance, they all ran to the windows to look as the helicopter flew low overhead. That was just before lunch. She was still trying to settle them down to work after afternoon playtime when some of the children began to hear a rumbling, like distant thunder. For some time Mrs

Burke managed to keep them at their desks. But when Father Gerald was seen hurrying along the school lane, then everyone was at the windows again, necks craning, and there was nothing more she could do about it. The diggers were on their way. They could see them now. The roar of the engines was rattling the windows, and the classroom itself seemed to be throbbing and pulsating, so much so that Jessie had to clap her hands over her ears to stop them hurting.

She was the only one who stayed behind in her place. She did not need to see. She did not want to see. She looked up out of the window at the Big Hill, and through the mist of her tears she thought she saw someone standing there, right at the very top. She went over to the window. The figure was still there, and beckoning her. She knew at once who it was, and she knew at once what she had to do. She blinked her eyes to rid them of the tears, to see better. When she looked again, there was no one up there.

By this time, every child was fighting for a place at the playground fence. Mrs Burke couldn't stop them, and Miss Jefferson didn't want to – she was too excited herself. It was Liam who opened the gate, and then they were all running down past the abbey ruins towards the road. There they were, all four giant Earthbusters trundling towards them along the coast road, a yellow convoy, billowing black smoke, orange lights flashing; and behind them a long line of Land-Rovers and pick-ups. In the fields on either side, the sheep scattered in terror, blundering into each other in their panic.

The children just stood and gaped, flailing at the pungent exhaust smoke and turning away to cough. Then Marion Murphy began to wave and cheer, and very soon they were all at it, all except Jack who had noticed by now that Jessie was not there. He went back inside the school to look for her and found her still standing by the window, still gazing out. She turned as she felt him behind her.

'It's what Mum always said,' she said. 'Ever since this thing with the Big Hill began, she's always said it. You want something badly enough, then you've got to do it yourself. No use waiting for someone else to do it for you. You believe in something, then sometimes you've got to fight for your beliefs, you've got to fight for what you care about, like Grania O'Malley did, like you did when you fixed their diggers. Well, now it's my turn.'

'What do you mean?' Jack asked.

'I thought Grania O'Malley would do it for us, but I was wrong. Maybe she's done all she could, maybe now she wants us to help ourselves. So that's what I'm going to do, help myself.'

She fetched her coat and bag from her hook and then called to him across the classroom. 'You coming?'

'You can't just cut school.'

Jessie looked around her and shrugged her shoulders. 'Well, everyone else has,' she said. 'Come on. We've got to hurry. We'll go across the fields. We can still get there before they do.'

Jack helped her through the fence at the back of the school and then over the ditch at the bottom of Miss Jefferson's wild-flower meadow. Once into the bracken beyond, they were on the track that would take them around the bottom of the Big Hill towards Mister Barney's shack. Jessie led the way, fending off Jack's questions with the same grim determination that drove her tottering legs. She would need all the energy she could muster, all the breath in her body. She could spare none for talking. All the while they could hear the rumble of the convoy as it wound its way out of sight, up the hill past the abbey ruins. Jessie could see them in her mind's eye coming up the road past the end of the farm lane. Panda would be going berserk. She smiled as she thought of him trying to sink his teeth into one of those gigantic digger tyres.

'Jess, what's happening?' Jack was asking again, for the umpteenth time. 'Where are we going?' But she hardly heard him. Her eyes were focused on the ground at her feet. She had to be sure she did not trip. Her heart and her mind were fixed on her plan. It might take fifty days. Fifty days, she'd heard somewhere, was about as long as you could go without food. You had to have water, but there was lots of water where she was going.

Without warning, her knees buckled and then she was struggling to get up. Jack was there, arms under her shoulders, helping her to her feet, then holding her steady. Cross with herself, she shook herself free of him and staggered on. Brambles tugged at her coat, tore at her neck. She bobbed and weaved, trying to dodge them and duck them. She coughed out a fly that she had swallowed and battled on.

It seemed an eternity before they emerged from the track to find themselves in the middle of the grassy clearing, the place where the tracks met. There was the main track up the Big Hill, winding its way through rocks and bracken to the top; and there, just across the clearing from them, stood Mister Barney's shack, the smoke rising from the chimney. They could see the yellow convoy quite clearly now. It had stopped down by the road at the bottom of the hill. And beyond the yellow convoy, nose to tail behind them, were the islanders in their Land-Rovers and pick-ups. And there were people on bikes, and on foot too, dozens of them, all hurrying along the high road and the coast road. The whole island was converging on the Earthbusters.

It was some distance away, but Jessie could see her mother. She was standing in front of the leading digger, talking to the driver. And then she was pushing at it, kicking at it, drumming her fists on it. Jessie's father put his arms round her from behind and turned her towards him. The diggers towered above them, snorting black smoke from their chimneys. Her mother had stopped struggling now, and her father was stroking her hair, then leading her away, her head on his shoulder.

'That's your mom down there, isn't it?' said Jack. Jessie didn't reply. There wasn't the time. The diggers were on the move again.

Jessie couldn't run properly. She'd never been able to run, not like the other children could, but she was as near to it then, going across the clearing, as she'd ever been. She was going so fast now. She couldn't understand why she wasn't falling over, but somehow she wasn't. Somehow her body kept up with her legs and she didn't topple. Jack was having to run to keep up with her. She had worked out the exact spot to do it: where the main track up the Big Hill left the clearing. There were granite posts on either side, and boulders all around – it would be the perfect place. They would *have* to stop. They would have no choice. The diggers were still crawling up the hill. Jessie felt a great surge of joy as she knew for sure that she was going to make it to the clearing before them. There would be time enough too to catch her breath and tell Jack everything she had in mind, her whole plan. Nothing could stop her now. Nothing.

The driver in the first digger was the same driver who had talked to Jack down on the quay a few days before. He was still shaken by what had just happened down by the road. Until recently he had never given a lot of thought as to what his Earthbuster did. He had operated diggers all over Ireland and in England, motorway work mostly, and quarry work sometimes. He loved the power of them, the smell of them. There had been some talk back in Mrs O'Leary's pub where he was staying about the few cranks on the island who didn't want the gold mine. He'd laughed it off like all the other drivers; but after the machines had been tampered with that night, they had all taken it a lot more seriously. He was genuinely puzzled that someone out there hated his machine that much.

And then, just a few moments ago, there was this woman, eyes blazing at him, screaming at him to go back, that what he was doing was an obscenity, a sacrilege. She'd stood there, pushing at his digger, kicking it. He hadn't known what to do, what to say. She'd looked up at him one last time and begged him. 'Please don't do it. Please . . .' He'd revved up his engine so he didn't have to hear any more. He was still thinking about her, wondering what was so special about the hill up ahead that she wanted to save it. He peered up at it. It looked ordinary enough to him, just rocks and gorse and bracken. What was she making such a fuss about?

The boy came out of nowhere, and was waving him down. He braked hard, as hard as he could, and slithered to a stop. He hadn't noticed the girl until then. She was sitting right in the centre of the track over on the far side of the clearing, legs crossed, hands on her knees and still as a statue. The boy was shouting up at him now, and that was when he recognised him. It was the same American lad he had shown over his engine down by the quay. He remembered he had been impressed by how much he knew about engines for a boy of his age.

He turned off the ignition and opened the door of his cab to give him a piece of his mind, but the boy didn't let him get a word in. 'She says you've got to stop right there, sir. She says you can't go any further.'

The digger driver was suddenly aware of an old man emerging from the door of a shack on the edge of the clearing. He was inching his way down the garden path, balanced between two sticks. If the old man hadn't been there, the digger driver might really have let rip, language and all. He tried to calm himself. 'Will you tell the young lady to shift herself?' he said. 'We've got a job of work to do. We're days late as it is. You tell her, will you?'

'Won't do you much good,' Jack replied. 'See, she doesn't want you here. She doesn't want you digging up the Big Hill. Nothing will change her mind, not when it's made up. And it's made up.' The digger driver felt his anger boiling, but he held on to himself. The old man from the shack was leaning on his gate now, chickens pecking around his boots.

Neither of the children moved a muscle. 'Listen, son,' the digger driver thumbed over his shoulder as he spoke, 'there's three more of these behind. And we've got security men too, a dozen of them. After what's happened, the company's taking no chances. We don't want anyone getting hurt, do we now?' But he could see from their set jaws, their cold, defiant eyes that he was getting nowhere at all. He tried again, a gentler tack. 'Look, all this. It won't do any good, you know.'

Jack interrupted. 'She's not going to let you dig. Isn't that right, Jess? Tell the guy.'

'I'm not going to let you dig,' said Jessie.

'What did I tell you?' said Jack.

By now all the other Earthbusters and Land-Rovers and pick-ups had come to a standstill in a long line that stretched all the way back down the track to the road. Everyone was getting out to find out what was going on, what was holding everything up. They were swarming up the track past the machines and into the clearing. Father Gerald tiptoed round a puddle, his cassock tucked up under his belt. Behind him came Mrs Burke, teetering along in her tight skirt. Liam was there, and Marion Murphy too. They were all there now, every child in the school. They stood and stared, just like everyone else.

Jessie was looking for her mother and father, but she still couldn't see them. She noticed Michael Murphy talking animatedly to one of the digger drivers, and Miss Jefferson was picking up one of the infants – Jessie couldn't see which – who had fallen over and hurt his knee. Very soon the entire clearing was filled with islanders, and digger drivers in their orange overalls, and security men in their blue uniforms and shiny peaked caps – like the Garda, but they weren't. Last of all came Jessie's mother and father, pushing their way through the crowd to the front.

When she saw Jessie sitting there on the path in front of the diggers, she made to rush forward, but Jessie's father held her back. 'No, Cath,' he said. 'She won't come to any harm. I won't let her. But leave her be, eh? Let her do what she has to do.'

Jessie stood up – and that took some time. She had to turn herself on to her stomach and push herself up, first on to her knees and then on to unsteady legs. Jack did not help her. He knew by now that she only liked to be helped in private. As Jessie looked at the expectant crowd in front of her, she felt sick to her stomach and all her courage seemed suddenly to drain from her. Jack smiled his encouragement, but he could see from her eyes that she just could not do it. He knew then he would have to do the talking. There was no other way.

He took a deep breath. 'I guess you're all wondering what Jess and me are doing,' he began. 'Well, we're going to the top of the Big Hill, and we're going to stay up there for just as long as it takes, until the diggers go away. Jess and me, we've both been up there before.' He looked long and hard at Mrs Burke and smiled. 'I stood on top of that hill and I looked around me. Up there it's like you belong, like you're part of something that's been going on for thousands of years. It's special, real special, a living, breathing thing. You cut the top off the Big Hill and you'd be killing it for sure. You dig out the gold, you'd be tearing out its heart. But I guess you know that already.'

The sea sighed and the wind whispered, and the crowd stood stunned and silent. Jack went on. 'I've been thinking a whole lot just lately. My dad's sick, real sick. I've been thinking that maybe he won't make it, and he won't be around any more. And then I started thinking that that's what's going to happen to me too, to Jess, to all of us. It's like we're just passing through, but this hill is here for ever. And we've got to leave it just like we found it. We've got to leave good air to breathe, we've got to leave the fish in the sea, or else there'll soon be nothing left. I'm not making much sense, I guess, but you know what I mean.'

Jack took Jessie's hand in his. 'So Jess, she decided we're going right up to the top of the Big Hill, and once we're up there, we're not moving, no way. If they want that gold, then they'll have to go right over us to get it.' He caught Marion's eye, and smiled at her. 'You can come with us too if you want. You all can. We'd sure like that.' He turned to Jessie. 'Coming?' And they walked away together up the track.

The crowd looked on. No one moved. No one said a

word. A few paces up the track and Jessie felt weak all over. 'Jack,' she whispered. 'I'm trembling.'

'Me too,' said Jack. 'You've thought about this, haven't you? It's a long way to the top, you know.'

'I remember,' said Jessie. Suddenly she gripped his arm. 'Can you feel them, Jack?'

What?

'The ghosts, the pirates. They're here, they're all around us. And she's here too, Grania O'Malley. I can feel her. She's watching, I know she is!' Jack looked around him and then over his shoulder. He stopped. Jessie turned and saw what Jack had already seen. Old Mister Barney was following them up the hill, his white head bent between his sticks. He moved like a tortoise, every ponderous step a massive effort. He paused for a moment and lifted his head to look up at them.

'You mind if I come along?' he said.

Then Jessie's mother was breaking away from the crowd and running up to him. 'I'm coming too,' she said.

Mister Barney smiled at her. 'Just so long as you can keep up with me, Cath,' he said. He waved a stick at Jessie and Jack. 'Don't just stand there. We'll meet you at the top.'

Jessie was looking for her father and could not see him. 'Is Dad coming?' she called out.

'Later,' said her mother. 'He's gone back to fetch some food and drink.'

'Plenty of water up there,' said Jessie, and she turned, balanced herself against Jack and started to climb again.

They were only about halfway up the hill, just past the

waterfall, when Jessie felt her legs giving out on her. She was leaning more and more on Jack now, and stopping every few steps. 'I don't think I'm going to make it,' she breathed.

'You've got to,' said Jack, his arm tightening round her. 'She's watching, remember? Everyone's watching.' That was when she turned to look. Jack was wrong. True, some of them were still standing by the diggers and watching, but most of those wore the orange of the drivers or the blue of the security guards. Michael Murphy was with them, and a few other islanders – but only a few. Jessie was wondering where the rest had gone, when she saw them, dozens of them, coming around the bend in the track. Liam was running on ahead, waving to them. Father Gerald was alongside old Mister Barney now, with Jessie's mother. And Mrs Burke was just behind them, her skirt hitched up, Miss Jefferson striding past her. 'Will you look at that?' Jessie breathed. 'They're coming, they're coming with us.'

'So?' said Jack. 'What are you waiting for? Do you want Marion Murphy to beat you to the top?'

'She's not there, is she?'

'I don't know, but she could be.' That was enough of a spur for Jessie. She lurched on, calling out the rhythm as she went: 'One and two. One and two. One and two.' She scrambled on hands and knees over the rocky places, and then dragged herself to her feet, hauling on anything Jack offered her – an arm, a leg, trousers, anything. On she staggered with never a look behind her now. She could hear them coming. She didn't need to look.

In the end she wasn't first to the top. She had the first sight of it, and felt that warm tingle of exhilaration, of triumph, when Panda came bounding past her, knocking into her and sending her crumpling to the ground. She bellowed at him, but he never even stopped to look at her. Mole was trotting up the track towards them, his great ears pricked. When he saw Panda ahead of him, he raced on past them, head lowered, ears back, chasing him round and round the top of the Big Hill, Panda dancing away from him and barking wildly.

By the time Jessie and Jack got there themselves, Panda was lying down, panting and happy on the thrift, and Mole was browsing busily in the undergrowth near by, his tail whisking at the flies. Jack had a drink from the spring above the rock pool. He sat back on his haunches, wiping his mouth with the back of his hand.

'No earrings this time,' he said. Jessie was stretched out on her back still fighting for her breath.

'I can hear them,' said Jack getting to his feet. 'They're coming.' But Jessie could hear someone else, someone much closer. She propped herself up on to her elbows.

'Listen Jack,' she whispered. 'Listen.'

The voice was right beside them. 'Jessie? Jack? You've done fine, just fine.' It was *her*. It was *her*. The voice went on. 'We're all mighty pleased with you. But now you've got the high ground, you have to hold on to it, d'you hear me? Believe me, I know. Once you got the high ground, you don't give it up, no matter what. And don't let them talk you down. They'll try it for sure.'

'We won't,' said Jessie, looking around her, hoping she

would appear. 'We promise we won't.' There was no sign of her, so Jessie went on, 'It *was* you that dug up the treasure, wasn't it?'

The voice laughed. 'Well, as you know, the boys weren't at all pleased about the idea of parting with it in the first place. They were happy enough to dig it up. Lots of "I told you sos," but there we are, that's the luck of the game. I thought myself it was a fine idea, and it would have been too. All those rules and regulations. A lot of rot. Ah well, it was a nice try; but this is better, much better, and this'll work. So you just sit tight now, y'hear me?'

'Can't we see you?' It wasn't at all comfortable, talking to a voice.

'Soon enough, you'll see me soon enough, when you need to. I'll be seeing you.'

'Grania O'Malley! Grania O'Malley!' But there was no reply. Jessie turned to Jack. 'You heard her, Jack? You did hear her?' Jack was nodding, his eyes darting nervously.

'I wish she wouldn't go all invisible on us,' he said. 'It scares the hell out of me when she does that.' She took his hand and gripped it. She squeezed twice and he did the same. They were together in this, in this as in everything. Both of them felt it at the same moment.

And that was how Father Gerald found the two children some moments later, sitting exhausted but exhilarated, hand in hand beside the rock pool.

'You won't talk us down, Father,' said Jessie, as he came towards her.

'I wouldn't want to, Jessie, even if I could,' he said, his

sermon smile on his face, a smile Jessie had never believed was real, until now. 'There's half the island coming up the track. I don't know about them, but I've come to stay, and I'm staying put till the diggers go.'

'Where's Mum?' Jessie asked.

'She's way back down the hill with Mister Barney. Someone went back for his wheelbarrow – he just couldn't go any further, not under his own steam. He didn't like the idea of the wheelbarrow that much, not at first. "Jessie goes by wheelbarrow sometimes," says your mother. And he says: "Well then, if it's good enough for her, it's good enough for me." They won't be long. What you said about your father back there, Jack . . . Opened our eyes, so you did. You made us all do some thinking.'

Very soon the top of the Big Hill was crowded with people, all milling about in excited huddles. More would be coming, they said. Like Jessie's father, many had gone back for tents and blankets and food. Someone started clapping and then everyone was cheering. That was when Jessie saw her mother pushing the wheelbarrow up over the top of the hill towards her, Mister Barney waving like an emperor. They helped him out, and gave him his sticks.

'Well,' said Mister Barney looking around him, 'it's the first time I've been up here in over twenty years. And if they want to get me down again, then they'll just have to drag me.' He nodded towards Jessie and Jack and smiled, his eyes full of tears as he spoke. 'If I had my hat, then I'd take it off to the two of you. And I've not taken my hat off to anyone in all my life.'

Jessie felt Jack's hand-squeeze and responded in kind

without looking at him. She was tired. The muscles in her legs were cold now and cramping, but she had never felt so happy. Mister Barney had just finished speaking, and the clapping had scarcely died away, when they were aware of a dozen men standing at the top of the track, most of them in blue uniforms and shiny peaked caps.

'All right.' It was Michael Murphy, beside himself with fury. 'I've had enough. First of all you sabotaged the diggers, and now this. This is my hill you're on, and I've a legal right to do with it what I will. I've had enough of it, do you hear me?' He paused, and then added heavily, threateningly, 'You stay up here, and things could turn nasty. People could get hurt. Do you understand my drift?' He seemed to calm down a little. 'Listen, I'll let you stay here the night so's you can make your point, but I want you off this hill by the morning, you hear me now?'

For some time no one responded, everyone looking to everyone else. Then Jessie's mother walked right up to him.

'You're not welcome here, Michael Murphy,' she said. 'This may be *your* hill, but this is *our* island, and we all say we're not moving from here until your diggers leave. Now is that clear enough?'

It must have been, because Michael Murphy turned on his heel and walked away down the track, taking the men in blue with him, Panda yapping at their heels.

'I'm cold,' said Jessie, drawing her knees up to her chest and clasping them to her.

'You want me to rub your legs?' Jack asked. 'They hurting?'

But Jessie didn't get a chance to reply. Someone was standing in front of them, in a pair of pale green trainers. She looked up. It was Marion Murphy, and she'd been crying. 'I came, Jack,' she said. 'After what you said, I came. And I'm going to tell my dad to put a stop to it. I'll be back later. I'll bring back some chocolate, shall I? I've got a duvet at home, Jessie, if you want.'

'That would be great,' said Jessie, and she smiled at Marion Murphy for the first time in her whole life.

11 THE BATTLE OF THE EARTHBUSTERS

BY THE TIME DARKNESS FELL THAT NIGHT, THE TOP of the Big Hill had become a village of tents and makeshift huts. It was a fine, dry night, but there was a cold breeze off the sea and they were soon glad of all the cover they had built, and of the fire too. Father Gerald had appointed himself keeper of the fire, and sent every child he could recruit scavenging all over the hill. But the brushwood they found was too small and too dry, and burnt too quickly. There just wasn't enough of it to keep the fire going. So Jessie's father, who had already made several supply trips up and down the hill with the tractor and link box, went off back down the hill again to load up with peat.

Jessie sat in the mouth of her hut next to Jack, both of them swathed in blankets. The hut was built into the rocks, with a bracken roof and a bracken floor. She breathed in deep the warmth of the fire, and at last began to feel her feet again. She was watching the shadows round the fire, hoping always that one of them might materialise sooner or later into Grania O'Malley. But the shadows remained shadows and she didn't come. Mrs O'Leary had brought her barbeque up from the pub and was grilling hundreds of sausages over a bank of glowing coals, with Panda sitting, ears pricked and expectant, right beside her.

'Do you want one?' said Jack.

'Two,' replied Jessie, 'and that's just for starters.' And he left her there alone, gazing deep into the fire. She was conscious of the tractor coming back up the hill, its lights sweeping the bracken, and then her father's voice calling for help to unload. Mrs O'Leary was bellowing that the sausages were well done, that there were beans and bread to go with them, that everyone should come and get it. Shadows flitted past the fire towards the barbeque. 'And Mrs Burke's doing the drinks, by the rock pool,' Mrs O'Leary announced. 'And there's potatoes baking in the fire.'

'Quite a party,' said a voice. There was no one there, not at first; but then Grania O'Malley was suddenly sitting right beside Jessie, holding her hands out towards the fire and rubbing them together. 'That's a proper fire too.'

'They'll see you!' said Jessie.

'What if they do? And anyway who's looking? They're all after the sausages. And besides, to see me, you've got to want to see me; and what's more I've got to want you to see me. When they want to see me, and I want them to see me, then they'll see me, but only then – if you see what I'm saying?' Jessie certainly did not, but she wasn't going to say so. 'Listen, Jess,' she went on, 'I may not have time for this tomorrow. I want you to have this.' And she took Jessie's hand and pressed something into it, something hard and cold and sharp.

'What is it?'

'An arrowhead. No it's not Jack's. The boys and me, we looked for it everywhere. Couldn't find it. But maybe this one'll be just as lucky for him. You tell him what you like. You're good enough at the tale-telling – I've heard you. He won't know the difference.'

'Where did you get it?'

'America, just like he did. From the arrow the Indians shot at me. Missed me by a whisker, like I told you; but I kept it. My lucky charm, you might say. It worked a treat for me all my life, maybe it will for Jack.' She closed Jessie's fingers round it and smiled into the fire. 'The night before the battle, just like the old days. The times I've sat up here waiting for the enemy, and we always saw them off, always. I'll be with you in spirit tomorrow, Jess, you can be sure of that.'

'But there won't be a real battle, will there? No one'll really get hurt, will they?' Jessie asked. But when she looked, there was no one there to answer her.

Her father was walking towards her, dusting his hands off on his trousers. 'Strange,' he said. 'I was just unloading the peat a few moments ago, and suddenly there was this woman helping me – long hair, cloak round her shoulders. Don't know who she was. Never seen her before in my life. She said something though, like she knew me, like she knew you. She said I was a very lucky man to have a daughter like you. You know who she is? You seen her?' Jessie shook her head. Her father went on. 'A vision, I expect. She's right though, I am a lucky man. You're the daughter of your mother, I'd say.'

'And who else should she be the daughter of?' Jessie's mother said, coming out of the dark into the light of the fire. Jack was with her, and he was carrying a plate piled high with sausages and beans.

They called old Mister Barney over to join them, and he sat with them round the communal plate and dug in just like they did, fingers for the sausages and the one spoon to share for the baked beans. Jack pigged himself on the sausages. There wasn't a mention, Jessie noticed, of peanut butter sandwiches. When she pointed this out, Jack smiled wryly and said in his best Irish: 'Bog off, why don't you!' They were still laughing when Liam came round with potatoes. They were supposed to be baked, but they were more burnt than baked. They ate them all the same.

'Like the feeding of the five thousand,' said Father Gerald as he passed by. He wasn't far wrong too. The food seemed to have arrived miraculously, enough for everyone; and, from the spring above the rock pool, all the water they needed to wash it down. Mister Barney burped, apologised, and drank some more water.

'That's the best water in all the world, make no mistake,' he said. 'If I live to be a hundred, and it's not far off now, it'll be because of that water. Life-giving, that's what it is. They get digging with their infernal machines, and they'll poison it for ever. Have some, Jessie, have some while you can.' And he passed on the mug to Jessie. Jessie had never thought much about water before. Water had always been just water. It came out of the sky, and there was always plenty of it. She'd drunk it often enough, but now she was tasting it for the first time. It wasn't bitter like other drinks, it wasn't sweet like other drinks. It was cold and it was clean. Whether it was the water or not, Jessie did not know; but she felt a sudden and over-powering sense of complete well-being.

The sausage and bean feast went on well into the night. No one talked of what might happen the next day. With everyone in such high spirits round the fire, Jessie thought she must be the only one even thinking of tomorrow. She could see Jack fooling around in the darkness beyond the great fire with Liam and all the others. She wanted to get him on his own, to give him Grania O'Malley's lucky arrowhead, and to warn him about the battle. When the sausages and beans were exhausted at last, Miss Jefferson got out her squeezebox, and they sang all the songs they knew, and a few they didn't as well. Then there was the dancing, everyone clapping out the rhythm as the feet flashed and flickered in the firelight. In the dying of the fire it warmed their hearts, and their bodies too.

But it was a different matter when it was over. They crawled into their tents and their huts, and wrapped themselves up in their blankets against the cold and the damp. Once the urgent whisperings and the suppressed giggles stopped – and it wasn't long – then the night was filled with a heavy, ominous silence. Jessie snuggled up to her mother on the bracken. Her father and Mister Barney were lying head to toe beside them; and Jack was stretched out at her feet, head in the crook of his arm and facing away from her. He was asleep already, but she didn't want him to be. She kept prodding his side with her toe. She had to find some way to talk to him, she had to. Then she heard him snoring, and knew there was no point any more. She would tell him everything in the morning. Her last prayer that night was to Grania O'Malley, that if there had to be a battle, then please, she didn't want anyone to get hurt.

She was woken suddenly. Someone was calling her name. Marion Murphy was inside the hut and bending over her, tear-stained and crying.

'What is it, Marion?' said Jessie's mother, sitting up.

Marion was looking at Jessie. 'I couldn't come last night. I tried, Jessie, honest.' She was breathless with crying. 'My dad, he caught me with the duvet. He locked me in my room. I wanted to come.'

'It's all right, Marion,' said Jessie's mother.

'No.' Marion was shaking her head vigorously. 'It's not, it's not. You don't understand. They're coming. They've got over more of those men, those security men. They came last night on the ferry. There's a whole army of them now, and they're coming for you. I heard them plan it, the Earthbusters first, like tanks, and everyone else behind.

They're coming, they're coming now. They want to surprise you. I jumped out of my window. I hurt my arm.' Jessie's father was already pulling on his boots and crawling out of the hut. He patted Marion's head as he passed.

'Good girl,' he said. 'Good girl.'

Jessie smiled at Marion. 'You staying then, are you?' she said.

'If you want me?' Marion was looking at Jack.

'Course we do, don't we, Jack?' said Jessie. 'If there's going to be a battle, then we'll need all the good fighters we can get.'

'Who said anything about a fight?' Jessie's mother spoke sharply. 'This thing's got to be settled peacefully. I don't want anyone else getting hurt. Now let's have a look at that arm, Marion.'

There were no sausages left for breakfast, and no beans – they'd eaten them all. So everyone chewed on a cold charred potato or two, then cupped their hands under the spring, and had a long, cool drink of water to wash away the taste. Where the baseball bat appeared from, no one knew; but Liam was brandishing it around his head. And that wasn't the only weapon Jessie had noticed. There were garden forks, iron pokers and several long sticks sharpened into lances. They watched and they waited. There was, in the cold light of that dawn, a sense of awful expectation. When they heard the engines starting up at the bottom of the Big Hill, they gathered together, as sheep do, for protection. Jessie was frightened, frightened by what she had started, by what might happen. There was no stopping it now.

Her mother spoke out, her voice ringing with authority. 'We'll drop the weapons, all of them. We'll not be needing them. There'll be none of that.' Liam took some time to drop the baseball bat. When at last he did, then all the others, grown-ups and children, followed suit. 'We'll join hands, shall we?' said Jessie's mother. 'We'll make a circle, a circle round the top of the Big Hill that no one can break.' Jessie found Jack beside her and took his hand. She had her father on the other side. She clung to both of them, and just hoped. Only Mister Barney did not join in the circle. Leaning on his sticks, he stood in the middle like some ancient chieftain, Jessie thought. They could see the first puffs of black smoke now above the bracken and glimpses of yellow as the Earthbusters came grinding on slowly, inexorably, up the hill towards them.

Some, like Father Gerald, closed their eyes and prayed, while the gulls wheeled overhead, screaming, echoing the fear in their hearts. Then a voice came from behind them, clear and firm. It was Mister Barney. 'We'll see them off. We'll see them off, so we will. Stand firm, hold the line, and we'll send them packing.'

And then they saw the first Earthbuster rearing up the track towards them. Panda barked at it furiously, hackles raised. There was an initial, instinctive step backwards, but that only served to close the circle and tighten it. With arms linked now, they watched the first digger move on to the top of the Big Hill, crushing the bracken, bumping over the rocks towards them. It wasn't long before they found themselves completely surrounded. Michael Murphy was there, flanked by hard-faced security guards, a small army of them, just as Marion had said. The engines died and a stillness fell over the hill. Even the gulls were silent.

Michael Murphy was flushed in the face even more than usual, and it was the flush of rage. 'What the devil's the matter with you people?' he began. 'You all agreed, didn't you? Well, almost all of you anyway? How come you changed your mind, eh? Just because of what Jack said? He doesn't even live here. Haven't I told you and told you? This gold mine will bring us all work, keep the island going, just like the salmon farm did.' No one spoke. They only stared. Michael Murphy felt the resentment in their eyes, and their fierce determination. There was desperation in his voice now. 'For God's sake, didn't I say we'd put it right after? You won't even notice the difference, I promise you. The Big Hill will be here, just the same, and everyone will have their share of the gold, just like I promised. What more do you want?'

Then Mister Barney spoke up: 'But aren't I right in thinking that you'll be getting a bigger share than anyone else, Mr Murphy?'

Michael Murphy was blazing now. 'It's my hill, isn't it? I own it, don't I? And it's my money brought these diggers here, so it's my risk. Yes, so I'll do well out of it, but so will everyone, we all will. But I'll not stand here bandying words with a mad old fool like you. Now, are you moving or not?'

'Not,' said Jessie's mother firmly. 'What are you going to do, Michael? Set your men on us? You always were a bit of a bully, you know that?'

Suddenly Marion broke the circle and ran crying towards her father. 'Dad, please, please.' She was pleading with him, tugging on his arm, but he wouldn't even look at her. He waved a command to the Earthbusters. The engines fired up again, exhausts belching, then great yellow arms unfolding and stretching out, scoops lowered and poised for digging.

High in the cab, the driver of the first Earthbuster recognised the lady in front of him. She was the same one who had screamed at him and kicked at his digger. The boy was there too, the American boy, and the girl with the limp beside him, arms linked. He lowered his scoop to the ground like the others, an eye on Mr Murphy, watching for the signal to stop. The plan had been clear. They would dig round them, and then move in slowly, scraping away the earth at their feet, just close enough to scare them. But it wasn't working. Frightened or not, they weren't moving. None of them were. Some of the children were crying, mothers and fathers holding them now, trying to comfort them. The digger driver thought of his children back home in Dublin, and he did not like what he was doing. He wouldn't do it. He wouldn't go on.

He was reaching for the ignition key when he saw them out of the corner of his eye. From out of nowhere they seemed to come: twenty, thirty men maybe. Swords drawn, they were striding through the circle, but somehow without breaking it. Then some of them were heading straight towards him. The digger driver knew them at once for what they must be, even though it was impossible in this day and age, quite impossible. Pirates,

pirates straight out of the books he read his children. Baggy breeches, barefoot, some of them bearded, and even one with a black eyepatch. They were charging now, swords slicing the air, and yelling a bloodcurdling war-cry that sent warm shivers of fear up his back. The digger driver could not move. He wanted to run, but terror had frozen him to his seat. He looked towards Michael Murphy for help; but Michael Murphy was standing there, aghast, the blood drained from his face.

There was a flag fluttering from the centre of the circle now, a black flag with a red pig on it; and beside the flag stood a tall figure of a woman with a mass of black hair, and there was a sword in her hand too. The pirates were all around his digger now. They were climbing up on to it. One of them had his hand on the cab door, and wrenched it open.

'Nice morning,' said the pirate. 'I wonder if you'd care to step down for a little while?' There was an unpleasant smile on his face. He had very few teeth, and those he did have were like yellow claws. 'Out,' he said. The digger driver did not hesitate, and neither did any of the others. Every digger was soon occupied by pirates, who clambered all over them, waving their swords in wild abandon and whooping in triumph. Michael Murphy and his uniformed army were entirely surrounded by pirates, who tickled them with the points of their swords, under their arms, under their chins, teasing them with terror.

That was when the woman by the flag spoke up. 'Easy boys, easy boys, easy . . . We wouldn't want to frighten them, would we? Well, maybe just a little we would, but not so it hurts, eh?' She turned to Mister Barney. 'Hello, Mister Barney. And how are you this fine morning?' Mister Barney tried to say something. His mouth moved but no sound came out. 'Mister Barney knows well enough who I am – we've met before – and so do Jess and Jack.' She smiled at Jessie.

'By the look on your faces, there's some of you maybe wondering who we are. Well, I'll tell you. My name is Grania O'Malley. And these are my men, my boys. This is our island. This is our hill you're standing on, mine and my forebears', mine and my descendants'. And you,' she went on, sweeping her sword all around her, 'you are my descendants. You are too, Michael Murphy, and you should be ashamed of yourself.' She was pointing her sword straight at him. 'No one owns land, Michael Murphy. You look after it, you protect it for those who come after you, that's all. Can you not understand that? That is why I'll not let you cut off the head of this hill, why I won't let you tear the heart out of it, not for a pot of gold, not for anything.' Jessie wanted to run to her and hug her, out of sheer relief, out of pure love.

'Now, as I see it, Michael Murphy,' Grania O'Malley went on, 'the good people of Clare have given this a lot of thought. Maybe some of them have come to their senses more slowly than others, but no matter. They have decided they want you to leave and take your machines with you, that they want to keep the Big Hill as it is. They asked you nicely – I heard them. But you didn't listen. If you had listened, then there'd have been no need for me to go sticking my piratical nose in, would there now? As it is, I'm going to have to give a little helping hand.' And, with a wink at Jessie, she said, 'You'll enjoy this, I think, Jess.' Then she whipped up her sword and flashed it above her head. 'Right, boys. You know what to do. But take care now.'

All the engines started up at once. Every digger had a crew of pirates, one in the cab and others sitting on the sides, legs dangling. Grania O'Malley took up her flag and strode forward. 'They've been dying to do this ever since they saw those machines. Little boys at heart, just little boys.'

The Earthbusters were on the move, manoeuvring so that they were soon lined up and facing towards the cliff-tops, the pirates hanging on to anything they could. The engines revved to full, thunderous throttle; and then, as if unleashed, they lurched forward into the bracken, bumping over the rocks, in a helter-skelter race for the cliffs. The pirates leapt off this way and that, diving off the sides and out of the cabs, into the bracken and rolling away. Everyone was rushing to look. Jessie was just in time to see the first of the Earthbusters flying out over the cliff and somersaulting through the air. The others were soon to follow. Jack was hoping there would be massive explosions, but there weren't. Instead, there were four spectacular splashes, and a lot of steaming and hissing, as the diggers sank slowly into the sea and disappeared.

It was a moment or two before they all realised what had happened, before the cheering began. When it did, it was deafening. Everyone jumped up and down and hugged each other, everyone that is except Michael

Murphy and his blue and orange army. Jessie felt herself swept off her feet, and then she was swinging in the air, round and round and round until she was giddy with it and begged to be let down. Grania O'Malley set her on her feet and held her fast by the shoulders so she didn't tumble over.

'I think,' said Grania O'Malley, 'I think the enemy has decided they've had enough. Take a look.' And sure enough, there wasn't a sign either of Michael Murphy, nor of his blue-uniformed security guards, nor of the orange-overalled drivers. The battle was over, over before it had begun.

One by one the pirates gathered around Grania O'Malley from all over the Big Hill. One of them said he had never had so much fun in all his life – nor since, he added with a laugh. Grania O'Malley was talking to Jessie's mother and Mister Barney. Everyone else, Jessie noticed, was keeping their distance from her. They stood together in hushed and huddled groups, eyes wide with wonder and fear.

'Well, you'll not be needing us any more, will you?' Grania O'Malley was saying. 'I think we'd better be going. No sensible ghost wants to outstay her welcome. Now where's that daughter of yours, and where's Jack?' She turned, saw them and held out her arms. Like it or not, and he wasn't at all sure he did, Jack was clasped in an enveloping hug. 'Give my best to America when you see it, Jack,' she said, and she released him. 'Maybe I'll pay you a visit one day. How would that be?'

'Great,' said Jack. 'I know a lot of people who'd like to meet you.'

'We'll see, we'll see,' said Grania O'Malley. And she smiled sadly down at Jessie. 'All good things have to come to an end, Jessie. Look after the place for me, won't you?' She bent down, put her arms round Jessie and held her close. Jessie clung to her. 'I'll be seeing you,' Grania O'Malley whispered. And then, quite suddenly, there was nothing to cling to any more. Jessie looked around her. Grania O'Malley was gone, and her pirates with her.

Everyone thought they had gone for good. They were still standing, stunned by all they had seen, by all that had happened, when Marion grasped Jessie by the arm and pointed out to sea. The galley, under full sail, was moving out over the mist-covered sea towards Clew Bay, towards Rockfleet in the distance, the oars dipping together. Grania O'Malley was standing in the prow of the galley, her flag fluttering above her, her hand raised in farewell. The galley sailed on, drawn slowly into the mist, until they saw it no more.

Jessie felt Jack beside her. 'We won't see her again, will we?' she said.

'Never can tell, not with her,' Jack replied.

'She wanted me to give you this,' said Jessie, taking his hand and laying the arrowhead on his open palm.

'Where? Where did she find it?'

Jessie shrugged her shoulders. 'She didn't say.' She thought it safer to change the subject before he could ask any more about it. 'We've done it, haven't we?' She looked up at him and smiled. 'We've saved the Big Hill.' But Jack turned away and looked out to the open sea.

'I don't want to go home,' he said. 'I don't ever want to go home.'

'You haven't got to, not yet,' Jessie replied. 'You've got three weeks still.'

Mrs Burke was standing there, barefoot, her shoes dangling from her fingers. 'Well, Jessie Parsons,' she said. 'You *can* climb the Big Hill, and I'm going to have to eat a lot of humble pie, aren't I? I'm going to write you a hundred lines, Jessie, and do you know what they'll say? "There's more things in heaven and earth than are dreamt of in your philosophy, Mrs Burke." That's Shakespeare, you know,' she added with a smile. And Jessie remembered then that Grania O'Malley had once quoted Shakespeare to her, and tried to remember what it was. Then it came to her, and she said it out loud.

' "Parting is such sweet sorrow," that's Shakespeare.'

'So it is,' said Mrs Burke, wide-eyed with amazement, 'so it is.'

Mrs Burke was a changed woman after the 'Battle of the Earthbusters', as it came to be called. She ended term a day early – 'by decree,' she said, 'by Burke's decree' – and of course no one argued. So Jack had almost three weeks of baseball and rollerblading and fixing Clatterbang. He was happiest chatting away to Jessie, with his hands deep inside Clatterbang's clapped-out engine, trying to repair the unrepairable.

Marion came over often now. It was very strange, Jessie thought, how fascinated Marion Murphy had suddenly become by carburettors and exhaust systems and brake pads, very strange indeed! Jessie didn't mind so much now. She couldn't bring herself to like Marion, but at least she had stopped fearing her. Much as they might have liked to, neither Marion nor Jessie could keep Jack entirely for themselves. Everyone else wanted him on the baseball field, particularly now that the gloves, and the New York Yankee caps had arrived from home, along with a real baseball ball.

Of course the newspapers had a field day. Journalists came from all over the world. Clare Island became known as 'Ghost Island'. Everyone had a story to tell. Ghost-hunting tourists came over in their droves and went on treks up the Big Hill. But journalist or tourist, they all went away disappointed, concluding that the islanders were all conspiring together to spin them a fantastic yarn, that there had been no ghost pirates at all, that the islanders had simply dressed up as pirates, terrified the digger drivers and then run the Earthbusters off the cliffs themselves. In time, even some of the islanders themselves began to doubt the evidence of their own memories.

There was a last baseball game on the field – the Pirates (the children, including Jack and Liam and Marion) against the Earthbusters (the grown-ups, including Jessie's father, Father Gerald and Miss Jefferson). The Pirates won, but only because Jack hit four home runs, and pitched with such venom that the Earthbusters barely saw the ball. Pirates 4, Earthbusters 0. As Father Gerald pointed out, exactly the same score as the Battle of the Earthbusters.

After the game, they had an American-style barbeque on the field with fried chicken and beefburgers and Coke – and peanut butter sandwiches. Almost everyone was there, and it didn't rain either. Even Mister Barney came along. They all watched and clapped as he drank down his very first Coke. He said afterwards that it would be his last, quite definitely his last. It was like bog water, he said, with sugar in it; but that all the same, it had given him an idea, a wonderful idea. He would keep the idea to himself, he said, until he had it all worked out.

The next day, Mister Barney was there on the quayside, along with everyone else, to wave Jack off. Jessie had insisted on going with her mother to see Jack on to his plane at Shannon. It was a grey drizzly day, with the waves heaving and the mainland invisible behind the mist. Jack told Liam he had to keep the Pirates going, he had to make them practise, because he would be back. And Jessie knew he wasn't just saying that. For the first time in his life, Liam didn't seem to know what to say. Marion just hugged Jack quickly, and ran off. Jessie's father thanked him for all he had done, and for his work on Clatterbang.

'I won't say it goes a lot better, Jack,' he said. 'You'd need a miracle for that, and I think we've used up all the miracles due to us, don't you? But the exhaust sounds different, I'll give you that. Ruder.'

As the ferry moved out of the harbour and into the swell of the ocean, the goodbyes dying on the wind, Jessie began to wish she had stayed at home. Jack seemed so sunk in himself. He kept turning the arrowhead over and over in his fingers, and hardly looked up at all. Once back on the mainland, they sat side by side in the back of the car. She had so much to say, but could say nothing. They would catch each other's eye from time to time to try to smile, but they couldn't. Jessie was crying inside already. She just hoped she would be able to manage a smile when the time came to say goodbye.

At the departure gate at Shannon Airport there was a panic about his passport before Jessie's mother found it in a sidepocket of his bag. 'A pity,' she smiled ruefully. 'We could all have gone home again for peanut butter sandwiches and Coke. We're going to miss you so much, Jack. Give my love to your dad, won't you?' And she hugged him tight. 'God bless,' she said.

Jack put his baseball hat on Jessie head, fixed it sideways at the proper angle, and said, 'See you, Jess.' He walked backwards for a few steps. 'I'll write you,' he called out. He waved once and was gone. And she hadn't even said what she had meant to say, that she hoped his father would get better.

He did write, but not for some time. Jessie searched through the post whenever it came, but it was over a month before Jack's letter finally arrived. Jessie ripped it open and read:

> Dear Jess,
> I had a great time. I met just about the best friend I'll ever have too – and I'm not talking about Liam or Marion. They're

good guys, but I'm talking about you. Are you sure what happened up on the Big Hill really did happen? Sometimes, now I'm back home, I think the whole thing was just one wild dream. It wasn't, was it? I'm glad it wasn't only you and me that saw her – her and her pirates. I guess if everyone else saw them, then it really did happen, didn't it?

I've still got the arrowhead, only it isn't mine, is it? I thought it was, but mine had the point chipped off. But I figured it out. It's Grania O'Malley's, isn't it? She gave it to you, and you gave it to me, and you had to pretend it was my lucky arrowhead, the one I lost. Well, if you see her, will you tell her thank you, and tell her that her arrowhead is a lot luckier than mine was. When I had mine, Dad was sick and getting sicker. Now he's a lot better after his surgery, and better every day. He's smiling again. He says the new valve in his heart is real state of the art, and better than anything I've got in my VW Bug. Some arrowhead!

After what happened with you, the treasure and the Big Hill and all, I don't believe things just happen. I think maybe we can help make them happen. Next year I want you to come over to Long Island. I've asked Dad, and he says yes. I'll show you my VW Bug. OK, so I know you're not that interested, but I'm going to show you anyway. We'll go sailing and I'll take you rollerblading in Central Park. But I can't promise you ghosts.

The other day I told Mrs Cody – she's my teacher, remember? – that during the vacation I found out it was the Irish, an Irish pirate called Grania O'Malley, who discovered America first, and not the Dutch, not the French, not the British. She told me it was all just wishful thinking – the Irish blood in me. She'd never even heard of Grania O'Malley. One day I'm going to prove it, not just to her, but to everyone, then no one will be able to argue.

I hope you're getting along with Marion – she wasn't too bad after all, was she? Say hi to your folks and to Liam and all the guys. And a big hi to you and to Mole and to that stinky old dog of yours.

Love,

Jack.

Jessie sat down and replied at once, on Miss Jefferson's word processor which she had been practising on, and which she now found a lot easier than writing by hand.

Dear Jack,

Thanks for your letter. A lot's happened. You'll never guess. It's about the Big Hill. It was old Mister Barney's idea. My dad took him (and me) along to see Marion's dad, because he's the only one with the money to set it up, and because Mister Barney says you can't be blaming him for ever, that it was everyone's fault, not just Mr Murphy's. Anyway, we went to see him. He wasn't too happy at first. Then Mister Barney told him his plan, and he got happier by the minute.

Mister Barney said how he'd been thinking about Coke and how horrible it was, but how everyone else in the world seemed to love it. And there was the best and purest water in the world, pouring down the Big Hill and going nowhere in particular. How about we set up a bottling plant, and sell it? We'll call it 'Grania'. We'll have her picture on the label and sell it all over the world. we'll make a whole pile of money for everyone on the island, including Mr Murphy – lots of jobs and all that – and we'll not have to shift a single rock on the Big Hill.

Mr Murphy offered him a whisky and old Mister Barney said he'd rather have water – you live longer, he said. I can't help thinking that Grania must have put the idea into his head. After all, she did just about everything else, didn't she? I'll send you over a bottle of 'Grania' soon as they start bottling it – probably be next spring, Dad says.

We've still got lots of people coming over to Clare looking for ghosts. There were some Americans here last week. They came for tea, so we gave them the last of the peanut butter. They didn't seem to like it much. They asked me lots of questions and they had a recording machine on. Afterwards they told us they were from Los Angeles, and they made films. They said they might make a film all about the ghost of Grania O'Malley and the Big Hill, and if they did they'd film it here on the island. Dad says it's a pipe dream. Grania O'Malley smoked a pipe, didn't she?

Mole and Panda send you lots of love and so do Mum and Dad (and Marion of course) and so do I. And yes, I'd love to come to Long Island as long as I don't have to get oily hands, if you know what I mean. Mum says it's a bit expensive, so maybe I'll come over by boat, by galley, and surprise you. We've got someone here who's been before remember? So she knows the way. I'll ask her when I next see her, shall I?

See you soon,

Love from Jessie.

PS I haven't seen her again, but she's been here. I was

changing Barry's water last Sunday, and I found my two earrings under the stones. I wear them all the time. Dad says I look a million dollars. And he's right too.

POSTSCRIPT

Grania O'Malley and Clare Island

Of all the characters in this book, the only one who *really* lived was Grania O'Malley herself. She was a pirate queen who, for many years, held sway all along the coast of Mayo and Galway, and in Clew Bay in particular. In her long life – she lived from 1530–1603 – she had many galleys, many castles (amongst them one on Clare Island and one at Rockfleet, both still there), and she had many husbands too. The English called her Grace O'Malley, the Irish Grany O'Malley – pronounced Grania. She *did* have a son called Tibbott and he *was* imprisoned by the English. She *did* go to Greenwich in London to seek his release from Queen Elizabeth. So the two pirate queens met. No one knows what passed between them, only that some months later Tibbott was released.

An Armada galleon *was* wrecked off Clare Island in

1588, and there *was* treasure on board. In April of 1994 I went to Clare Island with my wife. We were not looking for treasure, but to see where Grania O'Malley had lived. We found a kindly people who took us in out of the driving rain, fed us and helped us with our research. Many of them were called O'Malley. We saw the 'Big Hill', as they call it. We went into the ruined abbey. We saw Grania O'Malley's grave. There's a school close by. We visited her castle. We heard there'd been gold found on the nearby island of Inishturk. We found the spirit of Grania O'Malley alive all over the island. That's why I came back home and wrote this story.

None of the Clare Island people in the story are real of course, but the place is; and as for Grania O'Malley, she's as real as you or me; as real as you want her to be.

M.M.
September 1995